GAZPACHO IN WINTER

JAMES TREVOR

iUniverse, Inc.
New York   Bloomington

Gazpacho in Winter

iUniverse books may be ordered through booksellers or by contacting:

iUniverse
1663 Liberty Drive
Bloomington, IN 47403
www.iuniverse.com
1-800-Authors (1-800-288-4677)

ISBN: 978-1-4401-1872-2 (pbk)
ISBN: 978-1-4401-1873-9 (ebk)

Printed in the United States of America

iUniverse rev. date: 6/25/2009

ACKNOWLEDGMENT

I would like to thank my sister Domenica for all the help that she has given me on this book. I would especially like to thank her for her generous offer to take out a second mortgage on her house to put me through professional ballroom dancing school. I would also like to thank Bill Myers, Grant Bracey, Joshua Perkins and Gwyneth Box for their help. Thanks to Mark "Bones" Sklair for his cover design. And, of course, thanks to mom.

BOOK I

THE GINMONGER'S SLATTERN

A tavern was in sight now. Through the mist, Ashton and Thornton could see the orange-lit window that held the promise of a coal stove and a snifter of brandy, which would serve to ease the memory of the frightful events of the evening as well as to invigorate them for the trek back to the motorcar upon the arrival of the mechanic.

They were on their way down from their student lodgings at Oxford when their motorcar broke down and the two had spent the previous forty-five minutes in the freezing rain with the bonnet up trying to suss out what the devil could be the matter with the blasted thing–a task which soon revealed itself to be as foreign to their abilities as translating Ovid would be to any one of the filthy churls whom Ashton and Thornton could now make out through the tavern's greasy window. They felt, though, that the worst of it was over.

At the entrance they did what they could to scrape the mud from their shoes. Such graces would, of course, not be appreciated–or even noticed–in such a place; but the strength and beauty of a proper upbringing and a public school education are in the maintaining of propriety and dignity, even–if not especially–when they are seemingly most superfluous.

The ever so slight, almost imperceptible, twitch of Ashton's right eyebrow was the only hint of the surge of revulsion that washed over him when the warmth of the tavern, mixed with the overpowering stench of cheap tobacco, unwashed labourers and stopped-up, overflowing, fetid, rancid acrid filth, hit him with the force of a ten-tonne lorry. Ashton stiffened his resolve and stepped crisply to the bar as Thornton inquired about the telephone.

As Ashton strode toward the bar (lamenting that both quaff and the receptacle in which it would be served were, for obvious sanitary reasons, quite out of the question) his muddy shoe made contact with a fresh mound of dog vomit. He slipped and crashed to the floor and into the Rover-retch.

Ashton propped himself up on his elbows and, in an attempt to recover his senses, began to vigorously shake his head in the fashion one sees in animated motion pictures. His confusion was furthered, however, by the thunderclap of laughter that burst out around him from the stout-stoked rabble. Ashton's confusion quickly turned to outrage and he poised himself to spring to his feet and demand a halt to their impudence. It was then that, out of all of those barbarian barks, he heard one laugh that left him breathless, as a kick to the stomach does. It was a deep, hoarse, gruff, hacking laugh. Ashton knew, however–immediately, instinctively, maybe even mystically– that it was a female laugh.

Upon hearing that laugh, that horrible laugh, all the rest of that ruffian roar meshed into a muffled din that served as a muted chorus to the godless aria of that devil diva. Ashton searched the room, tracing the source of that sadistic siren song until, as if crashing upon the rocks, he saw her.

Ashton gasped an inverted groan that resembled the sound of a laughing hyena, which egged the room on to another explosion of laughter, the patrons having now concluded, given his stupefied expression, and the fact that he appeared to be laughing while wallowing in a mound of dog vomit, that Ashton was an imbecile.

Ashton was oblivious to all of this. His stare was locked on her. She was a godforsaken horror. The massive mound of her bosom heaved with each guffaw. Her gaping mouth–exposing her craggy, rotting teeth–rivaled Dante's account of the entrance to Hell. Her grime-sodden smock encased her corpulence like a pig intestine does a sausage. Her bulbous nose was a roadmap-like red-and-blue crisscross of drink-ruptured capillaries. Her thick, swarthy hide hung from her primate skull, to which were plastered greasy clumps of matted hair. And from the corner of that dantenscan mouth came a greenish-brown string of drool that trickled into the simmering cauldron of mutton stew as, all the while, she beat her callused, meaty fist in unreserved revelry on the swill-coated bar.

She was a beast whose utter repulsiveness burst into high relief even against the background of the pestilent, festering gob of human phlegm in this tavern–and this from the perspective of a man wallowing in a puddle of puppy puke. She was the rubbish heap of the Almighty's errors. She was the repast that mummy and daddy flies compelled their maggot offspring to finish before they got their excrement for dessert. She was … She was …

"… *dog vomit!*"

Ashton looked around slowly. The roar had dissipated to a smattering of chuckles as the regulars went back to their ale and darts. Ashton began to come around from his dream-like– or was it nightmarish?–stupor.

"Huh? What?" Ashton muttered as he looked up, glassy-eyed.

"I said," Thornton enunciated with the strained staccato of impatience, "don't you think it would be a smashingly good idea if you were to get up out of that puddle of *dog vomit?*"

"Oh, right … Righto!" Ashton said, feigning confident attachment to the mundanity to which he had now returned. But attempting to push himself back onto his feet, Ashton stuck his hand back into the mutt muck and slipped back onto the floor, which provoked a few more weak, scattered chortles from the now laugh-sated louts.

"Good God, man!" Thornton exclaimed as Ashton finally managed to get to his feet. "You look as if you've seen a ghost!"

Ashton, wobbling on rubbery legs and dripping in hound hork, again tried to make light of it all.

"No, really," he muttered, his head reeling. "I'm fine."

"You seem terribly out of sorts, old man," Thornton said, hooking his arm under Ashton's and leading him to the bar. "You'd better toss back a stiff one and let's hope to God that blasted mechanic shows a bit of life and gets us out of this festering hellhole in short order."

Ashton, leaning on his old school mate, managed to hobble up to the bar and rest his weight on it before his knees could give out.

"Frightful spot of bad luck this all is," Thornton said. "Here I invite you down to the house for a chummy weekend, and it's been nothing but a muddle all the way."

Ashton was beginning to come around now. He scanned the room, though he knew not quite why, vainly searching for that blowzy siren who, having had her laugh, had gone to the kitchen to decapitate chickens for tomorrow's stew.

"Sorry 'bout that, gov'nor," the short, dumpy, balding, ruddy, filthy, flyblown ginmonger said, addressing himself to Ashton. "A gent'man like yourself oughtn't a 'ave to suffer such indi'nities."

Thornton, who was born and, during the off months from school, bred in this region, was well familiar with the sort of sarcastic twaddle that these local sorts tried to put over on men of standing.

"Shut your blasted gob and bring us two brandies, you blithering twit, and a rag–preferably not disease ridden–for Mr. Chesterfield."

"Righ' 'way, sir. Din't mean at all to upset ya, sir," the ginmonger truckled. "I'll just slip off on down to the cellar where we keep the best, and at no extra charge at all for you gent'men."

The ginmonger scuttled down the rickety stairs. With feline precision he moved through the penumbra, his only guide being the instinct he had developed through years of slinking through its cavernous interior–an instinct so honed that not once since the electric light had been installed down there fifteen years before had it ever occurred to him to turn it on. He glided past the barrels of real ale, stout and lager until he reached the dust-covered oak cask in which the armagnac ripened. Virtually untouched by the regulars, the ginmonger stocked it for the occasional fox-hunting party that came through. Though he served it infrequently, the ritual was second nature. From the shelf above the cask he took down two palm-sized snifters and carefully wiped the dust from them. Tilting them under the spigot, he generously filled them. Holding one in each hand, he then inhaled deeply, as if savoring the sweet bouquet. He then unleashed two voluminous wads of phlegm, one into each snifter, and carefully swirled them until the contents blended nicely.

"Here we are now, gents," the ginmonger said upon returning. He was careful to maintain a cheerful, yet docile tone. "Sorry to keep you waitin', but, as you gent'men know, a good brandy can't be rushed now, can it?" He presented the brandies to them with a broad, simple grin.

"Perhaps I was a bit rough on the old bugger," Thornton said to Ashton after the ginmonger had left them. "They're childlike and mischievous," he said, pausing to warm the snifter in his palm, swirl the contents beneath his nostrils, inhale deeply and swallow a formidable draught. "But they mean us no ill will."

Ashton absentlmindedly swirled his sputum-tainted potion. Though out of sight, that swarthy she-Satan was most certainly not out of mind. Fortunately, Ashton's restive musings were interrupted by the arrival into that moldy mire of the mechanic.

"Right, then, someone 'ere call for a mechanic?" barked the short, burly man in the greasy blue overalls.

"It's about bloody time!" Thornton exploded.

"Well, well, Mr. Fopwanker. You'll 'ave to understand that I been right busy draggin' out of the coals the fancy-pantsed arses of bourgeois pigs like yourself whose inbred brains are too addled to know the difference between the gearshift and their willies."

Thornton reared himself to put this insolent churl in his place.

"T'aint easy, no t'ain't," the mechanic continued, "being the only mechanic for a hundred miles 'round."

Thornton applied the brakes and exhaled slowly. With great difficulty he contorted his lips into a smile.

"No, no, I'm sure that it isn't," he managed to say, straining the bounds of his patience.

"Right then!" the mechanic said, assured that the hierarchy had been established. "Stop bloody well wasting my time, then, and lead me to daddy's car so we can get ya off to the club before the other useless bastards there gobble up all the cucumber sandwiches."

Thornton flung some change onto the bar and, though boiling inside, quietly followed the mechanic out. For all of the benefits of the technological advances of the day, Thornton couldn't help but feel that they put at a terrible disadvantage those like himself who were hereditarily unsuited for doing anything for themselves.

"Ashton, old man, look lively," he called. "We've still got to put a bit more into it before this dreadful nightmare is over."

Ashton turned in Thornton's direction, the mist gradually dissipating from his eyes. "Right, old boy," he replied with feigned nonchalance, putting his untouched brandy on the bar. "Let's get at it," Ashton said, heading toward the door. At the threshold he paused and looked once more toward the kitchen. With the squawks of the moribund chickens in his ears, he turned and walked out of the door.

Ↄↄ

Howling, Ashton sat straight up in bed. Cold sweat streamed down his face and back.

It seemed an eternity until the morning sunlight and the clean white sheets were able to coax Ashton into denying the undeniable. *It hadn't happened*, Ashton subconsciously told himself as his panting subsided and his muscles relaxed. *It hadn't happened*.

Ashton arose and drew his own bath, as cold as he could tolerate. He slid into it and, teeth chattering, tried to concentrate on the day's activities, which were to commence with a morning ride.

After drying himself, he donned his breeches and boots. Normally, such attire would have been quite unacceptable at breakfast, but Thornton had decided that, given the brevity of their sojourn, some exceptions could be made for the sake of expediency. His parents and sister had been forewarned and, under the circumstances, were disposed to overlook the irregularity.

Ashton abandoned his chambers and, turning the corner to the staircase, surprised upon the upstairs chambermaid. Though young, she was obese and unkempt.

"Mornin' to ya, sir," she said with a curtsy, which resembled the bobbing of a dead whale on the high sea. Ashton grasped the railing to steady himself. After a moment, he mustered his composure, nodded curtly to her, and swiftly descended the stairs.

"Ashton, old man!" Thornton exclaimed as he rose from the breakfast table to greet him. "We were about to send out a search party."

"I do apologize," Ashton said. "I shan't try to excuse my tardiness on the change of climate or air. I'm simply as lazy as a stable hand near retirement."

"None of that, now," Lord Wingate said cheerfully as he stood and extended his hand. The older man had a full head of silver hair and a moustache of the same hue. He was short and stocky and wore a salt-and-pepper tweed suit, indicating that his day's business would be conducted on his country estate. "After what Thornton has been telling us of last night's mis-adventures," he added, "a few extra minutes of rest are most certainly excusable, as well as advisable. Such a night, com-bined with the quotidian nocturnal activities of young men, as I remember them, would wear out a bull," he added with a wink.

"Wentworth," Lady Wingate intervened dryly. "Whatever the 'quotidian nocturnal activities of young men' might be, I'm sure they need no encouragement on your part."

"Where are my manners?" Thornton said. "Ashton, I'd like to present by dear mother. Mother, I'm sure that my copi-ous anecdotes of life at university supersede any introductory comments I could make with regard to Ashton."

Like Thornton, Lady Wingate had an aquiline face, with the added feature of appearing to have had all of the blood drained from it. Her faded hair was piled in a practical manner upon her head and she wore an old fashioned black dress with a high collar that held a cameo at her throat.

Ashton approached Lady Wingate and lightly clasped her bony liver-spotted hand.

"Lady Wingate," he said, bowing slightly, "It is a pleasure indeed to make your acquaintance. Thornton has spoken so affectionately of you."

"You're too kind," she replied with habitual ease.

"And last, but most certainly not least," Thornton said, "It is my pleasure to present my sister, Aurelia.

Aurelia was demure–or was it boredom? She had regularly suffered this sort of contrivance since her debut and feigned spontaneity was rote now. She brilliantly alternated eye contact with gently averted downward gazes as she offered her silky hand to Ashton. Aurelia's peaches-and-cream complexion, which leaned luminously to cream, was devoid of any imperfection. Her breastless, shapeless form, draped chastely in a modest dress, was a citadel of decency.

"My brother has often spoken of you, Mr. Chesterfield," she said in a delicate voice, with a trace of a smile.

Ashton went through the motions, saying something brief and meaningless–too brief, too meaningless. A hint of consternation wafted through the room; Aurelia had never before failed to enchant. Had this encounter taken place only twelve hours before, Ashton would have been hopelessly enamored. He was indifferent.

Nonetheless, it was a pleasant breakfast. The conversation was light as was the repast, a copious meal and a morning of riding hardly being congruous. Thus, Ashton and Thornton limited themselves to fried bacon, fried sausages, fried black pudding, fried eggs, fried tomatoes, fried mushrooms, fried potatoes, beans, toast, tea and brandy. Ashton culminated his indifference to Aurelia with his failure to inquire as to whether she was planning to join them on their ride, leaving all with the impression that he was a queer one indeed.

The crisp breeze slapped Ashton's face as he galloped briskly through the countryside. His malaise, which he forced himself to attribute to a hangover, was seemingly alleviated. (The previous evening, once in dry clothing and seated in the Wingate's library before the roaring fireplace, over which hung a portrait of the Wingate's illustrious ancestor the warrior king Laurel the Hardy, Ashton and Thornton had mercilessly attacked a bottle of forty-year-old Chivas.)

The countryside was splendid. The swaying grass of the rolling meadows gave Ashton the sensation of galloping through a bright green sea under the deep blue sky. The air was cool and fresh. It was a glorious day. As they reached the gate of the pigsty at a local farm, Ashton could no longer restrain his enthusiasm.

"Thorty, old boy, last one to the end of the fence is a bloody Cambridge man," he shouted, giving vent to his recently recovered spirits.

Ashton dug his heels into the flanks of his mount and charged off. Giggling with abandon, Ashton slapped the haunches of his horse with his crop and raced cleanly past the end of the fence. Reining his mount to an abrupt stop, Ashton spun it around.

"Well, Thorty, it seems that once again the better man has …"

Ashton cut himself short. There, a full clip back, he saw Thornton stopped alongside of the pigsty. With a lost, vacant stare he was looking at the pigs.

Ashton indulged in a warm bath before dinner. Whilst his morning bath had served to cool his passion-racked body, this one would serve to ameliorate what tomorrow would surely be a jolly sore behind. Ashton was enjoying the sensation of having spent an exhilarating day of physical culture combined with the expectation of what would surely be a splendid dinner. He amused himself with the thought that his dinner jacket would undoubtedly be a few sizes too large, given the pounds that he surely had shed that morning.

Ashton gave some brief thought to Thornton's rather rummy interest in the pigs. Admittedly, Thornton was a bit of an odd bird. He was pasty-skinned and had a long, aquiline nose. His gangliness made him useless at sports and, adding to that his frequent moodiness, he was rather unpopular with the other chaps. Ashton, by contrast, was sturdy and handsome. He was a jolly sharp cricket player and, given his easy nature and generosity, well liked by the other fellows. He took quite a bit of ribbing from them for his friendship with Thornton, but Ashton felt there was some good in all people, and he stood by his friends.

The dinner was indeed splendid. As a special treat for Ashton, Lady Wingate had planned a typically regional meal. There was succulent boiled meat, exquisite boiled potatoes and a sublime dish of boiled vegetables. The only extra-regional addition to the delightful repast was the Beaujolais.

"What is your opinion of the wine, Ashton?" Lord Wingate queried.

Ashton swirled the glass beneath his nostrils, took a sip and rolled it over his tongue.

"It's naïve," said Ashton, "yet not stupid. Fluffy, yet it doesn't leave hairballs at the back of your throat. It's bold, yet it doesn't make a complete wanker of itself. It's witty, yet it doesn't cause you to burst out laughing so hard that it dribbles out of your nose. It's a wine of exceptional character, yet it isn't beyond peeking through the bushes every now and again to watch little girls change into their bathing costumes."

The Wingates were impressed by his vinous connoisseurship, none more so than Aurelia. She gazed at Ashton. Indifferent to her this morning, sophisticated this evening; Ashton was beginning to intrigue her.

The after-dinner conversation flowed glibly. As it was a reduced dinner party, the gentlemen refrained from excusing themselves to the library and enjoyed their port and cigars in the charming company of the ladies.

Aurelia's youthful grace proved her a delightful dinner companion, flowing with humorous anecdotes concerning the ladies' college which she attended. Lord Wingate's digressions into the world of public affairs were deftly deflected by Lady Wingate and, thus, the evening hummed with good humour and gaiety.

The morning ride, as well as the glow the port brought on, edged Ashton into a comforting attraction to the charming Aurelia. He entertained the idea of requesting the Wingates' permission to accompany Aurelia to services tomorrow. But, Ashton and Thornton had a spot more of the old laugh-it-up ahead of them this evening. So, what tomorrow would bring would be seen tomorrow.

Lady Wingate and Aurelia had retired to their rooms for the evening and Lord Wingate saw Thornton and Ashton off.

"Well, lads," Lord Wingate said as he personally held the door open for them, slapping them on the backs, "Don't do anything I wouldn't do, which I dare say shouldn't leave you too cramped." Lord Wingate impishly looked over his shoulder, checking to make sure that Lady Wingate wasn't hovering about ready to scold him.

"Well, it's off in the Bentley," Thornton said as they headed for the car park. "Father was awfully good about giving me the loan of it until those dashed fools get my motorcar into order. It's a bugger that I've got to wait two solid years until I finish university for father to give me a proper one to zip about in."

"Shall we be returning to the same place as last night?" Ashton asked, trying to sound nonchalant, though he was not quite sure why he was asking the question and why he was trying to sound nonchalant.

"Ashie, dear Ashie, some of us *do* have ancestors who crawled out of the primordial ooze and climbed down out of the trees for some good purpose. If it's dog vomit that you so desperately crave, then when we get to the club you must simply get a couple of scotches into old Colonel Weston and then ask him to recount for the one-thousandth time his exploits during the Burma campaign."

Ashton feigned a chuckle.

The club was quite full, though not unusually so for a Saturday night. Thornton and Ashton had no trouble finding a table, as the Wingates had had the same one reserved at the club for well over three hundred years. Brandies were brought with no need to order them, as the Wingates had always taken brandy at this time, on this day, for well over three hundred years.

"Are you quite sure you're all right?" Thornton asked. "You really seem quite off your form."

"Never better," Ashton replied, too quickly, polishing off his brandy in one prodigious gulp.

"Oh, Manfred," Thornton said, directing himself to the waiter. "I think you had better bring another one for Mr. Chesterfield–a full one this time."

"Yes, sir," Manfred droned in servile recognition of the quip.

"You know, Ashie, if you'd allow the brandy to glide momentarily over your tongue you might find the taste rather agreeable."

"I'm sorry," Ashton said. "But with the ordeal last night and today's ride and what not, I suppose I am feeling a shade out of sorts."

"I'm terribly sorry to hear that, old Ashie. We've really tried to make you feel at home here and …"

"Oh, you've all been more than good to me. I really can't remember when I've had a better time."

Manfred returned with a fresh snifter. Ashton forced himself to take just a sip and set the snifter back down.

"That's a bit more like it, Ashie."

Ashton, bolstered by the brandy, asked the question.

"Who was she?"

"Who was who?"

"The woman."

"Which woman would that be?"

"You know," Ashton fumbled, "she … uh … was … you know, the … uhm … the sort of … horrible one at the … uh, tavern last night."

"'The sort of horrible one at the tavern last night!'" Thornton mocked. "My dear Ashie, you are going to have to be a bit less parsimonious with your adjectives if I am to have any clue whatsoever as to which of those 'sort of horrible' wenches you are referring to."

"Well, you know, uh, the large, filthy, sweaty, repugnant, loud, disgusting, greasy, revolting, mangy, repulsive, flyblown, sickening, lice-ridden, stomach-turning, hideous, beastly … you know, the … the sort of horrible one." Ashton drained his snifter.

"Ah, yes," Thornton said, leaning his head back in a gesture of sudden recognition. "The ginmonger's slattern."

"The ginmonger's slattern?" Ashton repeated with a vague interrogative lilt.

"Yes, Ashton. The ginmonger's slattern. Which is to say, as further explanation seems to be in order here, that she is the wife of the ginmonger."

"The wife of the ginmonger?"

"Well, we seem to be catching on," Thornton jested as he gently crooked his finger for Manfred's attention. "Perhaps a drop more will help you to sustain this stunning repartee."

Manfred arrived with a fresh snifter.

"Manfred, break out a bottle of your finest. It's a celebration this evening. It seems that our dear friend Mr. Chesterfield here has fallen madly, passionately, head-over-heels in love."

"Yes, sir," Manfred droned in servile recognition of the quip.

"Oh give it a rest!" Ashton snapped. "Sometimes that rot which you fancy a sense of humour can be bloody annoying."

Thornton lifted the snifter and rolled it gently under his nose. "Just what is it about this hag that has you so worked up?" he asked, peering coolly over the rim at Ashton.

"Nothing, nothing really," Ashton replied. "I just … it's just that she was so … so … horrible."

Thornton signaled to Manfred. Ashton's snifter was empty.

Ashton gripped the rim of the toilet firmly with both hands to ready himself for the next spasm. He tried to swallow, but gagged.

"Buaawuuughawumf!" Ashton opined. "Urp!" he reiterated.

His arms trembled as he tried to maintain a grip on himself as well as the rim of the bowl. He slowly opened his eyes. Looking straight down, a shudder of sudden, horrifying, awareness wracked his body. He saw there, in that bowl, what he now knew to be his destiny. It was as if his dignity, his brilliant future, his family and friends and seven hundred years of sterling ancestry had been heaved up from his soul, leaving only the vomit. Oh, the irony! This had all begun with his slipping in a pile of vomit, and now he would wallow in it for the rest of his days.

So be it.

Struggling to his feet, Ashton spun around and crashed into the wall. He fumbled for the doorknob, flung open the door, and stumbled out of the men's room.

"Are you awright, sir?" a scullery boy asked Ashton as he reeled through the kitchen, sending dishes and pans crashing to the floor.

"Get out of my way!" Ashton roared, shoving the boy aside and barreling out of the back door.

Ashton stumbled and crawled through the fields. He was soaked with sweat and dew. His face, hands and knees bled from the branch-lashing and tumbles he took. Though ignorant of the region, he would find her. He could sense her. He was like the fly, and she the carrion. He would find her.

The rolling meadows that had so soothed Ashton this morning were now like the barbed wire and broken glass that stood between a prisoner and freedom. He struggled on until, suddenly, he slipped (could it be dog vomit?) and tumbled down the steep slope of a hill. Banging his knees against rocks, smashing his face against tree trunks, Ashton rolled and bounced to the foot of it. He sat up and, in that same cartoon-like fashion, wagged his head in an attempt to recover his senses. And then he saw the tavern.

Ashton slowly rose to his feet. His clothes hanging in rags, his eyes wide and blazing, and the stiff, clomping walk forced by his bruised and battered knees gave Ashton the semblance of a zombie. With every step he took, she was one step closer.

Ten yards from the tavern, he stopped. Not out of doubt did he falter, but out of strategy. What would he do? Within a moment he was heading for the kitchen door. There he would hide and wait for her.

Ashton slipped in. The kitchen was dimly lit by the cooker flame. Hiding would not be difficult. He crept through the kitchen and, after a brief reconnaissance, nestled in behind a hanging sheep carcass. There he waited. Seconds, minutes, hours did he wait? Ashton did not know–nor did he care. One hour more, one year more, Ashton would not have budged. Patiently, quietly, devotedly, he waited.

The door from the taproom to the kitchen creaked open. Ashton's heart leapt. His skin tingled, his mouth went dry, his ears perked up, and his hands began to sweat. He heard the shuffling of feet, the clink and clang of pots, a slightly raspy breathing. One step out, Ashton thought, and she would be his. He eased the sheep carcass aside and slithered out from his lair. Inch by inch he slid along the wall, until he came to the corner around which she awaited. Without a breath, he gingerly moved his head around the wall. Ashton slowly opened his clenched eyes.

It was the ginmonger!

Of course it was the ginmonger! There would always be the ginmonger! Ashton was furious at himself for not having considered that before. He then turned his fury on the ginmonger. How dare he! How bloody dare he stand in the way! But then Ashton's fury suddenly evaporated into the Zen-like tranquility of those who are one with their destiny–those who accept their fate. Those who fear not what they must do.

Ashton crisply stepped from behind the wall.

"Ginmonger!"

The ginmonger spun around. "Ay! Ya startled me a bit there ya did, sir. Are ya all right sir? How can I help ya, sir?"

"How can you help me?!" Ashton bellowed as he neared the ginmonger. "You can die!"

In one swift, sweeping movement, Ashton snatched up the meat cleaver from the cutting board, raised it into the air and swung it down upon the ginmonger's head. The man crumpled to the floor.

Ashton realized that the ginmonger might only be stunned; thus, he calculatedly hacked away until there could be no doubt left. The ginmonger was dead. She was his.

Ashton clomped off to the taproom.

"Oh my God!" someone shrieked.

The horror in the voice silenced the tavern's merry din. Ashton's tattered clothing steamed from sweat and fresh blood. The cleaver dripped with warm gore. The fire in his eyes turned their blood to ice and the hush cooled into immobile terror. Ashton slowly panned the room until his eyes fell upon her. She stood frozen. Ashton's lips began to tremble. They parted slowly. Ashton spoke:

"I love you."

☙

By counting off "one elephant, two elephant," Ashton was able to determine that the hammer-blows from the gallows that echoed through his cell were coming at one-second intervals. Thus, had Ashton chosen, he would simply have had to ask the jailer for the correct time and then accurately count his way down to the exact moment of his execution. He chose not to. His choice was not an attempt to disassociate his mind from the inevitable—for Ashton had resigned himself to the inescapable certainty that at six that next morning, he would be hanged by the neck until dead. More than resignation, it was a longing. The fear of the afterlife, or lack of it, tortured Ashton less than the agony of her absence. The seconds spent without her accumulated to wear away at his soul the way that grains of sand accumulate to form a desert that eradicates any vegetation in its path.

No, it was not for fear of death that Ashton had chosen not to clock the last snippets of his life. He knew that to cleanly wrap up his life, his epilogue must be concise and direct. It had to answer that one question that had eaten away inside of him with almost the same passion as his love for her; Why?

Why, in the space of less than twenty-four hours, had the most average of university lads metamorphosed into an unrepentant cleaver-murderer burning with desire for a creature that was barely human? Why, when Ashton would never again see the sun, or walk through the woods on a crisp autumn afternoon, or hear a note of Mozart—Why was his only thought the thought of her?

He called up to duty the last shreds of his will to hold at bay the thought of her. Later, as he stood hooded and with the antithesis of the umbilical cord secured around his neck, then, and only then, would he unleash the thoughts of her to flood over him and smother him with euthanasiac bliss. And with that reprieve, he must concentrate. To concentrate as only a condemned man can. The question was simple–Why? The answer was elusive.

Like a moving-picture editor at his viewing machine, Ashton watched his life scud along. The images flickered through his mind until, inexplicably, they skidded to a halt. Ashton, as a discriminating editor would, immediately deemed the scene irrelevant and tried to fast-forward. His subconscious firmly resisted moving on. Aston relented and pondered the scene. It was from his early childhood.

There was the image of Ashton, at age five, leaving a Sunday afternoon garden party at the Prescotts'. The Chesterfields had taken their leave and were heading for their coach. The coachman, unaware of their approach, continued chatting with the Prescotts' gardener. As they neared, the coachman burst into a hearty guffaw. Ashton stopped in his tracks. Never had he heard such a sound. Until then, Ashton had lived in a world of titters and snickers. In a world of giggles and tee-hees. A world in which a polite mouth was covered when an upward tilt of its corners was sensed.

Was this the sound that people made when they died? Ashton thought. *Or maybe the sound of the devil himself?* Whether death or devil, Ashton wanted no part of it. He was already five, thus he was old enough to dominate almost completely any expression of emotion. The overly pert blink of his eyes, however, was immediately detected by his father.

"You blithering idiot!" Captain Chesterfield roared as he lashed the coachman across the face with his crop. "You've frightened the child half to death!"

"I'm sorry, m'lord," the coachman spluttered as he lay on the ground, nursing his lip.

"You will take us home immediately," Chesterfield responded. "Whereupon you will pack your belongings and be gone!"

"Please, sir," the coachman yelped. "I've twelve lil' ones an' an ailin' wife …"

"Well, one must really take these things into consideration before one goes about terrifying children and humiliating one's master," Chesterfield interjected, bringing the point home with one more resounding crop-blow. The coachman struggled to his feet and, with some trouble, managed to open the door of the coach for them. Chesterfield, meanwhile, was expressing his deepest apologies to the Prescotts for the coachman's behaviour. The Prescotts were fully understanding of the unfortunate affair and, feeling themselves partly responsible, summarily sacked the gardener.

Ashton sat in his cell, perplexed. He replayed the scene. What could it be? Garden party? Coach? Horses? Nothing unusual there. The sacking of an impudent servant? Quite routine. Nothing rung a bell. What did it mean? Ashton was at the end of his tether. Only a hair's breadth from extermination and he was unable to budge his thoughts from an insignificant incident where an impertinent coachman had guffawed.

Guffawed! *Eureka*!

Of course! It was the guffaw! That bloody coachman had guffawed! Oh, how wrong he had been as a tot! That booming laugh was not the sound of death! It was the sound of *life*! It was not the sound of the devil, but of an angel–his angel!

That repulsive slattern was alive! She was an angel! She did not titter or snigger or giggle or tee-hee. She bellowed, roared, barked, hooted, howled, cackled, split her sides, slapped her knee! She guffawed!

The clang of the outer cell door served as an exclamation point to Ashton's discovery. Had so much time elapsed?

The hall reverberated with jingling keys and footsteps, which came to a halt outside of his cell. The riddle had been solved and Ashton was ready.

"Is it time?"

"Eh, ya got plen'y a time," responded the jailer. "There's just someone 'ere to say 'ello–or, should I say, 'goodbye.'"

The jailer let out a guffaw. The remark was meant to be the stab, the guffaw the twisting, of the knife. But it filled Ashton with warmth.

"Ashton."

Ashton stared at the floor, basking in the jailer's miscalculated mirth.

"Ashie."

Ashton slowly looked up. "Thornton! Dear Thornton!"

He jumped to his feet and sprang for the cell door. Abandoned now by his family, Ashton hadn't counted on one last affectionate encounter. Confinement, however, had had an atrophic effect on him and his spring immediately degenerated into a slow, shuffling stumble. With determination he shambled forward, arms outstretched, head hung low with fatigue. His lips, however, retained enough strength to form a vague smile and there was an indubitable gleam in his eyes.

Three yards from the cell door Ashton stopped suddenly, as if hitting a wall. His neck straightened and his gaze hardened.

Thornton smelled like a pig.

Thornton smelled like a thousand pigs. He smelled like an open, pestilent sewer. He smelled like a horde of a hundred thousand Huns. Thornton smelled like a thousand pigs, an open, pestilent sewer, *and* a horde of a hundred thousand Huns.

Thornton smelled like her.

The exquisite stench flushed Ashton's mind clear–and he understood. Thornton had been with her. Thornton had always been with her.

She and Thornton had killed the ginmonger–and Ashton would pay the piper. Oh what a crime–for it was a crime! They, however, would not hang. They would not sup once on the gaol fare of stale bread and warm water. They were free even from being scolded and sent to bed without their pudding.

The perfect crime. As the worms nipped away at Ashton's corpse, they would live on in each others' arms.

Thornton stared impassively at Ashton. He knew that Ashton knew. Ashton knew that Thornton knew. Thornton knew that Ashton knew that Thornton knew. Ashton knew that Thornton knew that Ashton knew that Thornton knew. It was all very clear.

Ashton grew calm. He understood that Thornton had been driven to this betrayal by the madness of absolute passion and pure love. Thornton's perfidy would have been, by all that Ashton up until recently had firmly believed, worthy of the highest condemnation. But Ashton knew that Thornton had done what he had done to be with her. Ashton knew that he would have done the same.

Though fair play and loyalty were the backbone of England and the hitherto unquestioned foundation of Ashton's creed, he would have shed them in an instant had he thought that it would have meant even the briefest of moments spent in her embrace. Truth, justice, decency, honesty, loyalty–what did they matter if the reward for discarding them were even the most ephemeral wisp of her affection?

That Thornton was sacrificing a dear friend instead of a complete stranger, as Ashton had done, was irrelevant. The passion that she inflamed was capable of crumbling the foundation of even the most soundly constructed edifice of friendship. Ashton would not have hesitated in doing the same if necessary. Realizing all of this, Ashton's voice was devoid of invective when he calmly addressed Thornton.

"So it was all planned from the beginning, wasn't it? The car breaking down just outside of the tavern?"

"Well, if I had known that would involve dealing with *that* hideous mechanic I would have rethought that part," Thornton said, turning his attention momentarily from the subject of his heinous treachery toward Ashton as he recalled how irksome the mechanic's insolence had been.

Ashton moved closer to Thornton–not to do him harm, but from a longing for one last whiff of her. Though Ashton understood that the ginmonger's death, as much for Thornton as it had been for himself, was necessary, and that any means were acceptable, he still needed to know why it was he who had been condemned to carry out the horrible deed.

"Why me, Thornton?" Ashton asked impassively.

Thornton, contemplative, was slow to respond. "Do you remember Freddy?" he finally uttered.

"I'm not quite sure what Freddy has to do with …"

"Do you remember Freddy?" Thornton interrupted testily.

"Of course I do."

"Did he ever confide in you his opinion of me?"

"Yes he did," Ashton replied curtly.

"And what was it?"

"As I am to die shortly, tact would be rather superfluous, wouldn't it? Freddy thought you were the biggest wanker he had ever met."

"Yes," Thornton responded knowingly. "And Bilby?"

"Bilby," Ashton continued with the same unbridled honesty of the condemned, "often opined that you kept venery well within the immediate family."

"Yes, yes–and Reggie?"

"Reggie concurred with Bilby."

Thornton sighed. "I knew that. I knew that without even having to ask."

He was silent for a moment, then exploded in rage.

"Why *you*?" Thornton suddenly burst out with such fury as to cause Ashton to take a step back. "Why you, you ask? Who else? Who else would have accepted my invitation to come down here? Bilby? Freddy? Reggie? I believe we've firmly established that they despised me rather a bit more than, oh, say–dog vomit! Yes, Ashton, everybody has always despised me. Dear charming mother. Jolly old father. Sweet, sweet Aurelia. What an award-winning performance you were witness to. They despise me more than anyone, which is saying rather a lot, as everyone else despises me quite a bit." Thornton's fury subsided. "Everyone, that is, except you, Ashton."

Thornton's gaze lingered on the floor for some while before he continued.

"Who else would have accepted my invitation? There was no one else, Ashton. It had to be you."

Thornton lifted his eyes and looked forlornly at Ashton.

"You see, Ashton, you are the only friend that I have ever had."

THE FOURTH WAY

Prime Minister Thornton Wingate sat in the backseat of the limousine that was taking him from 10 Downing Street to Parliament. He was preparing his notes for the speech he was to deliver there in which he would present his plan to encourage investment through an enhanced capital gains tax credit which would be financed by putting an end to government subsidized milk for school children from low-income families. He thought he would approach it from the angle in which the children would benefit by learning the all important lesson that there is no such thing as a free lunch. To counter any charges that would likely come from the Liberals that this measure could result in serious short- and long-term health problems for hundreds of thousands of children, Thornton had commissioned a study that "proved" that a child's supposed need for calcium is a wildly inaccurate misconception. The study was conducted through the Bradford Foundation, a medical research think tank that was fully funded by the osteoporotic prostheses industry–an industry that contributed heavily to the Conservative war chest.

Thornton looked in the rearview mirror to rehearse his summation. The lean and hungry look he had had as a youth had aged into an emaciated, bitter visage with the sides of his bald, bony scull wreathed with grizzled hair.

Thornton cleared his throat and spoke:

From the milk queue to the dole queue (dramatic pause). We are teaching our children that their hands are not designed for productive labour but, rather, to be held out in supplication to the government in the expectation of having any fleeting whim instantly gratified. No, my learned colleagues, this country was built by those bold and courageous enough to pick up their telephones and tell their brokers to invest in Britain! Are we going to let these people down? Are we going to turn our backs on those great patriots who ask for nothing in return other than not to be taxed on their windfall profits? Small thanks, I say, for such selfless …

The mobile phone in his breast pocket quivered. Thornton, annoyed at the interruption, pulled it out and flipped it open testily.

"Yes?"

"Prime Minister Wingate," came his secretary's voice, "Lady Throppe is on the line."

"Oh, fucking hell!" he hissed.

Thornton had squandered his trust fund cavorting about Europe with the ginmonger's slattern, the spree ending when she abandoned him in a small southern Italian village moments after he had spent his last farthing. Wingate made it back to England, broke, estranged from his family, and more bitter and ruthless than before—qualities that his great aunt, Lady Throppe, had recognized as valuable assets for a political career that she, ever since, had financed and guided.

Though her exact age was unknown, she was, by any calculation, very, very, very old. But, quite from slipping into senility, with every passing year, Lady Throppe's mind grew only more cunning.

A woman of her own mind, she was in many ways ahead of her time. She refused, for instance, to change her last name when she married Bertrand Uppspew. The union itself went against convention, as she was well into her thirties at the time, while Bertrand, to whom she had been governess, was barely twenty. Bertrand died in mysterious circumstances only weeks after they were wed, leaving her with a title and a vast fortune.

While Thornton and Lady Throppe despised everybody, they despised each other in a special way. They were, however, inextricably linked in their ambitions and integral in each other's success.

"Thornton?"

"Yes, Aunt Anne?"

"Thornton, we have a problem."

Thornton sat forward in his seat. Lady Throppe did not rattle easily, and for her to describe something as a *problem* bespoke grave danger.

"What is it?" Thorton managed to gasp.

"I do not wish to speak about it on the telephone. When can you come to the house?"

"I have my speech to the Parliament; I could be there immediately following," Thornton said, his voice quavering slightly.

"Good God, Thornton, pull yourself together. I can practically hear your knees knocking. After all, we've certainly weathered a storm or two in the past, haven't we?"

Thornton knew that she was referring to that sticky patch a few years back when he had barely escaped being charged with crimes against humanity.

"Anyway, Thornton, I am close to finding a solution to it. I am, after all, the person to whom Sherlock Holmes, to his dying day, referred to as *That Female*."

"Aunt Anne," Thornton said, his voice shifting from sheer terror to the most patronizing tone that he could muster, "Sherlock Holmes was a fictional character."

"You forget, Thornton, that we are too."

Thornton flushed with anger. Every time he felt that he had got the better of his aunt, she flung it right back in his face.

"I shall see you after my speech," Thornton said curtly, snapping the flap of the phone shut.

Thornton Wingate was an exceptionally intelligent man. He had a keen mind that lent itself to cunning and intrigue. Had Machiavelli penned his magnum opus a few centuries later, he would have undoubtedly titled it *Thornton*. Thornton was well aware of his gifts and took great pride in them. Aunt Anne, however, made him stupid. It's not that she made him *feel* stupid but, quite literally, she *made* him stupid, for she also possessed his gifts, but in a far, far greater measure. In her presence he was reduced to a drooling, lip-twiddling imbecile.

In most cases, when confronted with such an intractable nemesis, Thornton simply had the person whacked. Aunt Anne was far too clever to allow that to happen, though. She was old, however, very, very old. Thus, Thornton accepted that his only path to her money was to allow time to take its course. *But time*, Thornton thought now, as he often thought when thinking about Aunt Anne, *is bloody well taking its time.*

THE SENTIENT SOLUTION

"Watson, would you come here?"

Dr. Watson rose from his chair near the fire and went to the window where Holmes stood. He measured his pace to ensure that he wasted not a second of the Master Detective's time, yet not with such haste as to upset the furniture.

"Yes, Holmes?" spluttered Watson, somewhat winded for the exertion, as well as flustered from discomfiture; for he was prescient that he would, as was the custom in his relations with Holmes, presently be made an ass of.

"Watson," said Holmes, looking out onto Baker Street, "what do you make of that woman on the corner?"

Watson swallowed hard and directed his gaze whither Holmes indicated.

"She appears to be ... well ... somewhat young," stammered Watson.

"*Touché*, Watson," said Holmes, turning to look at him. "*How* 'somewhat' young?"

"Well ... *rather*... somewhat young," elaborated Watson.

"She is three and twenty years of age," pronounced Holmes.

"But how on Earth could you know that, Holmes?" Watson ejaculated, his voice abubble with astonishment.

"If you observe, it is clear, Watson, that she is not wearing a wedding ring. What requires more careful observation is that her complexion begins to turn ever so subtly to the sallow.

Given these two factors, it is simplicity itself to determine her age; because it is precisely at this age when a spinster enters upon her wizened fate."

"But she is, nevertheless, a rather handsome woman."

"Then tell me, Watson, why has she not, at such an advanced age, plighted her troth?"

"I am really at a loss to say, Holmes."

"Observe her attire and comment upon it to me."

"It seems to be of fine quality, Holmes, though not of the latest in fashion."

"Which would indicate?" Holmes prompted Socratically.

"Well, because … uh … she chooses to dress so?" Watson offered, with some trepidation that this was not the response which Holmes had sought to elicit from him.

"No, Watson, the female never *chooses* to ignore the dictates of fashion. The antiquated garments would indicate that our young spinster has suffered a decline in fortune. And that would result in?"

Watson furrowed his brow, raised his eyes to the ceiling and stroked his chin with purpose. After a time, a spark shone in his eye and he slapped his right fist into the palm of his left hand.

"By Jove, Holmes!" Watson cried with epiphanic glee. "That would result in the dearth of an adequate dowry to attract the interest of a gentleman of her same station!"

"Well, bugger me, Watson! You've got it!"

Watson tingled with pride. This proved to be short lived.

"And you find it of no particular significance," continued Holmes, "that a woman of such station should be wearing a cloak, the front of which is covered in swine ordure?"

Watson winced. He looked afresh at the woman.

"Well, yes, Holmes, one might surmise that the particular … uhm … state of her apparel could be of some … significance." Watson's voice ebbed to a mumble.

Holmes glowered at Watson.

"Yes, Watson, one *might* surmise that. One might also surmise that the circumstances which have resulted in such a misfortune are very much related to the matter which brings her to us." Holmes returned his attention to the woman. "Her pacing is growing less restless; thus, she will have begun to gather her courage and shall be ringing our doorbell presently. Go and inform Mrs. Hudson that, upon taking the lady's cloak, she is to convey it straight away to the Chinaman's. He is to be expedient in its lavation, and to return it here by the close of my interview with the woman."

"At your service," said Watson, leaving the room in search of Mrs. Hudson.

Holmes continued to observe the woman, who was now crossing Baker Street in the direction of 221-B. Watson, having completed his errand, returned to the parlour. Forthwith the doorbell rang, followed shortly by a knock at the parlour door.

"Enter, Mrs. Hudson," instructed Holmes.

The door opened and Mrs. Hudson showed the young woman in.

"A Miss Anne Throppe to see you, Mr. Holmes."

"Thank you, Mrs. Hudson," said Holmes as Mrs. Hudson abandoned the parlour, closing the door behind her.

Holmes approached the woman.

"How do you do, Miss Throppe," he said, clasping her hand. "Allow me to present to you my friend and confidant, Dr. Watson."

Watson bowed.

"It is a pleasure to meet you Miss Pigshit ... I ... ur ..."

"Watson."

"Holmes?" Watson said crisply, feigning dignity.

Holmes flicked his forefinger in the direction of a small stool located in the far corner of the room.

"Yes, Holmes," Watson said with a marked lack of crispness, and slunk thither.

"Please, be seated, Miss Throppe," said Holmes, waving to an armchair near the fire. Miss Throppe took her seat and Holmes sat opposite her. He took a small turquoise box from the table, opened the lid and proffered it to her.

"Cocaine?"

"No, thank you, Mr. Holmes. But a cup of tea would be most restorative."

"Watson."

"Yes, Holmes?" Watson said, jumping to his feet.

"As Mrs. Hudson is away on another matter and we require tea, I am entrusting you to procure it. Do you believe yourself a match for the task?"

"Oh yes, Holmes. Quite surely, Holmes!" Watson, confidence regained, scurried out the room.

Holmes watched him leave, briefly pondering upon the whimsy of fate and why it should have deemed fit to have furnished him with Watson as his one and only friend. He quickly, however, returned his attention to the matter at hand.

"Tell me, Miss Throppe, what brings you from Prigston with such flurry?"

"How ever did you know that I have come from Prigston?" Miss Throppe exclaimed, leaning forward in amazement.

"Excrementally, Miss Throppe. I observed you from the window, noting that your cloak was coated in porcine unpleasantness. Judging from the freshness of it, I deduced that its application could not have been made but more than fifty minutes prior to your arrival here. A flustered female will walk at the rate of one mile per twenty-seven minutes. She will also, on unfamiliar terrain, and wearing unsuitable footwear, stumble once every seventy-three yards, adding thirteen minutes to the cumulative time. The site of your meeting with this mishap, therefore, could not have been farther than one point two miles away; that could only be Channing stockyard, which lies thirty-six degrees northwest of here. It can be easily surmised that you are not a swineherd's wife but, quite the contrary, a woman of station, albeit of withered means. So, drawing a direct line from here through Channing stockyard leads to the only district appropriate for a woman of your class–Prigston."

"Why, Mr. Holmes, you are even greater that your reputation would have it!" Miss Throppe exclaimed.

"Miss Throppe, you have seen nothing yet," Holmes said, flicking a speck of cocaine from his cuff.

A terrible crash of shattering china and the metallic resonance of a tray falling to the floor sounded from the other side of the door.

"It would appear, Miss Throppe, that tea shall be delayed."

There came a light tap at the door.

"Come in Watson, go quickly to your stool, sit and be silent," directed Holmes.

Watson quietly complied.

Holmes now eased back into the chair, crossed his legs, touched the tips of his fingers together and closed his eyes.

"But now, Miss Throppe, let us hear your tale of woe; spare no detail."

Spinster Throppe collected herself. Her tale was thus:

"Mr. Holmes, I am descendant of the Dorkshire Throppes, whose ancestry can be directly traced to England's greatest of warrior kings, Laurel the Hardy. In the early years of the last century my family entered into the commerce of slaves, which enjoyed great custom and established us well. With the deplorable betrayal of the Whigs in Parliament, and the ensuing abolition of said commerce, we were forced to abandon that endeavour and to seek another. My family then embarked upon the burgeoning opium trade. My grandfather, Alexander Pope Throppe, was a confidant of Prime Minister Melbourne and was instrumental in prevailing upon him the prudence of compelling China to desist from obstructing its importation. The attendant conflagrations were woeful, but our family thrived quite satisfactorily from the outcome.

"My father, Colonel Winthrop Throppe, was a distinguished officer in the Eighth Hussars. As a man of commercial affairs, however, he was in want of acumen. Often was the sad occasion when my father would find himself in the hands of the Jews. Resultant was the waning of our fortunes. Upon his passing, I was legated a meager income that I have seen necessary to supplement with the fruits of my labor. For the past two years I have been in the employ of Lord Heathrow Uppspew of Prigston in the capacity of governess to his children Ernest and Bertrand and ... and ... I ... I ..." Miss Throppe grew silent.

"Please continue, it is crucial," Holmes implored the spinster.

"Well, actually, I have rather forgotten what the whole point of my coming here in the first place was," said Miss Throppe, whereupon she indulged in a moment of silence to gather anew her thoughts. "Oh yes, of course!" she ejaculated upon recollection. "Upon awakening this morning I found, beneath my bed, the body of a dead man."

Holmes elevated his eyelids.

"It is a rather singular occurrence," said Holmes, "for a man, alive or dead, to be beneath or, for that matter, anywhere in the vicinity of the bed of a spinster governess. Was this man of your acquaintance? More to the point, was he, shall we say, an *ami de coeur*?"

"Mr. Holmes! What do you imply?" Miss Throppe stiffened her back. "Only one man has ever trespassed upon the sanctity of my chamber—and that man was quite unknown to me—and quite *dead*!"

"Miss Throppe, I imply nothing," Holmes said with weary annoyance at this intrusive burst of female emotion. "I am solely concerned with establishing the circumstances which have led to the presence of a dead man beneath your bed. In this domicile, the responsibility for indignation at the hint of a wavering of society's standards of moral rectitude is left wholly to the pedestrian mercies of Dr. Watson."

Watson nodded slightly, careful not to be excessive in his enthusiasm, given that he was at a bit of a loss as to whether this commentary constituted flattery.

"Tell me, Miss Throppe," continued Holmes. "What do the police make of this?"

"I have not, as of yet, informed them."

Holmes fixed his gaze upon her.

"Neglecting to inform the police of the discovery of a corpse beneath one's bed is rather unorthodox, would you not agree, Miss Throppe?"

"Well, Mr. Holmes, as is all of England, I am well familiar with Dr. Watson's chronicles of your adventures. The portrait painted of Scotland Yard is that of a rather ineffectual, dare I say bumbling, lot. I thought it best that you should be the first to examine the evidence in its pristine form."

"Wisely done, Miss Throppe. The police shall have ample time to bungle this singular affair." Holmes rose to his feet, as did Watson, followed by Miss Throppe. "But now let us proceed without further delay to the scene of this most intriguing mystery."

There was a knock at the door and Mrs. Hudson entered.

"The Chinaman has returned Miss Throppe's cloak," said Mrs. Hudson, helping her on with it.

"Mrs. Hudson, would you be so good as to engage the services of a cab."

"Yes, Mr. Holmes," said Mrs. Hudson, taking leave of the parlour to effect this request.

"Thank you so very much, Mr. Holmes," said Miss Throppe as she, Holmes, and Watson abandoned the parlour. "My cloak was in such a deplorable state."

"It was my pleasure, Miss Throppe. I am well aware of the interest that a lady of three and twenty takes in her appearance."

"You flatter me, Mr. Holmes."

"How so, Miss Throppe?"

"I am not three and twenty, Mr. Holmes, but rather nine and twenty."

"Indeed?" said Holmes, his countenance betrayed by an uncustomary hint of perplexity. "I do seem to be rather off the mark."

Holmes ushered Miss Throppe out of the door and closed it behind him.

The hinges creaked thunderously as Miss Throppe pushed open the heavy oak door and led Holmes and Watson into her chamber. In contrast to the grandeur of the rest of the Uppspew manor, it was a small room, measuring but fifteen by twenty feet; devoid of frivolous decor and spartan in its furnishings. In the northeast corner of the room stood a wardrobe and to the left of it was a washstand with bowl and pitcher. There was a window on the west wall of the room beneath which was a writing desk and wooden chair. The remaining piece of furniture was the bed set in the southeast corner of the room, unremarkable in any way save for the two boot-shod feet protruding from beneath.

"Miss Throppe, would you be so kind as to allow Dr. Watson and myself to conduct our investigation alone. These matters are best expedited with a reduced assemblage."

"Certainly, Mr. Holmes. I shall be just outside if you require me." Miss Throppe left the room, the door closing behind her with an ear-splitting creak.

Holmes and Watson approached the bed and crouched down to examine the lifeless man beneath it.

"What do you make of it, Watson?"

"Well, Holmes, he is undoubtedly dead."

"It comes to mind," said Holmes, turning his gaze upon Watson, "that I have never actually *seen* this medical degree which you profess to have taken." He sighed, and returned to his examination. "It seems he has been thrashed rather thoroughly about the head." Holmes rose to his feet. "But we shall return presently for a more detailed examination of the corpse. For now, there are a few other questions which require my immediate attention."

Holmes went to the window. With magnifying glass in hand, he methodically went over every inch of the frame, sill, and exterior. He then began a study of equal fastidiousness of all four walls. Crouching on his haunches, and standing on a chair at times, Holmes left no spot unexamined. Upon completion of this task, Holmes returned the magnifying glass to his coat pocket. He stood in ponderous silence for quite some time before he spoke.

"Watson," said Holmes at last. "Do you notice anything queer about these walls?"

"No," Watson responded in a weak peep.

"Keenly observed, Watson!" exclaimed Holmes. "If a struggle to the death had taken place here, we would invariably find these walls bathed, splashed, splattered—at the very least speckled—with blood. On these walls there is not a trace of the crimson liquid of life."

"So you are saying, Holmes, that the murder could not have taken place here?"

"Or, if it had, it was at the hands of someone against whom this wretch harboured no mistrust; thus being taken completely unawares."

"Do you believe he might have been brought to this room posthumously; through the door or, perhaps, even through the window?"

"Through the window not, Watson. There is no recent marring of the frame or sill, neither are there hairs nor clothing fibers. Whether the body had been brought in through the door remains to be determined upon further investigation of the house and interviews with the members of the household. I shall now, however, occupy myself with a more extensive examination of the corpse."

Holmes prostrated himself and crawled under the bed.

"Let us see," came Holmes' voice from beneath the bed. "Our victim was two and thirty years of age, an ostler by trade, lived in the East End, had a common-law wife, and was the father of five children."

"Truly amazing!" Watson cried as Holmes crawled out from under the bed. "But I am sure you will once again explain how it was that you deduced such information with a description of your method that will make it appear simplicity itself."

"Yes, Watson, simplicity itself," said Holmes as he handed Watson a sheet of paper. "In his pocket I found this document, upon which is written all the information that I have just related to you. The name to whom it is addressed, however, has been smudged over with blood and is illegible. The letter is from a solicitor. It appears that the victim had been remiss in his responsibilities toward the woman and children. This letter proposed to remedy the situation through the garnishment of his wages. What is unclear, Watson, is this."

Holmes opened his hand to reveal a small, hard, white chip. "I retrieved this from the most prominent of several lacerations on the victim's head. What do you make of it, Watson?"

"It appears to be some sort of a stone," said Watson upon examining it.

"A stone it is not. Look at the luster, and the ridge pattern. Observe that its weight does not correspond to its size, were it a stone. No, Watson, this is not a stone, but, rather, a piece of the protective covering of some sort of mollusk."

"*Mollusk?*" repeated Watson, his voice awash in bafflement.

"Yes, Watson—*mollusk.*"

Miss Throppe led Holmes and Watson down the stairs and into the game room. They had requested an interview with Lord Heathrow Uppspew, and it was there where he was always to be found. The game room was oak paneled and imposing. Its walls were lined with cabinets containing scores of hunting rifles, above which were mounted the trophy heads of many a formidable beast, which bespoke frequent safaris through the Dark Continent.

In the centre of the room was a magnificent billiard table. Standing next to it was a man of medium height and hearty build. He had the sort of thin mustache that was popular with the sporting gentlemen; beneath which was a large mouth containing large teeth with large gaps between them. His black hair was oiled and combed back close to his head. He wore a blue blazer with a crest over the left breast pocket, white trousers and a red cravat–the sort of bold and extravagant attire which was coming into fashion among the jaunty and gay fellows of London. They found him engaged in the task of disassembling a billiard stick and placing it into a fine leather case.

"Lord Uppspew, may I have a word with you?" Miss Throppe said as they entered the room.

"Oh, hullo," said Uppspew. "How jolly nice to see you Miss … Miss ..."

"Throppe, Your Lordship."

"Ah, yes, yes, of course–the governess, I believe? I do hope you're getting on and aren't too terribly put out by any mischief on the part of ... of ..."

"Ernest and Bertrand," interjected Miss Throppe, helpfully reminding Lord Uppspew of the names of his progeny. "Your Lordship," she continued, "this is Mr. Sherlock Holmes and his assistant, Dr. Watson. They wish to have a word with you concerning a rather distressing occurrence."

"And what would that be?"

"The discovery," said Holmes, now appropriating the interview, "of a dead man beneath the bed of Miss Throppe."

"A dead man! I say! That's a bit rummy, isn't it?" Uppspew blurted. "Rather incommoding for Miss Throppe, one might gather," he added.

Uppspew directed his eyes to the ceiling in what appeared to Holmes to be a vague attempt at reflecting upon the matter at hand. "Well," he said, appearing finally to deal squarely with the issue, "off to the club." He reached for his cue stick case.

"Lord Uppspew," said Holmes. "If I may impose upon your tenuous attention span for just a brief moment longer."

"For what purpose?" Uppspew inquired with mild bewilderment.

"Just a few questions."

"Concerning?"

"The matter of the dead man beneath Miss Throppe's bed, actually."

"Are you still on about that, old chap?" Uppspew remarked quizzically. "I must say, Holmes, I find this morbid obsession of yours with this whole dead body matter to be rather disturbing." He consulted the clock upon the mantelpiece. "Well, I'm dreadfully late for a snooker match with Charles Dippington. Rather a grudge match, actually. The dear old boy shan't enjoy a moment's peace until he prevails against me. I shan't say *that* day will be soon in coming." Uppspew tittered smugly.

"Lord Uppspew, do you have any idea why there should be a dead body beneath the bed of Miss Throppe?" Holmes inquired, attempting to refocus Lord Uppspew's attention.

"Haven't the foggiest, actually. Don't really fuddlemuck about much with the day-to-day goings on about the place. Rather the reason one has servants, isn't it?"

"So you heard nothing unusual coming from Miss Throppe's chamber last night?"

"Wouldn't, really. I seem to remember that her chamber is on the other side of the house from those of the family. I somewhat recollect that Miss Throppe, at one time, occupied one that was closer but, if memory serves me correctly, she found the howling somewhat irksome."

"The howling?" Holmes said, arching an eyebrow.

"Yes, rather queer family trait; we Uppspews howl in our sleep. Something or other to do with six hundred years of marrying our cousins. Rather off-putting for Miss Throppe, being the light sleeper that she is and all. I remember quite clearly when I was informed of this because I could not but think how rummy a condition that was. Not once in my entire life has anything *ever* disturbed my sleep."

"Thank you, Lord Uppspew, you have been most helpful," said Holmes. "Perhaps I could now have a word with Lady Uppspew."

"Of course," said Uppspew, searching for the cord to the servant's bell. Finding none, he bellowed.

"Ewinthrall!"

A short, thin, white-haired butler shuffled into the game room.

"Yes, Your Lordship?"

"Ewinthrall, send Lady Uppspew in."

"Your Lordship," droned Ewinthrall, "Her Ladyship passed on seven years ago."

"Really?" Uppspew said with a lilt of bemusement. "Was I informed of this?"

"Yes, Your Lordship," droned Ewinthrall. "On several occasions."

"Oh ... Well, right. I see ... Very well, Ewinthrall, thank you."

"Yes, Your Lordship," droned Ewinthrall, exiting the room.

"Frightfully sorry, Holmes," Uppspew said after a moment of confused silence. "Wish I could be of more assistance." He snatched up his cue stick case. "Right, must dash! Wouldn't want to keep old Dippy waiting for his thrashing. Insult to injury, simply not on. Well, ta ta, carry on and all that," chirped

Uppspew, abandoning the game room with a spring in his step.

"Well, Holmes, that interview was most certainly a fruitless employment of our time," said Watson after Lord Uppspew's departure.

"*Au contraire*, Watson," said Holmes as he produced from his waistcoat pocket a small box, opened the lid, took a pinch of cocaine, lifted it to his nostril and sniffed crisply. "*Au contraire.*"

Suddenly, that familiar gleam that Watson recognized so well appeared in Holmes' eyes.

"Watson!" cried Holmes, "let us betake ourselves to the nearest public house!"

"Holmes, do you believe that we shall find the key to this riddle there?"

"No, Watson, I believe that we shall find whisky there."

Holmes marched out of the game room with Watson at his heels.

The Slothful Beagle was smoke-filled and raucous. As Holmes and Watson made their way through the crowd, a short, grizzled old man, in want of razor and teeth, approached Holmes.

"Fitiz damarderer whatya belookin' fer, aynew whota basserbe," rasped the old man.

Holmes, scowling at him, removed his timepiece from his waistcoat pocked and snapped it open. "Sixteen minutes to the hour of seven," he said, snapping the timepiece closed, returning it to his pocket, and continuing on toward the bar. "Ginmonger, we require two whiskies with soda," he commanded.

"Two whisky 'n' soda, Gov," responded the ginmonger.

"Holmes."

"What is it now, Watson?"

"Well, as you are aware, my former career was that of assistant surgeon in the Fifth Northumberland Fusiliers."

"And hearing this yet once again would be of some possible interest to me because–?"

"Whilst serving in Afghanistan," continued Watson, "interaction with the soldier class was unavoidable, many of whom were of the very sort we are now amongst in this tavern. In my daily contacts with them I was able to develop a rough, yet passable, understanding of their plebonic vernacular."

"Rose to the challenge, did you Watson? Commendable."

"Well, the point, Holmes, is that the old idler who approached you a moment ago was not inquiring as to the hour of the day but, rather, indicating to you that he had information relevant to the matter concerning the murdered man beneath the bed of our hapless spinster."

Holmes spun on his heels to face Watson.

"By God, Watson! There's a drop of utility in you after all!"

Watson beamed.

"Come, Watson," said Holmes as he strode towards the old man, who was now seated at a table near the hearth. Holmes stopped before the table.

"Old man, how do you know of this murder?" asked Holmes. "It has not yet come to be of public knowledge."

"Aye guttah nefyoo woot warkfer t'Uppspews asa fuumin. Toolmi 'boot demardar'ndet Mistah Holmes 'er beaht ta 'oossnewpen 'boot."

"He has a nephew in the employ of the Uppspews as a footman who informed the old man of the murder, and that you had been at the house to investigate it," translated Watson.

"And what is it that you know, old man?" Holmes asked.

"Wootay noo kint be tild witoowta paynta bittah tah sooze miparch't trote."

"He's thirsty and would like a pint of bitter before he speaks."

"Ginmonger, a pint of bitter," shouted Holmes, as he and Watson took seats at the table.

"Coomin' rait uup, gov," said the ginmonger, pouring out a pint and bringing it to the table with the whiskies. The old man, with a shaky hand, put the pint to his withered lips and took a hearty draught.

"Now that your uvula has been bathed in its unguent, tell us what you know about this crime," said Holmes.

The old man wiped the foam from his mouth with the back of his hand and told his tale.

"Einydaft fuh'enfool coosee twasacumin."

"It was common knowledge that this tragic event would come to pass," translated Watson.

"Elucidate," instructed Holmes.

"Eh?"

"Woota fuhkya tookin' boot?" translated Watson.

"Oh. Tastif wharshagen datart Throppe."

"You impudent scoundrel!" Watson shouted, slamming his fist on the table.

"Translate, Watson, translate!" Holmes interjected.

"The dead man, according to this reprobate," Watson said through clenched teeth, "was amorously involved with Miss Throppe."

"And who was the dead man?"

"Haywara Wilshm'n naymah Gynwrath Sufford."

"He was a Welshman by the name of Gynwrath Sufford." Watson paused, considering the content of what he had just translated. His face flushed with rage and he sprang to his feet.

"How dare you insinuate that a lady of Miss Throppe's breeding and position would be cavorting with a *Welshman*! Why, by George! I shall give you the thrashing that you so justly deserve, you ... you–!"

"Watson," Holmes said wearily, "you would confer a great service upon me if you would, for the remainder of this interview, contain your chivalrous zeal and confine your utterances to the translation this old idler's gibberish into the Queen's English."

Watson composed himself and relapsed into his chair.

"As a service to you, Holmes, I shall."

Holmes resumed his inquires. "And who would have killed him?"

"Tuuhderbloke wut wunah be shagenuh. Be awog naymah Ricardo Joya."

"His rival, A Spaniard by the name of Ricardo Joya."

Upon hearing Joya's name, the tavern erupted into clamorous demands that he be horsewhipped and hanged. Some supported the position that he be hanged and then horsewhipped.

"So, old man," said Holmes when the din had subsided, "you would attribute this crime to jealousy."

"Nay. T'oonar."

"No. To honour," translated Watson.

"Whose honour?" asked Holmes.

"Datart'soonar."

"Miss Throppe's honour."

The old man elaborated.

"Tis loykdis: Dastif'n datartah benahkin itouf ferataym. Joya, coarse, dint loykdis noon boot eh new nunkin bedune tachenge harhart, soo heeispetah disishun. Den, turnsouw dastif, Gynwrath Sufford, gah faive bassars witah nutterhuur. Wun Joya harkdis e'goos fuh'en nuhts. Sey taynt rit fer huur ta soofa sootcha hensalt. E cuumin'ear 'n waz ollarin, 'ayhm gwintah stumpiz boolyx'n den kiltaht basser Sufford.'"

Watson balled his hands into fists, took a deep breath and translated.

"The tale is such: The dead man, Gynwrath Sufford, and Miss Throppe had been involved for quite some time. Joya, understandably, was greatly miffed, but he knew he could not change Miss Throppe's heart, so he respected her decision. It came to light, however, that Sufford was the father of five children by another woman. When this came to Joya's attention, he felt it unjust that Miss Throppe should suffer such an insult. He became quite distraught and publicly pronounced his intentions to do grievous bodily harm, followed by murder, upon the miscreant Sufford."

"And where can we find this spirited Spaniard?" asked Holmes.

"Fooc tif aynoo. Noon've laydayz oopon 'im saynse tatafernune."

"His whereabouts are unknown. He has not been seen since that afternoon in here."

"I have no further questions," said Holmes as he rose from the table, tossing a shilling to the old man and starting toward the door with Watson in tow.

"Balderdash!" exclaimed Watson. "Not a word of truth to it."

"Truth, Watson, is what I must now seek alone. I shall see you back at the hearth later this evening."

Before Watson could utter a word, Holmes had jumped into a passing cab and was gone.

The howling wind whipped the rain against the carriage as it clattered to a halt outside of 221-B Baker Street. Watson had used to good advantage the absence of Holmes to attend to his medical practice, though it seemed to him that it had declined somewhat considerably since he began to inform his patients of his dedication to rooting out villains in the company of his housemate, The Greatest Detective the World Has Ever Seen.

Watson opened his umbrella to shield himself from the brutal elements and stepped into the squall. Pushing his way towards the house, he espied a figure in the doorway. As he approached, Watson made out a blowzy harlot bedecked in the most scandalous of attire. She wore a black skirt, which, oddly, appeared to be made out of leather and rode shockingly above the knee. On her legs were stockings of some sort of mesh. She had a large handbag slung from her shoulder and there was a tawdry faded pink boa around her neck. Her hair was a garish blonde color of the sort that would be produced by applying the chemical peroxide to it, her shoes had heels that resembled railroad spikes and her face had a thick application of white powder with blotches of rouge on the cheeks, and her lips were painted scarlet.

"Well, 'ello there 'ansome," said the trollop to Watson. "Lookin' for a good time?"

"Distance yourself from my home and my presence, slatternly strumpet!" Watson bellowed, secretly delighting in the opportunity to give free rein to his moral indignation without reproach from Holmes.

"Watson, you really must take a more objective view of the human condition," came the voice of Holmes through the painted lips of the tart. "If for no other purposes than those fundamental for the detective–understanding motive and *modus operandi*."

"Great blazes! Is that you, Holmes?" Watson stood agape for some short while before collecting himself to speak again. "I was aware of your talent for disguise, but this is really quite remarkable! Why are you dressed so?"

"This is not the issue at the moment, Watson. The issue is that I have forgotten my key and, lest I induce hysteria in Mrs. Hudson at the sight of me, I have chosen not to ring the doorbell but, rather, to await your arrival. You have now arrived, and we are but a few paces from our fire and pipes. I suggest, therefore, that we transfer the venue of our conversation to the parlour."

"You forgot your keys, Holmes? That's rather unlike you; then again, *this* is rather unlike you."

"Unlock the door, Watson," Holmes said, testily articulating each word.

"Oh. Right ho."

After only relative difficulty, Watson achieved the objective of opening the door, upon which Watson squished, and Holmes swished, to the parlour.

Reaching the fireplace, Holmes took his pipe from the mantel, filled it with tobacco and lighted it.

"Pray tell, Holmes. Where have you been and what have you learned from your seemingly rather queer adventures this evening?"

"I have been on the scent, Watson, beginning with the where, why and what of Senor Ricardo Joya." Holmes took a contemplative draw from his pipe and released the smoke slowly.

"And what have you discovered?" Watson inquired.

"One or two matters of some interest. I first searched out Joya's residence, a rather dreary flat located at 1996 Atlantis Way where he resided with his mother. There, I was fortunate enough to encounter Joya's landlady, a compatriot of his by the name of Senora Cotilla. True to her profession, she was exceptionally well informed of the minutiae of her tenants' lives, and most eager to recount to anyone willing to listen all that she knows. It would seem that Joya was a rather feckless chap. Frustrated in his attempt to incorporate himself into the Constabulary, he secured a position as a night watchman for an East End fish market. He was a socially inept lad whose principal avocation was to have himself photographed dressed as a Gurkha and sneering with bravado."

"But you speak in the past tense, Holmes."

"Astutely perceived, Watson, for Ricardo Joya has gone."

"The blackguard!" hissed Watson. "Murdered and fled!"

"It appears, Watson, that Joya was so keen in his desire to flee that he did so two full days before the murder."

"What?" cried Watson in astonishment.

"What I have discovered, Watson, is this: On the evening of the third of March, there was a great ruckus coming from the Joyas' flat. It was on that afternoon that Ricardo Joya had announced his murderous intentions toward Sufford in the Slothful Beagle. His mother had become aware of this, as well as of his infatuation with Miss Anne Throppe. She approved neither of his plan to slay Sufford nor, much less, of his passion for a Protestant. She insisted that they return immediately to their ancestral village of Lepe, Spain. She seems to have won the day because the next morning they booked passage from Plymouth to Santander and were on the ship that very afternoon. My sources in Spain have informed me that he did indeed disembark there at seven in the morning on the day previous to the discovery of Sufford's body beneath the bed of Miss Throppe."

"But ... who–?! How–?!"

"Watson, do stop blathering and listen. You will remember that when Miss Throppe first appeared at the corner of Baker Street I deduced from the stage of her wizening that she was three and twenty years of age. You will also recall that at the end of our interview Miss Throppe informed me that she was, in actuality, nine and twenty years of age. There is but one explanation for such a forestalling of the wizening process– Miss Anne Throppe is a spinster by only the strictest of legal definitions."

Watson regarded Holmes with a dull gaze.

"As an appreciation for subtlety seems to escape you, Watson, I shall speak the word–*venery*."

"For all that is sacred, Holmes! I can scarcely believe it! Miss Throppe is such a sweet flower."

"It is precisely that, Watson, which has kept her flower so sweet. But, to continue, venery requires company. It then falls to us to determine who that would be. All evidence indicates, and none contradicts, that that person was Gynwrath Sufford."

"So it was true, just as the old idler at the tavern had said."

"Precisely. You will also remember what else he said concerning Sufford."

"That it had recently come to light that Sufford had another woman and five children with her."

"Exactly. The old idler had posited the theory that Joya had killed Sufford over the matter of Miss Throppe's honour. However, Watson, there is a fury that burns even more ardently than that of a chivalrous suitor manqué–it is that of a scorned female."

"Yes, I do remember the Bard mentioning that they can be rather unpleasant."

"Now, Watson, let us hark back to our interview with Lord Heathrow Uppspew. You had concluded that this was a fruitless employment of our time, but he provided us with one piece of vital information–that Miss Throppe was a light sleeper. You will recall the thunderous creak that rang out upon opening the door to Miss Throppe's chamber. Had anyone entered there during the night it would not have gone unnoticed by her and, as I deduced upon my examination of Miss Throppe's chambers, the only possible ingress of a body, dead or alive, would have been the door.

"It is my conclusion that Sufford entered the chambers alive, of his own volition, and with the consent of Miss Throppe. There, within that chamber, is where he met his doom. That he was struck repeatedly about the head indicates that the arm that wielded the instrument of death was a weak one. Sufford fell to the floor and crawled under the bed in a vain attempt to escape. Death befell him within moments."

"But what was the instrument of death?" asked Watson.

From his handbag Holmes pulled a stone-like object the size of a rugby ball and set it on the table with a great thud.

"There you have it, Watson!"

"Great Scott, Holmes! What *is* that?"

"It is a conch, Watson."

"On the soul of the Queen!" Watson ejaculated. "You don't mean–?"

"Yes, Watson," Holmes said gravely. "Gynwrath Sufford was conchwhipped to death."

"Good God in Heaven, how awful!" gasped Watson, a shudder coming over him.

Watson and Holmes sat in mournful silence for some little time to regain their composure, so unsettled were they by the horror of so dastardly a deed.

"But where would this conch have come from?" Watson asked, breaking the silence.

"The mollusk," replied Holmes, "which inhabited this conch thrives only under conditions where the water temperature never rises above sixty-five degrees, nor falls below thirty-five; the depth of the sea must also be no greater than twenty feet. There is but one region of England which fits these requirements–Dorkshire."

"What a coincidence, Dorkshire is whence Miss Throppe comes," said Watson.

"I assume that you would also deem it a *coincidence* that I came upon it on a stroll from Prigston to here–by way of Channing stockyard."

"Wait one moment, Holmes!" said Watson, gnarling his visage and scratching his head–an indication that Watson's cerebral capacities were being strained to their limits. "Great Holy Child of the Most Perfect Union! *Miss Anne Throppe*!"

"Watson," said Holmes. "I find your interjections to be increasingly unfathomable and bizarre."

Watson squinted intently at Holmes.

"Aha!" Watson exclaimed. "So that is why you are clad in such attire."

"Your segue eludes me, Watson."

"You wanted to test your theory of how long it would take a woman to walk from Prigston to here!"

"Uh ... yes. Yes! Precisely," said Holmes. "Of course, that is the reason. Well, as I was saying ..."

"Though it does seem rather queer," Watson interrupted, "that you should dress as a tart to measure the speed at which a spinster would walk."

"Watson, could you wrest your concentration from the trivial and allow me to finish?"

"I'm sorry, Holmes. Please continue."

Holmes cleared his throat. "Well ..."

"It strikes me, also, as rather queer," interjected Watson, "that whenever your investigation calls for dressing as a woman you never invite me to accompany you."

"Dash it, Watson! I do not have time to explain to you my proclivities ... that is to say, my *methods*."

"I apologize, Holmes," said Watson slumping into his chair. "It is simply that I cannot make heads nor tails of this whole affair. Why on earth would she have come to *you*, of all people, Holmes?"

"Hubris, Watson. She would have believed that by coming to me directly she would have dispelled any suspicion. As far as my ability to implicate her in this sordid affair, it appears, she would have feared little. The reasoning powers of the male, any male–regardless of his reputation to the contrary–are disdained by the conchwhipping female. Yes, Watson, that would have been the reason she had come to me, had she committed this vile act. But I digress into supposition, dear Watson– because Miss Anne Throppe is innocent."

"Innocent!" cried Watson.

"Yes, Watson–innocent. The murderer of Gynwrath Sufford is Ricardo Joya. I have informed the police of this and they are, at this moment, initiating the procedures for his extradition to England–the first leg of his journey to the gallows."

"Holmes, I ... I ... I am befuddlement itself," stammered Watson, shaking his head slowly. "You have indicated that there is not a trifle of evidence to implicate Joya, yet the evidence against Miss Throppe is overwhelming. Why ... it seems obvious."

"The obvious, Watson, is what you are now overlooking."

"I don't understand, Holmes."

"Think back, Watson, to the old idler in the Slothful Beagle. What was his opinion regarding the murderer?"

"Well, Holmes, he was indeed convinced that the culpability clearly rested upon the head of Ricardo Joya."

"And the view of the other loungers in the tavern?"

"They were of the same mind."

"And you yourself, Watson, did you at any time harbour any doubt as to the guilt of Joya?"

"Until just a few moments ago, not a wisp of doubt."

Holmes grabbed the *London Chronicle* from the table and threw it to Watson."

"Read the headline!" bellowed Holmes, throwing one end of the boa over his shoulder, dropping into his chair, and crossing his legs with aplomb.

Watson read: "'*Wog Whacks Welshman.*' By Jove! Of course, Holmes, of course!" Watson shouted, bounding to his feet. "Popular opinion believes unquestioningly that he is the murderer *and* the press has denounced him! The guilt of Ricardo Joya is indisputable! How could I have doubted it for a moment? It is simplicity itself!"

"Dare I admit, Watson, that for a time, I, too, found my judgment clouded by the facts."

Watson breathed a contented sigh. Returning to his chair, he put his feet up on the ottoman and lighted his pipe.

"Ah, Holmes," mused Watson, "there is no greater leisure for a man than that which comes after a job well done"

"So true, my dear Watson, so true," concurred Holmes, kicking off his high heels and plunging a syringe-full of seven-percent solution into his arm.

And all of England slumbered serenely.

THE COWS COME
HOME TO ROOST

The door to Lady Throppe's victorianesque parlour opened and Ewinthrall shuffled in. Ewinthrall had been the butler for the Uppspews and Lady Throppe had inherited him, along with everything else, when Bertrand, who had been her charge as governess and, later, her husband, died within a few weeks of their marriage.

Though Ewinthrall had shuffled when he was with the Uppspews years before, now, at age one hundred and fifty-seven, his shuffle had lost some of its former spring. Lady Throppe never tired of holding up Ewinthrall's longevity as irrefutable proof of the salubrious effects of utter servility.

Though Lady Anne Throppe looked old, she was even older than she looked–and she looked *really* old. How old, no one really knew. Quite unlike Ewinthrall, however, her longevity was far from being due to utter servility. Though Anne Throppe had technically served in her life, specifically in her capacity as a governess to Lord Uppspew's children, Ernest and Bertrand, she had far more ruled than served. No, her secret for longevity was that tried-and-true method that has served so many others. She lived on and on because she was evil incarnate.

"Your Ladyship," said Ewinthrall. "His Prime Minister-ship is here to see you. Shall I show him in?"

Before Lady Throppe could answer, Thornton, having bored of this old-fashioned time-wasting nonsense, pushed his way past him.

"Get out of my way, you doddering old fool!"

"I am so terribly sorry to have displeased His Prime Ministership," Ewinthrall said with life-prolonging obsequiousness. He turned to Lady Throppe. "Shall there be anything else, Your Ladyship?"

"Get your wrinkled arse out of here before I kick it, with you attached, through the fucking window, you past-your-expiry-date piece of sniveling crap!" Thornton shouted.

"My ineptitude shames me," Ewinthrall fawned, tacking on a few more years. He turned and humbly shuffled out, closing the door behind him.

"When is that old git going to curl up and die?"

"Never, Thornton, if you continue to make him grovel so."

"Have you asked me here to elaborate on your theory of longevity? I certainly hope so. Because it would be such a shame if the prime minister's time were to be wasted on anything *trivial.*"

"Thornton," Aunt Anne said with the steady tone of exasperation she employed while speaking with him. "Referring to oneself in the third person is a mannerism which becomes men of Caesarean stature. One rather cringes, however, upon hearing it employed by a quivering, inconsequential worm."

"Aunt Anne, I am the prime minister of ..."

"Thornton, shut up. The problem which I have asked you here to discuss is of a rather serious nature and it would be of enormous help if, for once in your life, you could dedicate just a few brief moments to acting as if you had been blessed with an intellect somewhat rising to the level of that which God has seen fit to bestow upon your average hamster."

Thornton's legs began to tremble violently. It had been terrifying enough when Aunt Anne, in their telephone conversation, had referred to a *problem*. She was now terming it *of a rather serious nature*! Thornton just managed the two steps to the nearest armchair before his legs gave out and he collapsed into it. Lady Throppe sighed and then went to the drinks cart to pour Thornton a generous scotch with a parsimonious splash of soda. Thornton took the drink with trembling hands and drained it. He inhaled deeply, exhaled tremulously, and slumped back into the armchair to await the deluge.

"It seems, Thornton, that our ancestor, Laurel the Hardy, was not all that he was cracked up to be."

Laurel the Hardy had been the king of England in the late tenth century. History and legend had it that he had successfully repelled the invasion led by Gance the Able, the then king of Normandy, thus keeping England free from Norman rule for over a century and a half until the coming of William the Conqueror. The figure of Laurel the Hardy, for almost a thousand years, had been a great source of national pride and his name was still invoked by English football fans at matches between England and France (*Be it soon, or be it tardy, we'll kick the Frogs' arses like Laurel the Hardy!*).

Thornton had based his entire political career on being a direct descendent of Laurel the Hardy and, thus, the standard bearer of his stellar legacy. The poster for Thornton's first campaign had him, in full armour, lance held high, atop a fine white steed. The slogan on the poster read: *The Blood of the Warrior Courses Within.*

"What ... what are you talking about? Thornton stammered, having recovered somewhat from the initial shock.

"Thornton, you're speaking again, rather than listening." Aunt Anne cleared her throat and continued. "Something has been uncovered."

Uncovered was a word that terrified Thornton. He lived in constant fear of that word and his name appearing in the same headline. He began to tremble violently again.

"An unfortunate document has been discovered," Aunt Anne continued.

"What sort of … document?" Thornton managed to splutter out, his voice no higher than a whisper due to the constriction of his throat.

"A poem."

"A *poem*?"

"Yes, Thornton, a poem."

A wave of calm swept over Thornton and he began to laugh.

"Aunt Anne, a poem is hardly a *document*," Thornton said, continuing to laugh, both out of relief and, once again, with the feeling that he was finally able to prove Aunt Anne a fool.

"It is an historical poem," Aunt Anne said dryly.

"Oh, an *historical* poem," Thornton mocked.

"As such," Aunt Anne continued, "it is, or it is believed to be, based at least partly on truth."

As if being hit with a bucket-full of ice water, Thornton stopped laughing. The word *truth* had the same effect on him as the word *uncovered*. He, nevertheless, did not relapse into his previous state of terror. It was, he thought, still only a poem.

Aunt Anne went to her writing table and picked up a magazine, which she brought to Thornton. He took it and looked at its title: *Your History: The Magazine That Finds Old Stuff and Then Prints It.*

To Thornton, *Your History* sounded ominously like *you're history*. Nevertheless, he mustered what, in Thornton's case, could only vaguely be described as fortitude, and flipped through it until he found the poem.

THE SONG OF LAUREL THE HARDY

Whylom[1] waes in Aengland a chivolrous king,
The deeds o his noble lyf herein now we sing.
Fer honours so bestoed him, Laurel waes he naymd,
Fer brayvry in battaile, waes far and wyd he faymd.
Shirk nought he from joust, nar he from party,
And swa[2] he waes kowthe[3] as Laurel the Hardy.
Baptyse Laurel at birth did Charles the Chaplain do,
And later did confirm him swa Abbot Cousteleaux.
As a yong gome[4] fought he fiersly againes the hethen Moor,
The sweet savour o blood he quikly crayvd galore.

Retornd ta Chrisyandom, tho, he soone missd his sadel,
Pined he oh so despretly ta be againes in battaile.
Potterin adai[5] boute the garden at home
Nis[6] nought the lyf for a spirited gome.
Woe waes that hwen the Wars o Fayth they did cease
Thar camme oer the land an unfortunat peace.
However fer a king o his caractor

---

1   **whylom** Once upon a time.
2   **swa** so/such
3   **kowthe** known
4   **gome** man
5   **adai** during the day
6   **nis** isn't

T'wolde be a cynch incitin a war;
But ta facioun a force o victoryous might,
With another army he wolde haf ta unite.
Swa ta Mabel of Normandy his troth he did plight,
And with swa an allyance he redyd ta fight.
Now with his army, and that o his wyf,
Laurel the Hardy wended serchin fer stryf.

Ta Arbuckle the Fat, king of Denmark,
By ryder conveyd he this vexin remark:
"Wer it that myn hound hadde the fayce o thyn mother
Shave its arse and walk it backwards ik[7] druther."
Ta Eggihard of Gaul he did aver
His doughtar ta be slattern, his wyf ta be hur.
Nought unserprysin, ta Arbuckle it roild;
And nought neede it ta sey, Eggihard boild.
The Hardy decyded ta put them a-redy
Ta assure that the battaile be vishous and bledy;
Attakin them without theyr ful deployment
Nought wolde provyd swa much enjoyment.

Now goaded, the foes wolde prepar fer the fray,
The Hardy and host wolde soone wende on theyr way.
Unite they wolde with Gance the Able,
King of Normandy, father of Mabel.
They wolde feast and drynke and they wolde revel,
And then meet Eggihard ta scramble the devil.
After cwenchin themselfes with rivers o gore,
Wende they ta Denmark ta slaughter sum more.
A wunderful contryvance waes it this scheme–
At leest ta the Hardy swa it did seeme.
So plan he adais and eke anights[8]
Ta faren[9] abroad and endevour these fights.

---

7 **ik** I
8 **adais and eke anights** during the days and also the nights
9 **faren** go

Comme one dai, though, a thayne did call
Ta invyte the Hardy ta looke oer the wall;
The Hardy beheld hwat waes now within ken—
He colden't but notyce sixti thusand o men!
Hwen the armys and angry knyghts he espyd,
"Holy moly!" waes the blasfemus oath that he cryd:
"Rather than us venterin thither,
They han united and brought themselfes hither!"
On the horizen, but briskly proceedin,
Camme the foul foe, with Eggibert and Arbuckle a-leadin.

With cunning and wyl, Laurel thought fast;
He turnd ta the thayne, hwo waes lookin aghast:
"Quikly, gome, chapeth[10] thee a sturdy yong steede!
Fleeteth thee ta Normandy, proclaym oure grave neede!
Ta myn father'n law mayke him know oure morass,
And bid him speede commin ta sayve oure sad ass!
Oh knyghts and brave thaynes, man ye the walls!
It seemes a bit o misfortune is aboute ta befall us;
But with eager erls and loyle lieges
Smyte will ik the foes hwo besiege us.
Archers, aloft! Taut ye yourn bows!
Hail them with arows, let's see howe that goes."

Flye did the arows with a blood curdlin swoosh:
"Oh Eggihard, oh Arbuckle, take those upp yourn tush!"
The arows fellen like dead flys upon theyr shields;
Nary an inch o grounde gaind did the siegers thus yielde.
As the thick-armourd men marched on tward the moat
The Hardy decided ta get at theyr goat:
"In yourn heavy thick mayle act ye lyk otters;
Mayke myn day merry, comme swimme ye the waters."

---

10   **chapeth** mount

A thayne that waes cleped[11] Clovis Killmirth
Mayde known ta the Hardy the licoury[12] dearth:
"Sire, before thou geteth thyn hopes upp too highe
Thou might like ta wotte[13] that the moat is bone drye."

Laurel raysd his eyes ta the hevens and this he did swear:
"Oh Lord, colde ik get just a smidgen o helpe here?"
Laurel braught his arms doun and slappd at his thigh:
"Myn ideas are waynin, but let's gife this one a trye.
Bring out the cauldrons, fil them with oyl,
Light the fyre neath them, bring them ta boyl."
As the attackers clammourd upp the walls with a roar
The cauldrons wer tilted; the oyl they did pour.
Insyde the foe's armoure did bubble theyr gore.
"Quik," cryd the Hardy, "bring us somme more!"
"Ne can do," seyd Killmirth. "Oure oyl stock hath ben lowe
Ever saynce ya tolde the Sultan hwere he colde go."

The defenders abandond the empty oyl pot.
Unsheathd they theyr swerds ta repel the onslaught.
Roland Bloodglutton, Eggihard's vassal,
Waes the fyrst ta lepe oer the wall o the castel.
Swingin his broadswerd, throtes he waes slashin;
Wealdin his polax, heds he waes bashin.
The ithers soone followd and joynd in the fraye.
"Comme hither," seyd Laurel "mayke ye myn dai!"
So camme the moment of truth fer the knyghts,
And engayge did they alle in glorious fyghts.
The clang o steel and the shrekes o payn
Brightend the dai o the most melancolic thayne;
Flyin wer faingers, ears, and the odd piece–
More funn colden't be hadde hwilst wearin thyn codpiece.

---

11   **cleped** called
12   **licoury** watery
13   **wotte** know

Laurel beheded a knyght and tornd ta his right;
Thar he saw Eggihard a-redy ta fight.
"Well looke now hwo hath comme oer ta call,
Unwar[14] Eggihard, the gaule[15] frem Gaul."
"Prepareth thee ta die," seyd Eggihard, hissin;
Vengance wolde be his fer Laurel's foul dissin:
"Myn wimenfolk's virtu thee quastion *that*, lout?!"
"Quastion it, never–fer its lack nay ik doute."
Irkd by this insult, Eggihard did lunge;
This affront ta his honour he wolde expunge.
The swerd missed the Hardy by a foot'n a haffe,
Hearty and loud the Hardy did laffe:
"Eggihard, fer swerdwieldin nay thou seemeth fittin;
Hath thou ever considerd takin upp knittin?"
Eggihard lyfted the swerd frem his side–
"Stop!" cryd the Hardy. "Thyn shoo is untyd!"
Eggihard lookd down ta see if this wer the case,
Fergettin that armourd bootes han't no lace.
With a swoosh frem Laurel's swerd Eggihard's hed neetly split
"Eggihard, oh Eggihard, thou wert elways a twit."

Clever, however, waes Arbuckle the Fat;
Doin him in nolde[16] be swa easy as that.
The Hardy's men fought brayvly and true,
But comme none-tide[17] they wer just aboute through.
Hackd upp bodys and body parts,
Enuf ta fill a thusand carts,
Litterd the castel frem wall ta wall,
And scores o men continue ta fall.
Sadly waes ebbin the deffender's resistence
Hwen a clarion waes heard off in the distance.
The Hardy tornd his notice ta wence camme the sound,

---

14   **unwar** foolish
15   **gaule** scum
16   **nolde** wouldn't
17   **none-tide** midday

His heart pitter–patterd at the sight that he found;
Commin oer the horizen wer thusands o lances–
The standard they camme undar waes that o brayve Gance's!

Hwen the enimy saw Gance's men's pikes
They utterd as one a thunderous "yikes!"
Theyr horses did shreke and the men ludly wayld–
Ther aint much amusement hwilst bein impayld.
Nor waes it pleasent, they soone diskoverd,
Hwen theyr faces wer bludgeond and theyr extremitys severd.
But nary a knyght woned[18] ner did one sob–
For, after alle, a job is a job.

Hwat Eggihard and the Fat wraught on Laurel's men,
The Able waes givin back twyce oer again.
The moat that waes empty began now ta flood
With barrels and barrels o fallen men's blood.
The Hardy now saw doun by the stable
Mortal combat betwixen the Fat and the Able.
The Fat fought well but nought well enuff,
And anon the Fat's lyf the Able did snuff.

Now without leaders the invaders alle fled,
Leavin behynd them the dyin and dead.
Cheerd they the victors with a hip hip hoorah,
Standin knee highe in steamin hotte vissera.
"Now," seyd the Able, "that the vanquissed do flee,
Mighte ik haf a confabulashun with thee?"
"Gladly, dear father, thyn counsile ik treasure,
But first answer me this, if it is thyn pleasure."
Laurel askd Gance howe he hadde arrived thar swa quikly,
The answer Gance gave lefte him feelin a bit sickly:
"Given that thyn head is that of a dunder
Ik knew oure allyance wolde cause thee ta blunder;

---

18   **woned** lamented

64

Thus to halt wydowhood for Mabel, myn daughter,
Ik hurryd hither ta forestall certain slaughter.
And methinks that perhaps tis this thou sholde know–
Tis ik, Gance the Able, hwo is now runnin the show."
With Laurel's host in tatters, and the Able's throng strong,
He deemd it unwyse ta tell the Able he waes wrong.
Thus the Hardy did pledge ta seyrve the Gance loyally,
Fer a king ellways knows hwen he's been screwd royally.
Then camme ta Laurel's ear a disquietin babble,
The unmistaykable sound of a wyldly irkd rabble.
The few hwo survived the harrible butchry
Hadde in theyr mynds the followin sech query:
As if in one voyce, the peple did shout:
"Tell us, King Laurel–hwat waes *that* alle about?!"
Ta preyserve the honour of kith and kin
His proclamacion wolde neede elygant spin;
So with gifte o gabb and smermy smyle
The Hardy fiddld the peple's gyle:
"Neary nought thanke me fer preserving yourn lyves;
The deed that ik did fer ya ik wolde gladly repryze."

Quiker than Laurel colde even haf thought it,
Hook, lyne and sinker, the masses hadde bought it;
Hwat hadde moments before ben an unruly band
Wer now eatin with relish frem the palm o his hand.
"Thanke thee, oh Hardy, thyn brayvry is true;
Hwat wolde we do without a leader lyke you?"
"Nought neede mencioun it," ta them did he address;
"Now rolle up yourn sleefes and tydy this mess."
Hwen the peple wer done the playce waes swa cleane
Neary a fainger, nar nose, nar earlobe wer seene.

And swa is the tayle o the commin o Gance
Howe Aengland camme under Normandy's lance;
And thus of tonge and blood and custom we

Gazpacho in Winter

Ne longer purly Aenglish be.
And throughout the land, frem now til ferever,
Laurel the Hardy, ferget thee we'll never.

AFTERWARD

Since its discovery at the University of Dorkshire library where, curiously, it had been misshelved under the category of Bornean Fertility Rituals, *The Song of Laurel the Hardy* has posed one of the most impenetrable enigmas in the history of English literature, and has forced upon the scene one of the most cataclysmic alterations in our knowledge of English history.

When it was written and by whom are now the subjects of the most intense scholarly debate.

Some aspects of *The Song of Laurel the Hardy* can be inferred. For example, the spelling of the poem indicates that it must either have been written before the 15th century by an East Anglian clerk, or after 1995 by an American college senior. The latter possibility, however, was ruled out after its examination by Hugh Trevor-Roper.

Upon its discovery, the text was sent to Oxford where it was authenticated by Trevor-Roper, who determined that it had been written circa 1380, though it recounts events that occurred two hundred years earlier. Trevor-Roper presents no evidence as to why he believes this to be the case, but his track record in authenticating historical documents is so impeccable that no scholarly authority seriously questions his opinion.

The verse of the time tended to be composed in rhyming couplets of eight to ten syllables. That some lines of this poem contain up to fourteen leads some to speculate that it might be the work of Bartholomew the Longwinded (born Bartholomew Prescott, 1335?–1400). Bartholomew held a series of minor clerical posts in the court of Edward the Irascible, for the most part sinecures, his principal work being that of court poet. Later in life, Bartholomew was to fall out of favor with Edward as a result of the offense the king took at the closing lines of the hagiography Bartholomew had composed for his benefactor:

> And ner it be seyd o Edward the Irascible
> That his reign ne hath ben remarkably passable.

To his deathbed, Bartholomew insisted that he had always held King Edward in the highest esteem, but was working on deadline and having trouble finding a rhyme for "Irascible." The falling out, however, ended in Bartholomew's expulsion from the court and the beginning of his life as a troubadour. *The Song of Laurel the Hardy* seems to have been written later in his career, presumably to keep his repertoire sufficiently fresh so as not to find himself relegated to the position of an oldies troubadour.

The impetus to untangle the mystery of *The Song of Laurel the Hardy* came from the University of Dorkshire which, in order for a thorough study to be conducted, provided a two-year endowment to Charles Letton Ph.D., noted medievalist and author of *A Merry Minstrel Am I: Iambic Pentameter and Gender Identification.* The results were disappointing, however, which was later explained through the discovery that Letton had done little else during those two years other than play canasta on the Internet.

Camille Piglia, renowned expert on everything, dealt briefly with the text in her book *Singing the Praises of the Dead White Male: The Phallophilic Eurocentrical Cultural Oligarchy of the Late 14th Century Troubadour.*

> The antidisgynophobic duality of Laurel's disconcupiscent marriage to Mabel of Normandy to "double" his "forces" imbues the *zeitgeist* of an already bifurcated Otherness with what can only be seen as the highlighting of the Emasculating Tautology; a mammolithic somaticism, if you will.

Medievalists are evenly divided between those who disagree strongly with everything Piglia says, and those who disagree with it vehemently. However, with virtually nothing else to go on, she currently represents the accepted view.

Far more revolutionary has been the impact of *The Song of Laurel the Hardy* on our knowledge of English history. The long-held belief that Norman England began with William the Conqueror's victory over Harold in 1066 has now been repudiated by all except the few remaining recalcitrant medievalists who have not already committed suicide or gone mad.

Now submitted to public attention for the first time, *The Song of Laurel the Hardy* is expected to have a severe effect on the English populace in general, who, though never happy with the idea of having been defeated by the French, are expected to have a far more difficult time coming to grips with the notion of having been outsmarted by them.

One of the most groundbreaking discoveries scholars have made through *The Song of Laurel the Hardy* has been the use of words and phrases in the text that were thought to have been of modern coinage. Since there is no evidence of any continuity or constancy in their use from middle to contemporary English, linguists are arriving to the conclusion that there exists the possibility of dormancy in language followed by a seemingly inexplicable resurrection. A new branch of study, narcamorphonology, has developed to examine this phenomenon. In *The Song of Laurel the Hardy*, we see such examples as *twit*, *diss* and *running the show* used in a contemporary manner. This breakthrough has proved invaluable in unraveling such heretofore baffling texts as Geoffrey Chaucer's *Deff Jam*

Phat Citee inna Hous and William Langland's '*Tis a Pity She's a Ditz.*

The language of the poem is presented here exactly as it was written, though I have taken the liberty of adding a minimum of modern punctuation when its absence would have caused unnecessary confusion. The only other alteration to the original text I have made has been to completely rewrite the last few lines because I just didn't like the original ones.

James Trevor

WHEN TOASTERS FLY

Thornton was leaning forward in the chair with his forearms resting on his thighs. He slowly lifted his gaze from the magazine, which slid from his fingers and fell to the floor. He gazed at nothing in particular and his complexion had gone ghostly white.

"Oh, dear," he said at last.

"Oh, dear, indeed, Thornton."

"This is not good."

"No," Aunt Anne concurred, "It is not."

"In fact, it is very bad."

"Indeed it is," Aunt Anne replied. "Have you quite finished blathering, Thornton?"

"Why wasn't I aware of this before?"

"Because you're an imbecile, Thornton."

Thornton began gnawing on his knuckles. He then lowered his head and cradled it in his bony hands.

"I'm ruined," he said, his tone of voice somewhere between abject despair and bitter acceptance.

"Oh for God's sake, Thornton, you are not ruined," Lady Throppe said testily. "We've simply run across a bit of a sticky patch."

"*A bit of a sticky patch*!" Thornton leapt to his feet. "I've based my entire career on my bloody *blood*! On being a direct descendant of Laurel the Hardy! And now it turns out that he was the ass who was single-handedly responsible for handing the entire bloody country over to the bloody *French*!"

"In the afterward to the Song of Laurel the Hardy," Aunt Anne said, "there is one point upon which that twit Trevor is quite correct–it is one thing to be defeated by the French, it is quite another to be outsmarted by them. Admittedly, this will be a bit tricky to smooth out."

"*A bit tricky!*" Thornton screeched. "I can see the *Sun's* headline now: '*Bienvenues Froggies: Welcomes Wingate's Witless … Wadmal–? Wallydraigle–? Waesucks–?*'" Thornton concentrated on searching for a synonym for "ancestor" which began with *W*.

"Thornton, completing your alliteration is of rather little importance at the moment. Shall we return our attention to the pressing matter at hand?"

Thornton returned his attention to the pressing matter at hand.

"Oh, God! Oh, God! Oh, God! Oh, God! I'm ruined! I'm ruined! I'm ruined! I'm ruined!" Thornton moaned, his face turned toward the heavens and his arms held out in supplication.

"Thornton, defeatism was not the attitude that enabled me to prevail over Sherlock Holmes."

"I don't want to hear *another fucking word* about Sherlock *fucking* Holmes!" Thornton screamed.

Lady Throppe, who was facing Thornton, reached behind her where a conch was set on a small table. She grasped it and deftly swung it around against the left side of Thornton's head. Thornton did a half cartwheel, landing on the crown of his head. For just the briefest of moments, his upside down body did a perfectly perpendicular handless headstand before it crumpled to the floor.

The door to the parlour quietly opened and Ewinthrall shuffled in, carrying a basket. He had heard the familiar sound of conch cracking against cranium and was efficiently going about his routine. He took a fresh conch from the basket and placed it on the small table. He then turned to Lady Throppe.

"Will His Prime Ministership be one whom we shall be reviving, Your Ladyship?"

"Yes, I am afraid we shall have to," Lady Throppe sighed. "But not just now, I am so enjoying the peace that is afforded by the absence of his babbling."

"Yes, Your Ladyship," Ewinthrall droned as he picked up the broken pieces of conch from the floor and placed them into the basket.

Thornton began to twitch, and the corners of his mouth were frothing.

Lady Throppe heaved another sigh.

"Well, I suppose we must bring him to now lest that minuscule portion of his brain which he vaguely employs suffer permanent damage."

"Yes, Your Ladyship."

Ewinthrall shuffled to the drinks cart, took a seltzer bottle and shuffled back. Aiming the nozzle at the prime minister's face, Ewinthrall spritzed a reviviscent spurt.

The prime minister spluttered. He sat up slowly and held his head in his hands until he had recovered his senses sufficiently to allow speech.

"For God's sake, Aunt Anne," Thornton shouted. "I wish you would stop *doing* that!"

"Conches don't kill, Thornton, blathering idiots do."

Thornton mulled that one over for a moment but decided that trying to figure out the logic of it was contraindicated to the recovery of someone who had just been conch-conked senseless. It did have a calming effect, though, and he crawled back into the armchair.

"There is a solution to this, Thornton."

Thornton looked at her with bleary, yet beseeching, eyes.

"Do you remember Margaret's standing in the polls before the Falkland War?" Aunt Anne asked.

"Very low," Thornton answered weakly.

"Precisely. And during and after the Falkland War?"

"Very high," Thornton answered weakly.

"Precisely."

Aunt Anne said no more. She watched Thornton to see if he was capable of arriving at *four* from the summation of *two* and *two*.

"War against the French?" Thornton finally said, believing that this was what she was driving at.

Aunt Anne sighed. Thornton had added *two* and *two* and had arrived at *three*.

"No, Thornton. Our motives, if we were to declare war against the French in the wake of this revelation concerning our ancestor, would be *obvious*. Besides that, it would foster that much more animosity against the French, and, thus, that much more resentment against Laurel the Hardy, and, by association, you."

"Yes, I see," Thornton said, rubbing the side of his head. "But, then, war against whom?"

"It doesn't matter against *whom*!" Aunt Anne said, growing annoyed. "Just as long as the French are on our side, are our allies, are our friends."

"Our *friends*?"

"Yes."

"The *French*?"

"Yes, Thornton, the French."

The expression on Thornton's face was of the sort that most probably greeted Einstein when he began telling people that a toaster flying faster than the speed of light could quite likely end up in the Mesozoic Era. In his time, Thornton had betrayed friends. He had incited murder. He had committed crimes against humanity. He had engaged in acts of perversion that would have caused the Marquis de Sade to blush.

But make friends with the French?!

Aunt Anne understood that her suggestion should undoubtedly be met with horror and incomprehension; thus, she hastened to soften it.

"Well, not forever, Thornton. Just until the elections are over. And, besides, it's not as if such a thing has never happened."

Thornton looked at her dumbfounded.

"Most recently the Second World War," Aunt Anne said.

"The Second World War?" Thornton asked, mystified.

"Thornton," Aunt Anne replied with strained patience. "Do you remember in the latter part of the 1930s when you were about to be conscripted into the army and your father made a telephone call, whereupon you spent the following six years working as a colonial administrator in Gualla Bora?"

"Yes."

"That was the Second World War."

"Oh."

"If we were to unite with the French," Aunt Anne continued, "the notion could be woven that what Laurel the Hardy did was part of a long-term strategy."

"But how could we get the French to go along with it? What would they get out of it?"

"We must simply wait for France to tumble into chaos and anarchy, thus sending the French government teetering on the edge and scrambling for anything to grasp onto."

"But how long could that take? We don't have all the time in the world. The elections are coming up soon," Thornton said, his voice once again beginning to evince panic.

"How long could that take?" Aunt Anne said, taking her turn to chuckle patronizingly. "You seem to be forgetting something, Thornton."

"Which is?" Thornton inquired.

"Which is, Thornton, that the French have had to establish five republics when one republic, for those who approve of that sort of government, generally serves most people quite adequately. Which is, Thornton, that the French declared war on the Germans without the foresight of having an army on hand with which to greet them. Which is, Thornton, that in 1968 France was brought to its knees by rambunctious university youths participating in a somewhat amplified version of what I believe is referred to in the current vernacular as a 'rave.' Which is, Thornton, that the French awarded its highest honour for artistic genius to Jerry Lewis. Which, in short, Thornton, means that undue patience is not wanting in the matter of France's tumbling into chaos and anarchy. The French, after all," Aunt Anne concluded, "are the French."

THE OVERZEALOUS AMERICAN WHO BROKE THE SPIRIT OF THE NATION OF FRANCE

"*Avec le bon vin, il-y-a la belle vie!*"

Frank Slaughter chirped as he punctuated his bon mot with a "*pop*" *de resistance* that was unanimously acknowledged with a light round of applause by his dinner guests to be, yet again, a masterful un-corking–this time a Maison de Chat Beaujolais (1976).

Frank acknowledged the praise with a smooth chuckle and deftly splashed a dash of wine into his own glass to flush out any bits of cork, as well as to release the bouquet–Frank's fluency in these matters was *savoir faire par excellence*. He then poured a *tâte* for the guest to his left.

The guest, Maynard Mainott, the mayor of Duluth, Minnesota, scooped up the limited edition piece of 1876 Yvette Yalaiphe crystal stemware, as if it were a Budweiser can, jerked it around under his nose, took a slurp, rinsed his mouth and gargled noisily.

Obviously the man does not distinguish between a '76 Maison de Chat Beaujolais and Listerine, Frank thought as he smiled graciously at the peasant. *Let's just hope he doesn't spit it on the floor in a final display of vinous connoisseurship*. Mayor

Mainott nodded his approval. "Tray bien," he croaked with a fingernails-on-chalkboard mid-western nasal shrill.

"I'm glad you find it … yummy," Frank said. *Though a poor second to cheery Koolaid, I'm sure*, he thought.

The other dinner guests snickered at the barb, which, of course, had gone right over Mayor Hayseed's head.

"Perhaps another … glug?" Frank said as he kept his gracious smile fixed and filled Mainott's glass with more of the "tray bien" wine. (Which, in fact, was one of the finest selections from Frank's cellar–no small *pommes de terre*, for a private wine collection that Robert Parker had once described as "ass-kicking.") Mayor Mainott took another swig and Frank noted, much to his surprise, that Mainott did not belch after *every* gulp.

Frank let the matter drop. Normally, especially given such a fish in a barrel as Gomer here, he would have spent the evening subtly, yet unrelentingly, whittling away at this hoedunk philistine, to which the bumpkin would remain oblivious. This was a source of great amusement for Frank's regular circle. Few turned down an invitation to dine at Frank's when the guest of honor was a client from any of the fly-over states. Mainott was quickly proving himself to be the most splendid of fish, and all were aquiver with the expectation that Frank would, after this initial round, soon be blasting away into the barrel.

Tonight, however, would not be the night–for there was something that was pulling Frank's attention away from the sport. It was not something that he could put his finger on, but there was something that was drawing him away, drawing him in.

The evening wore on and, by the standards Frank had established for his dinner parties, was a dismal failure. It lacked the main ingredient that had come to be expected–Frank. His acerbic wit and suave repartee were glaringly absent. He was present in flesh alone. Recognizing this early on, the guests, much to Frank's relief, called it an early evening. The last one to leave, the peasant from Duluth, was still telling knock-knock jokes as Frank closed the door on him. Frank grabbed a bottle of Napoléon armagnac (1952) and a Yvette Yalaiphe snifter and went directly to his study.

As he sipped his Napoléon, it dawned on him. What had distracted him this evening was his own brilliance. He began to recognize that what he had been feeling was that Warm Glow. It was the Warm Glow that would come over him whenever he coined a Good One (of the Rather Clever variety).

Frank, who was in his mid-thirties, was a sturdily built man ($2000 a month health club membership) with a chiseled face (chin dimple, $47,000) and a rakishly bohemian coiffure (which, to maintain its look of unkempt indifference, required twice-weekly visits to Mario's at $350 a pop). A fleeting look at Frank's wardrobe spoke volumes as to the exquisiteness of his taste. On this evening he wore an Yvonne Abette sewer-sludge brown, soft-finished, worsted suit with pinstripes too subtle for the naked eye to perceive; a curdled-cream beige shirt, and a rust-colored crêpe de Kyrgyzstan necktie, both woven from the silk of free-range worms; and a pair of Enrico Massima close-soled, cap-toed, subtly polished, chestnut shoes that fit him in the insteps like a pair of condoms. To punctuate his ensemble, he wore a tie pin and matching cufflinks hewn from the gold teeth wrenched from the mouths of a select group of highly cultured Burmese political prisoners.

If a glimpse of his wardrobe did not suffice, the most cursory glance around Frank's Central Park West apartment–decorated in a highly individualized retro version of Neo-Classic Eclectic by designer Coco de Claunne and *decoré* with a harmonious *manage* of much-coveted Dismalist and post-Dismalist artwork–testified to his *savoir faire* in recognizing quality and strongly indicated, given the rarity of many of the pieces, his know-how in acquiring them.

As vice president of Carl Burnett, a top Madison Avenue ad agency, Frank's talent centered on coming up with Winners. He was the father of *You're a young, upwardly mobile kinda guy and you need an Oral-B toothbrush to fit your lifestyle*, and *Kraft Velveeta—for the woman of today who knows who she is, where she's going and what kind of aerosol-ejected processed cheese-like substance she wants*, and, what the industry considered to be his masterpiece, *Here at Enron, we're working for you*.

Frank's current specialization was in updating city mottos. Many cities were discovering that the mottos they had rallied behind in pioneer days or, in the case of many suburbs, the post-World War II years, reflected views of life that were virtually unfathomable to their modern-day denizens. Thus, for example, Frank had updated Chinuga Falls, Montana's motto from the mystifying *Through Courage and Perseverance We Shall Prevail* to the more readily comprehensible *Hey, I Don't Know Nothin' About It*. He had overhauled Rolling Fields, Illinois' increasingly enigmatic *Progress Through Community Participation* into the much easier to get behind *We Want It All, and We Want It Now*. And, for Frank's standard fee of $80,000, Duluth had now shed its crusty and crumbling *The Zenith City of the Unsalted Seas* for the peppier *Catch the Spirit!*

Frank's passion, however, was coining Rather Clever Ones. These earned him no money but, as Frank believed, vastly contributed to the advancement of humanity. These were the *bon mots*, the *phrases justes* that expressed the most profound thoughts and feelings of mankind, separating it, in its highest form, from the animal kingdom (or, at least, from the sort of people who lived in Duluth). He immediately intuited that *Avec le bon vin, il-y-a la belle vie* was a Rather Clever One of the *crème de la crème la plus haute*.

The dawn light backlit the Roger Doger pus-yellow drapes, which bathed the study in a diffused ecru hue. The morning found Frank, who had worked feverishly throughout the night, drained but content. He had mapped out the essence of the campaign, but details had to be worked out. Lots of details. Frank slipped his laptop into his Yvette Youdoux sacred-cowhide attaché case, showered quickly, threw on an everyday gray double-breasted Armani silk suit, and was off.

☙

"Hold all my calls and reschedule all my morning appointments," Frank snapped as he briskly strode past Nancy into his office and closed the door with curt determination. Nancy got the coffee percolating. She knew that this would be one of the mornings when Frank's regular breakfast of *café au lait avec croissant* would be substituted for an endless stream of American coffee.

Frank sat with resolution at his desk, snatched up the phone and speed dialed the Paris office of Publicité et Nous, a company Frank had dealt with for years, and which he trusted.

"*Allô.*"

"*Allô*, Robert Deuquí, *si vous plait*," Frank said in impeccable French.

"*Pardon, mais, avec lequel vous voulez parler?*"

"What?" (Frank's impeccable French had its limits.)

Eventually it was established who he was and to whom he wished to speak.

Frank liked Deuquí. He got things done. He also spoke English with such a thick accent as to pleasantly delude Frank into thinking that their conversations actually took place in French.

"*Oui?*"

"Deuquí?"

"*Oui.*"

"Frank *ici*, let's talk turkey, Deuquí."

"*Oui,*" Deuquí responded, aware of Frank's penchant and, thus careful to pepper his conversation with *oui, c'est bien, ou la la, c'est la vie* and a handful of other high school French words and phrases.

"We're talking the Bait and Wait approach, Deuquí. Billboards, full-page newspaper ads, prime time TV. *Comprendez vous*? White backgrounds, red letters. Are you ready for this, Deuquí? *Avec le bon vin, il-y-a la belle vie.*"

This was the first full sentence in French the Deuquí had ever heard Frank utter and, consequently, it didn't click in immediately.

"What do you want the ads to say?"

"What?"

"The ads."

"What ads?"

"Your ads."

"I just told you, Deuquí."

A pensive silence crackled across the line.

"Oh, the wine thing, you mean?"

"Yes, *the wine thing*," Frank hissed. "Are you paying attention Deuquí?"

"Yes, yes, I mean *oui, oui*. I got it, uhm '*Avec le bon vin, il-y-a la belle vie?*'"

"*Tres, tres bien,*" Frank replied sarcastically.

Frank discussed a few more details with Deuquí and then hung up. The first phase was in motion and must now run its course. The Bait and Wait approach was ideal for this sort of thing. Normally this consisted in clogging the media with something enigmatic. People begin to wonder. They begin to ask each other what it could mean. In short, they pay attention. In normal circumstances, the follow-up would come a few weeks later, clarifying just what product or service was being hawked. These, however, were not normal circumstances. There would be no follow-up in a few weeks, nor a few months, nor, for that matter–ever. The phrase would simply linger on and the curiosity would grow stronger until, finally, what would remain would be *Avec le bon vin, il-y-a la belle vie* indelibly engraved into every French brain, rolling off every French tongue. *C'est la vie, vive la différence, ou la la* and every other expression would take a backseat. *Avec le bon vin il-y-a la belle vie* would be the most spoken, the most heard, the most FRENCH of all *belles phrases*. And Frank would be its creator.

I'm getting ahead of myself, Frank thought, snapping out of his daydream. *Way ahead of myself.* He eased back in his chair, put his feet on the desk and clasped his hands behind his head. *I must wait. I must be patient. And when the time is right, and only then, will I implement Stage Two.*

❧

The weeks passed and the campaign was going along better than even Frank's most optimistic dreams. His moles were reporting back that *Avec le bon vin, il-y-a la belle vie* had now become the generic toast in cafés and restaurants throughout France. It was even being modified to express other concepts of well-being, i.e.: *Avec le bon snooze; belch; nose-picking; dump; etc., il-y-a la belle vie.* It was also being pilfered to promote products that, under normal circumstances, would have sent Frank scrambling for his lawyers. But these were far from normal circumstances, and Frank was walking on air.

The irony of it all was that what Frank considered to be a masterpiece of *belle phrase* was, as can clearly be seen, wholly unremarkable. What Frank saw as brilliance, in effect, shone most brightly for its triteness–which, of course, explains why it caught on so quickly and became so phenomenally successful. This was the sort of thing Frank would generally have recognized; but pride in the child will blur even the sharpest-eyed father–even when, to others, the offspring is clearly an obnoxious little shit.

Caught off guard by the speed with which it had taken hold, Frank found himself scrambling to put Stage Two into motion.

Stage Two centered on the "respectability" that any word or phrase would need to be truly French–the approval of the omniscient and omnipotent Académie de la Langue Française.

This prestigious body, which allowed *faire le looping* (to curl hair) into the dictionary only after eighty-seven years of debate, three duels, and a sizable contribution (from the hair dressing industry) to the Retired Lexicographers' Prostitute Fund, was, clearly, not easily, or at least cheaply, malleable.

Stage Two was divided into two steps:

Step I, which Frank codenamed The Piece of Cake, entailed getting *Avec le bon vin, il-y-a la belle vie* into a work of literature. No problem–shake a tree and easily compromised writers rain down on you. Frank's advance team had dug one up in a matter of days. A check for the equivalent of a month's rent and six cases of gin was sufficient to persuade Alex de Toquejoint, professor of contemporary culture at the Sorbonne, to include the phrase in his essay arguing the connection between the introduction of rear-view mirror fuzzy dice and the Algerian debacle.

Step II, which Frank codenamed the Tricky Bit, required getting the majority of learned members of l'Académie to vote it into the next dictionary. Given, first of all, the backlog of words on the docket (they were still trying to coin a French word for "jitterbug"), it could be decades before they even got around to reviewing it, let alone approving it. Frank, wisely, was not overconfident, but stoically plodded on.

As demonstrated in the case of de Toquejoint, one time-worn way to streamline its consideration and better insure its acceptance lay in bribery and its cousin, blackmail. Frank's reluctance to adopt these measures was not a mark of his ethical nature (he was, after all, in advertising) nor of a belief in the incorruptibility of the esteemed members of l'Académie. (When, after all, was the last time you ever saw the police drag someone out of an adult cinema who wasn't wearing a wrinkled tweed sports coat and horn-rimmed glasses?). No, what caused Frank to falter was the expense. But falter long he didn't. Just as Michelangelo had endured seven years flat on his back with paint dripping into his eyes and Pope Julius riding his ass, so too would Frank suffer for his art. Alas, in the interest of humankind, Frank put off having his weekend place in the Hamptons remodeled, and sunk the whole wad into *Avec le bon vin, il-y-a la belle vie.*

Initially, everything went smoothly and relatively inexpensively. That thirty-seven percent of the members of l'Académie had gambling debts that needed servicing or led lives of sufficient indiscretion as to incur only minor detective fees in ferreting out extortionable dirt led Frank to no false illusions. This was statistically in tune with all non-Amish societies. It was the remaining fourteen percent that would demand the greatest amounts of time, effort, money–and luck–especially given that a peccadillo would have to be pretty wonking for a Frenchman to feel the need to pay to cover it up.

The months had passed and, with hard work and perseverance, most had fallen. Most, except for at least one more member who Frank would need for a tie-breaking vote. Of the remaining members, nothing, *nothing*, could be found on them that even hinted at their receptiveness to bribes or their vulnerability to blackmail. Frank, as strong-willed a man as they come, was falling prey to doubt. Not only in peril was his contribution to French culture, but his whole concept of human nature. Could it be that "character" was creeping toward the majority level? Could it be that incorruptibility was overtaking cynicism, abuse of power, and moneylust? Was it possible that honor, duty, pride, dignity, loyalty, honesty, integrity, courage, generosity, fortitude, humility and decency were now the order of the day?

The phone rang.

"Slaughter here."

"Giggle, giggle! Tee hee hee! *Moutons*! Tee hee!"

"What?"

"Hee hee hee! *Moutons*! Eh … uhm, as you say in the English—sheep! Ha ha ha!"

"Sheep?"

"*Au cuir*! I mean in leather! Ho ho ho, ha ha ha!"

Through the laugh-contorted enunciations Frank recognized the voice of his chief investigator, Yves Drappe.

"Yves, what are you talking about?"

"Sheep in leather!"

Frank's mouth went dry. He was beginning to piece it together.

"Who?"

"*He*!"

"Who he?"

"Henrí, hee hee!"

"Henrí?"

"*Oui.*"

"Henrí *qui*?"

"Henrí Brie, hee hee!"

"*The* Henrí Brie?"

"*Oui.*"

"Gee!"

Frank hung up. Though stunned for a moment, it didn't take him long to realize that an armagnac and cigar were in order. He rose and went to the liquor cabinet and took out a bottle of Napoléon 1878; the grapes of which having been stomped by an elite squad of Bengali eunuchs. He poured a generous amount into a Yvette Yalaiphe snifter, returned to his desk and took a Manolo Suarez Embarco Especial pre-embargo cigar from the Maxwell Ekland olive-ashwood humidor. He rolled it between his fingers and passed it under his nose and, after savoring the rich aroma, snipped off the end with a Savinelli Giorgio platinum guillotine cutter. He then lit it unhurriedly with an L.B. Dupois black lacquer and palladium trim ligne. Frank sat and rested his feet on the desk.

Popular support. Institutional approval.

Frank had done it.

❧

The weeks and months passed (as did the days, hours, minutes and seconds, for that matter) and Frank had been working 24/7 on the long and arduous task of transforming Scramton, West Virginia's city motto from *God, Country, Toil and Truth* to the zippier, and more accurate, *Tippin' the Scales at 300 Pounds and Still Gobblin' Down Them Donuts*. Clearly, if anyone on this planet deserved a vacation, it was Frank. He thought this a perfect opportunity to pop over to Paris for a hear-see.

Frank had been getting bits and snippets back regarding the success of his baby, but he was unprepared for what he found on arrival. From every corner, *Avec le bon vin, il-y-a la belle vie* rang out. Edith Cresson had even modified it into one of her most popular catch-phrases, *Avec la disappearance des homosexuals anglo-saxones, Il-y-a la belle vie*. After an overpowering and exhausting day of drinking it all in, Frank had a light dinner of *sauté de rate* and called it a night.

Back at his suite, Frank flipped on the TV. The program was *Apostrophe*. He recognized the guest as Claude le Patritue, a balding, red-faced, rotund scholar of mid-Gaulish poetry, heavily into debt and flagellation. He was better known to the French as the country's leading curmudgeon, who would say anything to roil. The subject of the debate was "The role of neo-modern quasi-nihilists in post-Marxist cafés." Claude had the interviewer in fits by pronouncing that God was indeed alive and truly did like cleanliness. Frank tried to listen but, drifted into a pleasant sleep, bathed in the warmth of hearing Claude intoning *Avec le bon vin, il-y-a la belle vie*. Had Frank managed to stay awake, he would have heard the context in which it was used. A context in which, unbeknownst to Frank as he was flying out early the next morning, would send the nation of France hurling into the bottomless abyss. Frank slept soundly as the Gaulo-Armageddon entered upon its course.

As Frank slumbered, this is the course the conversation took:

Interviewer: "Come on now, Claude. *God ... existing*?!"

Claude: "Quite assuredly."

(Audience growls, hisses, boos, and makes that sort of *bouff* noise that only French people make.)

Interviewer: "This is unconscionable!"

Claude: "Well, if an American can come up with *Avec le bon vin, il-y-a la belle vie*, then anything's possible, don't you think?"

If a pin had been dropped in Alsace at this moment, its reverberation would have thundered all the way to Saint Tropez.

☙

Back in New York, Frank, having found contentment, no longer needed his work at Carl Burnett for his *raison d'etre*. He stayed there mainly because, now more than ever, he needed his salary to pay off the enormous debt he had incurred financing his campaign. It was his work, however, that would afford him his next opportunity to visit France.

Due to a triple-digit percentage increase in the consumption of sliced white bread in France, there was an assumption among manufacturers of processed foodstuffs that there would similarly be an increased demand for processed lunchmeat products. Frank was given the turkey-based bologna, or Bolurkey™, account. It could only be his complete indifference to his work which would explain his lack of even the mildest curiosity as to the root of this phenomenon.

✑

The gray Parisian air hung thick with the collective *ennui* of utter meaninglessness. Overnight, following Le Patritue's bombshell, France was plunged into a furious fit of stagnant malaise (seemingly an oxymoron, but you really had to have been there). The day following the broadcast of *Apostrophe*–more specifically the *lunchtime* following its broadcast–wine went unordered nationwide. Consequently, cheese followed suit. (What is cheese without wine? Even the French mice passed it up.) Baguettes, naturally, were the next to go–followed by each and every culinary item in the land of Voltaire. Frank did not know this.

At Orly Frank caught a taxi. Sitting in the backseat, mouth watering, he headed straight for his favorite restaurant, Le Dégueulis Frais, where head chef, Jacques Strappe, prepared what was universally accepted as the world's most sumptuous *Mouffette Écrasée aux Chemin*.

The taxi stopped on the corner of Le Boulevard Maginon. Though two blocks from Le Dégueulis Frais, Frank felt that the constitutional would open up a little more space for one of Jacques' *Mousse de Bûlouinquelle* for dessert. But Frank's heart, soaring as he rounded the corner, quickly plummeted until it splattered against the sidewalk–the windows of Le Dégueulis Frais were whitewashed and the door was boarded up!

Frank was dumbstruck. Had this been the States, the explanation would be simple; some competitor had devised a flash campaign to attract the clientele away to a better, equal or worse restaurant. (Frank was well aware that the quality of the product was quantitatively insignificant once advertising reared its head.) But that's there, not here! What advertising genius could possibly out-catchphrase Jacques' *Mouffette*?!

Frank walked down the street, though not aimlessly. Perplexity weighed heavily on him, but now so did hunger, thus, he was off in the direction of Andre's. Andre's was closed down–as was, as Frank soon found out, Les Deux Pugges, La

Putain Grosse, L'Auge, Le Chaland Gonfre, Les Boyaux and Boustifaille!

Frank entered into a state of panicked confusion. It was as if apples had started falling skyward and the sun was rising in the west! How could eight of the finest restaurants on Earth *just close down*? Frank pulled himself together for one last ditch effort. He hailed a taxi and gave the driver directions to La Mussett.

The taxi pulled away and Frank stood in the chilling rain, staring at the ghost-like emptiness that was once La Mussett. He staggered forward then collapsed into a weeping mass in front of the boarded-up door.

Frank awoke, perhaps hours, perhaps days later. He slowly got to his feet and began to wander aimlessly. His clothing, not designed for huddling in wet doorways of abandoned restaurants, was now in tatters. His post-modern coiffure hung in wet mats over his eyes, which Frank made no attempt to sweep away. He shambled through the streets maniacally moaning a dreadfully accented "*porquoi?*" The occasional passers-by were snapped out of their thousand-mile stare, walking-dead indifference and fled in terror when Frank glared at them and changed his tone from desolation to a fiercely accusative "*PORQUOI?!*"

"Oh my God!" Frank moaned, "*Mon Dieu!*" In a flash, Frank recovered his senses—or at least that was the way he saw it. Actually, he had suddenly taken complete leave of them, but was deluded by the ersatz clarity of the insane.

"An ad campaign, an ad campaign," he now sang as he chased the passers-by through the streets. Frank was a bit perplexed at their unreceptiveness to his one-point plan for national salvation.

"Yes," Frank yelled out as he punched his left palm resolutely. "Something is dreadfully wrong in France ... which rhymes with dance." Frank began to contort his body in what looked like a cross between the minuet and the cha-cha.

"Which rhymes with glance." He turned abruptly in the direction of the passers-by, who had taken safe haven on the other side of the street, and glared at them intensely

"Which rhymes with lance." Frank suddenly charged across the street wielding an imaginary spear, screaming "ugha bugha ugha bugha!" The crowd scattered.

"Which rhymes with happenstance." Frank poised himself to mime "happenstance" when he came to the realization that he had been in the throes of lunacy for the last half hour. Having come to that clear-headed conclusion, he was sucked back into the world of the sane.

I must eat, Frank thought, enjoying the subtly pleasant sensation that ideas could be just as meaningful, if not more so, when they echoed only in you head, and not off the surrounding buildings. Frank, having, of course, rejected the slop served on the airplane (Did those days really ever exist?), calculated (Isn't sanity wonderful? You can calculate and everything!) that he had not eaten for exactly quite a long time. Soaked to the bones, clad in shreds, and recently back from la la land, Frank's survival instincts told him that he must have food–any food.

Frank stood across the street from the McDonald's. It was not hard to find. As a matter of fact, it seemed to Frank that there were a lot more McDonald's in Paris than he remembered–a *lot* more. Frank dismissed this as a misperception caused by low blood sugar and the residues of his recent bout with insanity. But, on the other hand, Paris had certainly changed quite a bit restaurant-wise. Frank shook his head furiously to clear it out.

I'll eat first, Frank told himself. *Then I'll think.*

He began to drag his feet in the direction of the McDonald's, consciously shifting his plodding shuffle for a more dignified, crisper step as he approached it. He tucked in the shreds that were his shirt and spit-combed his tangled hair.

Frank entered the McDonald's with some difficulty. The place was packed. The long wait gave him time for observation and contemplation. *They're not tourists! They're all French! And badly dressed!* Frank watched as they docilely shuffled forward toward the counter, an image that he found strikingly reminiscent of the shift rotation scene in Fritz Lang's *Metropolis. Except it's in color now, garish colors!* Frank thought as he again noticed their dress. *Could it be the new fashion? That would explain why everyone was dressed that way.* Frank tried to convince himself that this was the case. He was unconvinced. Even as a post-modern anti-fashion statement it seemed unlikely. The clothing was just too bad–or not bad enough. *Wrinkled polyester?* Quality camp requires that you at least give the appearance of having spent a good deal of time primping in order to look that bad. But these people looked like they had just thrown these things on–maybe even slept in them. The men's unshaven faces were not carefully cropped, thirty-six-hour "guess who didn't sleep in his own bed last night" GQ stud-trim. They were six-day "guess who hasn't been back to the shelter for a while" Charles Bukowski wino-growths.

And the women! They all had their bra straps hanging off their shoulders! And this wasn't the titillating Cristina Aguilera variety of "Boy, I didn't even notice that one strap has slipped off my golden, silky shoulder and if you hold you breath long enough, maybe the other strap will also carelessly slip off and both of my supple, pert breasts will be in full view for just the briefest moment before I giggle innocently and pull the straps back up and ... oh my! You seem to be turning blue in the face."

No, this was the Kmart, bargain basement, curlers-in-hair, cigarette-ash-drops-into-the-voluminous-cleavage, tattoo-looked-better-before-cellulite-set-in, backhand-across-bawling-brat's-face, phlegm-hacking variety of slipped bra strap.

No, this was not carefully coiffured and coutured *mode-boheme*. This is how people look when they just don't give a damn anymore. Frank turned his attention to their faces–spiritless, lifeless, expressionless. Frank spontaneously shouted out:

"BRIDGETTE BARDOT'S RELATIONSHIP WITH FURRY LITTLE CREATURES GOES BEYOND THE PLATONIC!"

Not a head turned; not an eyelid batted.

He tried again:

"EXISTENCE *DOESN'T* SUCK!"

Nothing.

And a final salvo:

"JOHNNY HALLIDAY CAN'T SING, CHARLES DE GAULLE WAS A BIG POOPY FACE–AND JERRY LEWIS *ISN'T FUCKING FUNNY...* NOT EVEN IN AN IRONIC SENSE!!!"

Nothing.

It was Frank's turn to order. Were this still a country where people gave a damn, heads would have snapped around to look at Frank when he shrieked. It wasn't, so they didn't. Frank was alone in his horror–if "horror" is a strong enough word to describe what surged through Frank when his eyes fell upon the man behind the counter–none other than Jacques Strappe–the chef of Le Déguelis Frais! The man whose *Moufette Érasée aux Chemin* led renowned gastronomic critic, Arve Baston, to announce, upon finishing it, "I shall not profane my palette with anything lesser." Whereupon he picked up an oyster knife and slit his own throat.

Atop Jacques' head, where his *toque de chef* once majestically rested, was now a goofy little cap with golden arches on it.

"May I take you order please?" Jacques droned mechanically, his eyes staring a thousand miles into the distance.

Frank ordered–just what, he did not know. (Though, days later, upon Frank's disappearance, a Ronald McDonald Funland Get the Little Metal Balls into the Grimace's Eye Sockets game was found in his hotel room, which led investigators to speculate that he had most likely ordered a Double Cheeseburger Special™ or a Quarter Pounder Deluxe™, because such a nifty prize would not have been given away with just a regular burger, small order of fries and a small Coke.)

"For here or to go?" Jacques peeped.

"To go," Frank replied, too quickly, perhaps.

Frank pulled some soggy money from his pocket and smeared the bills on the counter. He took the bag and hastened toward the door.

"Stop!" Jacques croaked weakly, but with a certain gravity.

Frank stopped–as did his heart, his soul and his spirit. Defying everything inside himself that said he shouldn't, Frank turned slowly and faced Jacques.

The once celebrated chef looked up at Frank and strained to focus his thousand-mile stare on him. His lips began to quiver and, in what appeared to be the summoning up of his last shreds of will, he spoke.

"You must forgive me, for I have forgotten something," Jacques said forlornly.

Frank, wide-eyed and trembling, stared back at him. Jacques, unable to suffer Frank's horror-filled stare any longer, cast his eyes downward and said what it was that had to be said:

"Have a nice day."

D'ISTAING DEIGNS TO DISDAIN THE DANES

It was a warm spring day and the sun shone cheerily through the window of Thornton's office at 10 Downing Street. Warm sunny spring days depressed him. They reminded him of the only happy time of his entire life–when he was on the Grand Tour through Italy, Greece and the south of France with the ginmonger's slattern. Warm, sunny spring days also had the unfortunate effect on other people of inducing cheerfulness, the one quality in people which Thornton despised most–and there were many, many qualities in people which Thornton despised quite a rather lot.

Luck dictated, however, that Thornton's interlocutor this afternoon was not cheerful. In the past, President Valery Discard d'Istaing of France had rarely been cheerful, and, of late, just as each and every one of his countrymen, he was decidedly less so.

Monsieur d'Istaing had a large falconine nose, on either side of which were perched small eyes that, though three-quarters hooded by his eyelids, peered out with an indomitable mixture of Gallic haughtiness and *ennui*. He possessed a steely spirit which did not lend itself to defeat as quickly as had, in recent days, those of many of his countrymen. Beneath his nose stretched a vast, immobile area above a pouting frown which deigned to move only slightly to vocalize. His hair was thick, wavy and silver, combed back from a hairline that receded on the sides.

As Aunt Anne had predicted, it was only a matter of time before the French, being, of course, the French, would find themselves up *La Fleuve de Merde sans une rame*. President d'Istaing was in England on a routine visit and had no idea that Thornton would propose a solution to what was now referred to in France, by those who still clung to any semblance of caring anymore, as *Le Petite Dommage*. Word of this had spread across the Channel, and Thornton was ready to use it to his advantage.

"I understand you're experiencing some difficulties these days in France," Thornton said.

"Slight, ones, Thornton. Nothing that we're worrying too much about."

"Your whole bloody country has lost the will to live," Thornton shot back.

"Ah, that renowned English quality of understatement can be so comforting in troubled times," d'Istaing said, adding, "Perhaps learning to develop that quality was what drove Gance the Able to take advantage of your ancestor Laurel the Hardy's breathtaking stupidity and conquer England. I can't think of any other reason why he would be interested in this piece-of-shit soggy island."

Thornton, after years of dealing with Aunt Anne, was well used to being squashed like a bug whenever he attempted cleverness. Thus, he ignored the barb and continued on the theme.

"Yes, Valery, I too am in a predicament these days. But there is a way that the two of us can rally our forces and extricate ourselves from this mess and guarantee both of our re-elections."

"I'm all ears, Thornton."

"Nuke someone."

"Distract the voters' attention, and rally them behind the leader, by means of war? Well thank you for educating me on this arcane aspect of crisis re-election strategy," d'Istaing said. "Perhaps you can now help me with my colors and numbers," he snorted before continuing. "Now if you could give me the *name* of some country that would be incapable of retaliation that we could vaporize without pissing off our fucking ethnic communities and getting the international community crawling down our shorts–then *that* might be helpful."

"Denmark."

"Denmark?"

"Denmark."

President d'Istaing rose from his seat and went to the drinks cart where he poured himself a formidable glass of scotch.

"Uh, Thornton," d'Istaing said after a long pull of scotch and a moment of reflection. "Perhaps I haven't been keeping up as much as I should on current events, but Denmark as part of the Axis of Evil, arms proliferating, terrorist threat to our way of life has, to my knowledge, not really been the case for the last thirteen hundred years."

"Exactly."

"Well, except for the Swedes and the Norwegians."

"Who gives a fuck about the Swedes and the Norwegians?"

"That's true," d'Istaing said, taking another large swallow of scotch. "But, be that as it may, Thornton, I am still curious as to why, if nuking our way out of our respective *contretemps* is the solution, Denmark should be the target."

"Case in point," Thornton said. "Everyone hates the French for being arrogant pricks. Yet many, if not most, of the very same people who hate the French also love them for their cuisine, literature, wine, architecture and their singular ability to spend hours in a café rabbiting on about absolute bullshit." Thornton checked himself, remembering who his interlocutor was, and that the French were now his friends. "Uh … Of course these same mixed emotions are directed at the English, Germans, Americans and many other nationalities. As is well known, love and hate burn with such equal intensity as to make them almost kindred passions and, as such, not infrequently to overlap. Who among us has not strangled to death someone whom, just moments before, we had been begging not to leave us?" It occurred to Thornton that perhaps he was revealing, just a little too freely, details of his personal life best kept under wraps. He hastened toward his point. "Yes, Valery, you are quite correct, the Danes haven't significantly pissed off anybody for the last thirteen hundred years. As such, nobody of importance *hates* the Danes. Nor, however, have they done anything to particularly endear themselves to anybody. They're a clean slate. A slate upon which anything can be written, and which, with their complete annihilation, cannot be erased."

"And what shall we be scribbling on this slate?" d'Istaing asked, beginning somewhat to see the logic in this."

"Economic crimes against humanity."

"'Economic crimes against humanity?' What the hell does that mean?"

"It doesn't have to *mean* anything, Valery. It just has to be relentlessly banged into the voters' heads."

"That is true, Thornton. That is true. But we should be able to elaborate somewhat on it."

Thornton had thought about this too. "Do you remember Denmark's lone opposition to the EU's proposal to standardize the size and sugar content of butter biscuits?"

"Yes."

"Economic crimes against humanity."

"Yeeesss," d'Istaing said, raising his eyelids a nanomillimeter. "Yeess, yeess. I see what you mean."

Several concerns still weighed upon d'Istaing's mind, though.

"But does it have to be a nuclear strike? That's rather drastic, isn't it? Couldn't we do something a bit more conventional? You know, sort of pop in there with a few troops and tanks, slap them around a bit, declare victory; you know, that sort of thing."

"There are two problems with that, Valery. First, it would take time, and invariably, complications would arise. Time would give the opportunity to think, and complications would give ammunition to columnists and talking heads. No, what we need is an immediate victory and a surge of patriotism right before the polls open. The sheep march off to vote with the flag waving in their hearts, and when they get home and turn on their tellies, nothing but football and cooking shows. Denmark would be yesterday's news."

"Quite right, quite right. But we'd have to get Washington to go along with this. How could we do that?"

"Oh, I don't think it will be too difficult to talk Kenny into it."

"I don't think it would be too difficult to talk Kenny into buying the Brooklyn Bridge, if we could just pry Boris away from his side long enough to do so."

"Yes, Valery," Thornton said, taking a sip of scotch and leaning back in his chair. "That's where I'm going to need your help."

SOMEWHERE BETWEEN REAL AND REAL REAL

President Kenneth Bunkport was lost and confused. He had been separated from Secretary of State Boris "Bob" Rasputum a few minutes before and he now couldn't find his way back to the Oval Office. Currently in the sixth year of his first four-year term (he had been held back for a second year in a row due to poor performance) President Bunkport rarely had found himself in situations of such abject self-reliance, and he was not handling it well. His palms were breaking out in a sweat and he began to timorously hum a comforting lullaby that his nanny had sung to him many years before.

Realizing that he was on his own, the president took decisive action. He opened the first door he came to and stepped through it. President Bunkport found himself standing behind a podium. He didn't remember a podium being in the Oval Office. Nor did he recall the Oval Office generally containing several dozen people with cameras, microphones, tape recorders, television cameras and lights. The president's uncertainty that he was in the Oval Office was well founded–for he had, in fact, just wandered into the White House pressroom.

The reporters stared at President Bunkport with equal confusion. It was the first time they had ever seen him in the pressroom and didn't quite know what to make of it. Up until now, Rasputum had made sure that reporters never got closer than fifty yards to the president, and then only if he was conveniently standing under the deafening swirl of helicopter blades.

The silence didn't last long. Meg Jenkins from CNN pulled herself together and fired out a question:

"Uh ... How are you Mr. President?"

President Bunkport replied:

"You all look like happy campers to me. Happy campers you are, happy campers you have been, and, as far as I am concerned, happy campers you will always be. You look just like yourselves.

"Americans will soon observe the anniversary of my fellow astronauts Neil Armstrong and Buzz Lukens' walk on the moon. Buzz Lukens took that fateful step. For NASA, space is still a high priority. And thus, we must look towards Mars. Mars is essentially in the same orbit. Mars is somewhat the same distance from the Sun, which is very important. We have seen pictures where there are canals, we believe, and water. If there is water, that means there is oxygen. If oxygen, that means we can breathe. It's time for the human race to enter the solar system. But we are ready for any unforeseen event that may or may not occur. Because if we don't succeed, we run the risk of failure. There is no doubt in my mind that this country cannot achieve any objective we put our mind to. I recognize there are hurdles, and we're going to achieve these hurdles. By making the right choices, we can make the right choice for our future.

"As far as domestic matters, the Holocaust was an obscene period in our nation's history. I mean in this century's history. But we all lived in this century. I didn't live in this century. As such, we have a firm commitment to NATO. We are a part of NATO. We have a firm commitment to Europe. We are a part of Europe. I was recently on a tour of Latin America, and the only regret I have was that I didn't study Latin harder in school so I could converse with those people. The U.S. has a vital interest in that area of the country. I would also like to say that Hawaii is a unique state. It is a small state. It is a state that is by itself. It is different than the other forty nine states. Well, all states are different, but it's got a particularly unique situation. I also love California; I practically grew up in Phoenix. But we've got a big border in Texas with Mexico obviously–and we've got a big border with Canada–Arizona is affected. There's an old … saying in Tennessee … I know it's in Texas, probably in Tennessee that says Fool me once … shame on … shame on you … Fool me … Can't get fooled again. Of all the people in the world who understand Texas it's probably Australians. There are a couple of cows waiting for me. You know, when I first get back from Washington, it seems like the cows are talking back. But after spending some time in Texas they're just cows. Unfortunately, the people of Louisiana are not racists. It's wonderful to be here in the great state of Chicago. It's rural America. It's where I came from. We always refer to ourselves as real America. Rural America, real America, real, real, America. Somewhere between real and real real. I was known as the chief grave robber of my state.

"I have made good judgments in the past. I have made good judgments in the future. The future will be better tomorrow. We will move forward, we will move upward, and yes, we will move onward. We don't want to go past to the back. We want to go forward to the day when we're going to have the best-educated American people in the world. Quite frankly, teachers are the only profession that teach our children. When I picked the Secretary of Education, I wanted somebody who knew something about public education. She'll make a fine Secretary. From what I've read in the press accounts, she's perfectly qualified. What a waste it is to lose one's mind. Or not to have a mind is being very wasteful. How true that is.

"I also believe we are on an irreversible trend toward more freedom and democracy–but that could change. We're on an international manhunt for those who would do harm to America, or for anybody else who loves freedom. And free societies will be allies against these hateful few who have no conscience, who kill at the whim of a hat. It's in our country's interest to find those who would harm us and get them out of harm's way. And there's no doubt in my mind that we will fail. My friends, no matter how rough the road may be, we can and we will never, never surrender to what is right. The United States and the U.S. stand together. And, you know, it'll take time to restore chaos and order–order out of chaos. But we will. I think war is a dangerous place. I just want you to know that, when we talk about war, we're really talking about peace. Our enemies are innovative and resourceful, and so are we. They never stop thinking about new ways to harm our country and our people, and neither do we. You disarm or we will. More Muslims have died at the hands of killers than–I say more Muslims–a lot of Muslims have died–I don't know the exact count–at Istanbul. Look at these different places around the world where there's been tremendous death and destruction because killers kill. The vast majority of Iraqis want to live in a peaceful, free world. And we will find these people and bring them to justice. Justice ought to be fair.

"A low voter turnout is an indication of fewer people going to the polls. I like the idea of people running for office. There's a positive effect when you run for office. Maybe some will run for office and say, vote for me. I look forward to blowing up America. I don't know if that will be their platform or not. But it's–I don't think so. I think people who generally run for office say, vote for me. I'm looking forward to fixing your potholes, or making sure you got bread on the table. In this job you've got a lot on your plate on a regular basis; you don't have much time to sit around and wander, lonely, in the Oval Office, kind of asking different portraits, 'How do you think my standing will be?' I glance at the headlines just to kind of get a flavor for what's moving. I rarely read the stories, and get briefs by people who probably read the news themselves.

There's a gap between what my opponent promises and what he says he's going to do. And so, in my State of the–my State of the Union–or State–my speech to the nation, whatever you wanna call it, speech to the nation–I asked Americans to give four thousand years–four thousand hours over the next–of the rest of your life–of service to America. That's what I asked. I said two–four thousand hours. To whom much is given, much is owed.

"I understand how risky agriculture can be. It wouldn't be so risky if we could control the weather. That's one thing we haven't figured out how to do yet. It wouldn't be so risky if we could make it rain all the time. There would be hay to feed the cows. Somehow, that doesn't happen all the time. I know. We phased out the death tax, so America's family farmers can stay in the family.

"Japan is an important ally of ours. Japan and the United States of the Western industrialized capacity, 60 percent of the GNP, two countries. That's a statement in and of itself.

"And the time is getting worse. That's what people have got to understand up there in Washington or over there in Washington down there in Washington, whatever. Thought I was in Texas for a minute. So one of my visits–one of the reasons I'm visiting here is to ask the question to people. Because if there's–moving too slow, or people are saying one thing and the other thing is not happening, now is the time to find out. In terms of timetables, as quickly as possible–whatever that means. But it changes when you walk into a shut-in's home and say, 'Can I love you?' I was a prisoner too, but for bad reasons.

"I am a Republican. I am not part of the problem. Republicans understand the importance of bondage between a mother and child. Yes, that's a–first of all, Mom, you're doing–that's tough. But it's–I appreciate that. I appreciate the idea of you wanting to give your children the education from you and the mom … who's a parent, and a mom or dad. One of the hardest parts of my job is to console the family members who have lost their lives. Illegitimacy is something we should talk about in terms of not having it. Abortion, bussing, voting rights, prayers–I'm not interested in those issues and I want to stay as far away from them as I can. But we have a good Supreme Court. They're lawyers ... they're judges ... they're appointed for life. Abortion is not an issue with the American people. It is a figment of your imagination if you think that this is an issue that is talked about a lot. Most women do not want to be liberated from their essential natures as women. Speaking as a man, it's not a woman's issue. Too many OB/GYN's aren't able to practice their love with women all across the country. Us men are tired of losing our women. The loss of life will be irreplaceable. Would you like a puppy?"

Secretary of State Rasputum strode down the corridor toward the Oval Office. As usual, his pace bespoke purpose, and in his hand was a thick folder containing briefing papers. Rasputum had wavy, salt and pepper gray hair and wore the thick horn-rimmed glasses that had become his trademark. Though standing only five-four, he exuded, nevertheless, a commanding presence.

Rasputum was born in Russia. When he was twelve, Stalin visited his school on the occasion of The Day of the Revolutionary Junior High School Student. Little Boris had been chosen to present The Glorious Leader with a commemorative plaque and, after chatting with him for a few minutes, Stalin had determined that Boris was "totally creepy" and ordered him to be deported before puberty exacerbated the situation.

Upon arriving in the United States, Rasputum dedicated himself to his studies and soon shone as a brilliant student. He also developed into a fervent anti-communist. At age twenty-three he was awarded a doctorate, and an immediate professorship, from Harvard. His dissertation was on what he had termed The Tidily Wink Theory, which held that, once communism had been established in a country, its influence would flip up into the air and land pretty much anywhere. He also posited that, given the chaotic nature of this pernicious spread of communism, the defense against it should be equally as chaotic; thus, to combat it, it would be necessary for the Pentagon to spend sixteen hundred dollars per toilet seat, five hundred dollars per hammer, and hundreds of billions of dollars on a missile defense system that couldn't hit the broad side of a barn at ten paces on a sunny day. This theory proved enormously popular with many influential people in the military and in industry, and his rise from college professor to the upper echelons of government was meteoric.

For all of his qualities, Rasputum was beginning to feel that he was slipping. He would never before have allowed himself to let President Bunkport out of his sight.

As he was walking towards the Oval Office, Rasputum heard the president's voice coming from the Sub-Secretary of Corporate Welfare's office. Rasputum breathed a sigh of relief. He headed for that office and entered it. What he found, however, was not the president, but a television—and on it was President Bunkport *speaking to reporters*!!!

"We're all capable of mistakes," Bunkport was saying, "but I don't care to enlighten you on the mistakes we may or may not have made. The American people wouldn't want to know of any misquotes that Kenny Bunkport may or may not make. I stand by all the misstatements that I've made, no matter how often I'm misunderestimated."

Rasputum had always been of a purely cerebral inclination and had never demonstrated the slightest prowess at athletics. This would have come as something of a surprise to anyone who could observe him now legging it towards the pressroom at a cheetah-like clip.

"So that's … what … there's some ideas. And the–it's–my job is to, like, think beyond the immediate. I'm not into the detail stuff. I'm more concepty. You're all doing a heckuva job and I hope you leave here and walk out saying, 'What did he say?'"

Rasputum sailed through the door to the pressroom and interposed himself between the president and the microphone.

"Sorry, this press conference has to be interrupted. Technical difficulties," Rasputum said.

"What sort of technical difficulties?" A reporter, fast on his feet, shot back.

Rasputum cleared his throat curtly and then, without hesitation, and with the same adrenaline-fueled strength that had sent him sprinting here from the Sub-Secretary of Corporate Welfare's office at the unofficial time of 9.756 seconds, grasped the microphone and smartly snapped it off the podium. He then flicked a thin smile and shrugged slightly as if to say, *Ah, what can you do when you live in an age which is so at the mercy of fickle technology?* Rasputum then hooked his arm through President Bunkport's and, with a dignified yet expedient stride, got him the hell out of there.

"Public speaking is very easy, Bob," President Bunkport said, grinning with pride. Rasputum clutched the president's arm and led him back to the Oval Office. It suddenly occurred to Rasputum that the television that he had seen the president on was the White House closed circuit system–it was not a network broadcast! The networks wouldn't be airing it until the six o'clock news! Rasputum pulled out his cell phone and speed dialed Press Secretary Ron Siegheiler.

"Ron, Bob here. Get out to the press room *PRONTO* and tell the leeches that if they run one single solitary fucking word of what they've just heard I will have them all killed! What? I can't? Why not? Well … I don't give a good goddamn what you say. Tell them whatever the fuck you please–just make this thing go away! Got that? Good!"

Rasputum slapped his cell phone shut and turned to the president.

"Mr. President, do you remember what I said about reporters?"

"They give you cavities."

"No, sir, that was what I said about marshmallows," Rasputum said with practiced patience. "What I said about reporters was that you are never, ever to speak to them under any circumstances whatsoever without a written speech in your hand that I have personally given to you."

"Do all marshmallows give you cavities, or just mean ones?"

"All marshmallows are mean, sir. Just as all reporters are."

"Gosh!"

Rasputum led the president into the Oval Office and placed him in his seat at his desk. Rasputum's cell phone rang. It was Siegheiler. The news was good. He had contacted the heads of the major networks and promised them $70 billion worth of broadband spectrum for free in exchange for killing the speech–to which they had agreed. As for the print reporters, cases of whiskey and hookers would take care of them. Rasputum clicked the cell phone shut and, with that out of the way, moved onto the next item on the agenda. He turned to the president, who was gazing out the window and thinking about golf.

"Mr. President," Rasputum said in his deep, gravelly, heavily accented voice, "Prime Minister Ghreype Nehi of India is going to be here in just a few moments and I really need you to pay attention to just a few details."

Bunkport turned his attention to his secretary of state, and Rasputum knew he had roughly a one-minute window of opportunity.

"Mr. President, Ghreype Nehi, the newly elected prime minister of India, will arrive at the Oval Office shortly with his foreign secretary, Hydun Sikh. Nehi is a hard-line proponent of expanding India's nuclear capability. We are attempting to persuade him to adopt a more moderate approach."

"Does Mr. Kahblecugala like to golf, Bob?"

Rasputum took a deep breath and let it out slowly. He felt himself slipping again.

"I'm sorry, sir. Scrap that," Rasputum said. "When the prime minister arrives, simply shake his hand and, then, the foreign secretary's. Then simply ask the prime minister if he has had a pleasant trip. Then simply ask if his family is well. Please allow him to finish answering the first question before asking the second. I'll take it from there. Oh, and you'd better just refer to him as Mr. Prime Minister."

"Oodly doodly."

The president's phone rang and he answered it.

"Yyyyello. Okie dokie." He hung up.

"Has Nehi arrived?" Rasputum inquired.

Bunkport gazed vacantly at Rasputum. Rasputum took a deep breath and picked up the president's phone.

"Helen, Is Prime Minister Nehi on his way to the Oval Office? Uh huh. OK, thank you."

Rasputum hung up the phone.

"Mr. President, do you remember the conversation we had about the phone?"

"Don't answer it!" Bunkport responded, quickly and loudly, proud of having remembered the rule."

"Exactly, Mr. President," Rasputum said in his slow, calm, gravelly voice.

Rasputum went to the doors and opened them wide. Ghreype Nehi and Hydun Sikh were approaching the Oval Office.

"Welcome, Prime Minister Nehi. Welcome Secretary Sikh," Rasputum said, shaking their hands as they entered the Oval office.

"Mr. President, it is my honor to present to you Prime Minister Ghreype Nehi of India."

"That's funny," Bunkport said. "I used to be prime minister of India, too."

"Uh, sir," Rasputum whispered into the president's ear. "Actually, you were a *senator* from *Indiana*."

"Ya wanna play golf, Mr. Nawababiwagahoo?" the president chirped.

"Uh, why don't we all have a seat?" Rasputum interjected, quickly, and with as best an impression of a smile as he could muster. He led Nehi and Sikh to the two facing sofas with a coffee table in between.

The phone rang and Bunkport snatched it up before Rasputum could get to it.

"Yyyyello? Yes he is. Okay." The president handed Rasputum the phone.

"Mr. Secretary," Helen, the president's secretary said. "President d'Istaing of France is on the line and wishes to speak with you. He says it is a matter of utmost importance."

Rasputum hesitated. It was seemingly rude enough to receive Nehi and Sikh in such an unceremonious fashion. (A decision that had been taken as a way of keeping Bunkport away from the press–a lot of good *that* did.) But to keep them waiting while he conducted other business could be taken as extremely insulting. But, given that d'Istaing deemed this matter to be urgent, he could not ignore it.

"OK, Helen. Transfer the call to the small conference room. I will take it in a moment."

Rasputum hung up the phone and turned to the Nehi and Sikh.

"Prime Minister Nehi, Secretary Sikh, I apologize deeply, but I must excuse myself for just a moment to attend to a most urgent matter."

Nehi and Sikh were very gracious in accepting his apology and Rasputum couldn't determine just how upset they might be. He concluded that he would simply have to put the charm into overdrive for the remainder of their visit and hope that this would placate them. Rasputum then turned to the president.

"Sir, I will only be gone but a moment. You can talk about golf now, but please do not talk about anything else *but* golf. And you remember the discussion we had about the phone, don't you?

"Don't answer it!"

"Precisely, sir."

Rasputum walked the short distance from the Oval Office to the small conference room and picked up the phone.

"Monsieur President."

"Boris."

"Yes, sir?"

"Uh ... How are you doing?"

"Fine, Monsieur President, fine. It was my understanding, however, that there is a matter which requires my immediate attention."

"Yes. It appears that ... Oh, wait, a new development is just coming to my attention. Please wait for just a moment. This is a matter of the gravest importance. Please wait and I will be right with you."

President d'Istaing hit the hold button. He was sitting in the hall outside of Thornton's office, where Thornton could see him. President d'Istaing eased back in his chair, crossed his legs, picked up his snifter, took a sip and gave Thornton the thumbs up. Thornton picked up the phone in his office.

"So, what part of Indiana are you from, Mr. Nkglaptocrin-lownup?"

"Well, sir, I am not actually being from Ind ..."

The telephone rang. Bunkport picked it up.

"Yyyyello."

"Mr. President," Helen said, "Prime Minister Wingate of Great Britain is on the line."

"I didn't do very well in my high school Latin course," he said. "So would you get my interpreter?"

"I don't think that will be necessary, sir."

"Okie dokie."

"You're connected, sir."

"Hello, Kenny, Thornton, here," came the voice from the other end of the line.

"Hi, Kenny Thornton," the president said.

Prime Minister Nehi and Secretary Sikh could not but overhear Bunkport's end of the conversation.

"Uh, huh. Uh, huh. Well, if you put it that way, I'd have to go along with it. Oddle doddle. God bless. And good luck with the nuclear bombardment."

The president hung up the phone and resumed grinning at Nehi and Sikh, who were indulging in a moment of slack-jawed shock before both of them jumped to their feet. Nehi tried to swallow, but his mouth was dry. He mustered his courage and, in a hushed tone, asked the dreaded question:

"Nuclear bombardment? Is it India?"

Bunkport seemed to remember Kenny Thornton mentioning that the place began with a *D*, but then he also seemed to remember Bob mentioning that Mr. Gunabubana liked nuclear stuff. Folks from Indiana are nothing if not eager to accommodate their guests, especially if they're from Indiana too.

"Yes," Bunkport said with a pleasant smile. "Yes, it is."

Thornton, having hung up the phone, gave d'Istaing the thumbs up. President d'Istaing got back on the phone with Rasputum.

"I'm terribly sorry, Boris, for having kept you waiting."

"That's quite all right," Rasputum said, barely keeping a tone of impatience at bay. "What is the matter which you care to discuss with me?"

"Well, as you know, the NATO summit meeting is going to be held in Paris next month."

"Yes."

"Well, we need your advice."

"Yes."

"Uh ... Do you think we should we serve salmon or duck at the gala state dinner?"

Rasputum heard a crashing sound, like the doors to the Oval Office flying off their hinges, followed by the rapid thunder of footsteps heading down the corridor toward him. He dropped the phone and raced into the corridor. Ghreype Nehi and Hydun Sikh collided with him, sending him crashing to the floor. Rasputum got to his feet, head spinning, and looked in the direction where they had raced off in. He quickly turned to look toward the Oval Office. Sitting at his desk, with a vacant look in his eyes and a simpering grin on his face, was President Bunkport. Rasputum once again flushed with fury at himself. How on God's Earth had it occurred to him to leave the president alone with them! He turned to where Nehi and Sikh had raced off to and stumbled off after them.

Though disabled, Rasputum had the advantage of knowing the layout of the White House and, thus, was able to run out through a side door and head Nehi and Sikh off as they dashed out the main entrance.

"Whatever it is, it isn't!" Rasputum blurted out as he intercepted them.

"Bunkport has told us that India is under nuclear attack," Nehi said.

Rasputum knew that drastic situations require drastic measures. In this case, that would mean honesty. He looked around to make sure he wasn't overheard.

"Well, you shouldn't really pay much heed to anything President Bunkport says. You see, gentlemen, the president is, how can I put this, uhm ... an idiot."

"I did sort of get that impression," Nehi said, his voice sounding calmer. "So you assure us that there is nothing at all to this?"

"Of course not," Rasputum said. He could feel himself relaxing. "I mean, if there were any new developments regarding nuclear activity on the Indian subcontinent, don't you think the CIA would have been on top of it?"

As those last words passed his lips, the hairs on the back of his neck stood up. Nehi and Sikh's eyes bugged out. They briefly looked at each other and then dashed off down Pennsylvania Avenue. Rasputum slowly sat down on the steps and put his head in his hands.

If Rasputum had had any doubt whatsoever, he had none now. He was definitely slipping.

President Bunkport gazed out the window and took advantage of the sudden lull to engage in, for lack of a better term, thought.

Golly, Mr. Kawabunga sure seemed happy. Happy is nice. I like iced tea. That new titanium six iron really has improved my chip shot. I thought nuclear bombs were supposed to be bad. I wonder what time they're serving lunch today. Why do they spell "potatoe" with an "e" if you don't pronounce it? Ha ha ha ha, look at that funny squirrel in the tree there! It's too bad trees cause more pollution than cars, 'cause they're awfully pretty. What's the difference between a squirrel and a chipmunk, anyway? I'm pretty sure I remember hearing that nuclear bombs are bad. I wonder what month this is. I wish I was golfing. Nuclear bombs are probably even worse than trees. Boy, my dog sure sleeps a lot. If they drop a nuclear bomb somebody might get hurt. Wouldn't it be neat if spinach was bad for you and marshmallows were good for you? Maybe I should tell those folks that that guy on the phone's gonna drop a nuclear bomb on them. That'd be so cool if you could have marshmallows for dinner every night. What was the name again of that place where Kenny Thornton was gonna drop that bomb? I think it began with a D. Yes "de" place began with "de" letter D.

The president giggled at his joke and looked around for some of his Deke brothers to share it with. He found himself, not in Deke House, but in the Oval Office and, as so often it is at the top, alone. He then directed his eyes to the ceiling and scratched his head, a clear indication that he was mulling over a course of action. After careful consideration of this plan, and some analysis of his putting technique, he spun around in his chair and snatched up the phone.

"Nancy."

"Helen, sir."

"My name's not Helen, it's Kenny."

"I know that, sir. *My* name is Helen."

"Helen."

"Yes, sir."

"Get me the prime minister of Duluth!"

DULUTH MON AMOUR

Mayor Maynard Mainott stood at the window of his office at City Hall and watched Duluth burn. He unclasped his hands from behind his back and looked at his watch, and then turned his head upward to the skies. Still no sign of the nuclear attack President Bunkport had promised hours before. Mayor Mainott was growing impatient. After the initial bewilderment upon being informed that Duluth was going to be obliterated, Mainott's thoughts turned to the future–the future that would be built with **MASSIVE FEDERAL RECONSTRUCTION AID**. The prospect of that so overwhelmed Mayor Mainott's thoughts that it hadn't even occurred to him to ask the president who was going to annihilate Duluth or, for that matter, why. To the mayor's knowledge, not a screw was manufactured or an apple grown in or around Duluth that was destined in any way to the military industrial complex. There was no port, no airstrip of any strategic importance–no nothing, really. *Yes*, the mayor thought, *this bombing is truly manna from Heaven*.

Duluth had not been doing well for sometime now. The economy was down and spirits were low. Mayor Mainott had done all he could think of to improve the situation. Why, after all, hadn't he personally gone to New York to one of those fancy schmancy high fallutin' Madison Avenue ad agencies to commission a snappier city motto? It certainly wasn't his fault that *Catch the Spirit!* hadn't mobilized the masses. *Yes*, Mayor Mainott thought, *I have done all that can be done*.

Mainott turned his attention to the scene unfolding outside of his window. The sky was orange from the reflection of scores of flaming buildings. The streets were aswarm with the citizens of Duluth who were setting the fires, as well as smashing store fronts and making off with televisions, DVD players, computers and anything else they could lay their hands on. The mayor couldn't help but feel a twinge of pride in his citizenry's reaction to the news of imminent nuclear annihilation. It was oddly comforting to see that, when the occasion called for it, Lutherans could go berserk with the best of them.

Mayor Mainott could not help but feel himself partly responsible for this current state of affairs. (Mainott had taken the call from President Bunkport while being interviewed live for the weekly radio program *Dateline Duluth.* The mayor now thought that, perhaps, it was a bit unstatesmanlike to have blurted out, "Jesus Fucking Christ, Mr. President! What do you mean Duluth is going to be nuked?"

So, yes, Mayor Mainott did feel himself partly responsible and, thus, filed away in his brain the phrase that he felt would allay any criticism of his handling of the situation: *Yes, mistakes have been made.*

On the other hand, what difference did it make? Duluth was going to be wiped off the face of the map at any moment and his indiscretion which resulted in this riot would, in perspective, be deemed a flaw of judgment of flea-like proportion.

Mayor Mainott realized he was letting his train of thought drift from the main issue–**MASSIVE FEDERAL RECONSTRUCTION AID**. He refocused his concentration and looked beyond the flames and looting. What he saw was breathtakingly glorious: Eight-lane superhighways, towering skyscrapers, a football stadium seating a quarter of a million. What the hell! Might as well have a baseball park seating a quarter of a million too! In his mind's eye he saw bullet trains whooshing across town, an international airport, a state-of-the-art subway system, a series of architecturally ingenious suspension bridges–and maybe even an extra river or two to go along with them!

The mayor closed his eyes, took a deep breath, and trembled as he exhaled. No longer would Duluth be known as "Peoria without the Pizzazz." Mainott envisioned the city encircled by three-hundred-foot-high gilded obelisks with pictographs recounting for the ages the glories and triumphs of Duluth. He gasped in awe at the thought of pyramids rising from Duluth of such majesty as to make those of Egypt appear outhouses by comparison; hanging gardens that would make those of Babylon seem like a flower pot with a couple of sickly geraniums poking up; a cathedral that would make Notre Dame look like a poky piece of sniveling …

"Oh, golly! Oh, golly, golly, gosh!"

The mayor sighed. Once again his lofty visions had been wrested from him and hurled back down to the mundane by the arrival in his office of that most mundane of all creatures–Bert Gurt. Gurt was the thorn in the mayor's side. He was the city councilman who could always be counted on to chime in, "Well, let's not just jump headlong into this thing here," whenever a measure was brought up to allocate funds for the purchase of a new box of paper clips. He was the self-proclaimed, "Average fellow who knows the value of a hard-earned nickel." The only member of the city council who couldn't grasp the sagacity of spending $80,000 to change Duluth's city motto from *The Zenith City of the Unsalted Seas* to *Catch the Spirit!*

The mayor didn't bother to turn to look at Gurt. He had beheld the figure of that sixty-something spitting image of Jimmy Stewart enough times for any man's lifetime.

"Bert, I'm sorta busy here. So whatever little matter that should happen to be on your mind, maybe we could discuss it another time."

"Well, Jumpin' Jimminy, Maynard, the whole town's gone loco and you sent the dang police force out fishin'!" Gurt said, referring to the fact that Mayor Mainott *had*, in fact, sent the entire police force, less the couple dozen officers guarding City Hall, on vacation to rest up for the shoot-to-kill, summary-execution, order-restoration task awaiting them in post-nuclear Duluth.

"They're resting, Bert. They've got a big job ahead of them," Mainott said, making no effort to disguise the burden Gurt was inflicting on his patience. "In case you haven't heard, we're in for a little bigger trouble."

"That's another thing, Maynard. This darn bomb's gonna come a-fallin' down on us any minute now and there ain't a gosh blessed thing we're doin'! Whadda we oughta tell folks to do?"

"I dunno, Bert. Uh ... How about 'duck and cover'?" Mainott said distractedly, his attention having already returned to envisioning the Duluth of the future.

"Well, dag nab it!" Gurt said, with uncustomary harshness. "If you ain't gonna do nothin', I sure as shootin' am!"

"You go right ahead Bert," Mainott said with a chuckle at the thought of Bert Gurt organizing anything more complex than a game of horseshoes.

Gurt stomped out of the mayor's office. He almost slammed the door behind him, but upon reconsideration, concluded that there wasn't any call to be unneighborly.

The mayor looked at his watch and decided that it was probably about time to head on down to the bomb shelter below City Hall. He snickered at the thought that in the 1950s people were so paranoid that, in a city like Duluth–with absolutely no strategic or military importance–they actually built a bomb shelter. Suddenly, for the first time since the president had called, Mainott gave some thought to who it was that was going to annihilate Duluth, and why. He didn't think long about it, though. After all, you don't look a gift horse in the mouth. Soon he had returned his thoughts to **MAS-**

SIVE FEDERAL RECONSTRUCTION AID, and whistled a cheery tune as he headed out of his office.

He stopped at his secretary's desk.

"Shirley, I think it's about time to tell the staff and the City Council to go down to the shelter." Mayor Mainott reflected for a moment and then added, "Oh, and if it should happen to slip your mind to tell Councilman Gurt, I think we might not be surprised to find a handsome little raise reflected in our next pay check."

JUST 'CAUSE

President d'Istaing returned to Thornton's office after giving the instructions for the nuclear attack, codenamed "Just 'Cause," via his portable secure phone. Thornton was just finishing up his instructions.

"Alpha, delta, omega, rub a dub dub, Goldilocks is in the tub." Thornton then hung up the secure phone.

"'Rub a dub dub, Goldilocks is in the tub?'" d'Istaing repeated with a giggle.

Thornton was on a testosterone fueled high, of the sort only ordering a nuclear attack can give you, and was not about to have his code tittered at.

"Well, I can at least assure you, Valerey, that *British* bombs will arrive at their targets with precision and punctuality–and will most assuredly explode. I'm not quite sure we can say the same about French bom …"

"Thornton," d'Istaing interjected, "British *trains* don't even arrive at their destinations with precision and punctuality–though, admittedly, their record for exploding is awe-inspiring. The French TGV, however, offers safe rail travel at speeds of over 300 kilometers an hour and provides cars equipped with playground equipment and a buffet car which …"

"All right, all right," Thornton said. "Let's just forget about trains for the moment. Why don't you just pour us a couple of scotches and I'll put on CNN to see how things are going."

Thornton picked up the remote and zapped the television on. What was on was a montage of Middle Eastern types attacking different embassies around the world.

"Well, it looks like the Americans have ticked off the swarthy masses yet once again," Thornton said as Valerey walked over with the drinks. "They appear to be storming embassies all over the world. I haven't the foggiest what it could all be about though. What with putting all the final touches on the attack and all I've been rather out of the loop recently."

As the montage continued, Thornton and Valerey, almost as one, noticed that the flags flying over the embassies were not the Stars and Stripes. They had a red background with a white cross, the horizontal line of which extended from one end to the other and with the vertical part of the cross shifting to the mast side.

"Is that the Swedish flag?" Thornton asked, knowing full well that it wasn't.

"Could be the Norwegian," Valerey suggested, knowing full well that it wasn't.

"Possibly Icelandic," Thornton said, knowing full well that it wasn't.

After indulging in these few moments of denial, they finally had to admit it to themselves. IT WAS THE DANISH FLAG!

The Danish flag?

Thornton looked down at his drink and wondered why Valerey had slipped a hallucinogenic drug into it, not that the Frogs would actually need a reason, but … Thornton looked up at Valerey. Judging from the expression on his face, Valerey had either slipped the same drug into his own drink, or what they were seeing on the television was *actually happening*!

"Turn up the volume, Thornton, turn up the damn volume!"

Thornton did, and they were immediately apprised of the situation; the situation was this: In the space between when they had last read a newspaper and five minutes ago when they had unleashed a nuclear strike against Denmark, a Danish newspaper had printed a cartoon which had inflamed the entire Muslim world.

As has been amply demonstrated throughout this narrative, Thornton was apt to be a little slow on the uptake. On this particular occasion, however, I think we can all agree to cut him a little slack on this one.

"So let me see if I've got this straight," Thornton said. "After thirteen hundred years of not ruffling anyone's feathers, the Danes have enraged the entire Muslim world with a *cartoon*?!"

D'Istaing, who we have seen was usually quick on his feet, was also, understandably, nonplused.

"That would seem to be the case."

"The *Danes*?"

"It would appear to be so."

"A *cartoon*?"

"That is my understanding."

Thornton slowly rose from his chair and walked to the window. After spending a moment mulling the situation over, he fell to his knees and began to tear at his hair.

"I'm being undone by *poems* and *cartoons*! What will be the last nail in my coffin?! A bloody fucking fortune cookie message?"

D'Istaing had got over his initial bewilderment and now sought to calm Thornton.

"Thornton, I think we should …"

"Well they certainly picked a damned inconvenient time, didn't they?"

There was no irony in Thornton's tone. He was simply so distraught at the prospect of his plan going awry that he hadn't even considered that the country he had just ordered destroyed was under no obligation not to inconvenience him.

Lady Anne Throppe entered Thornton's office unannounced. One does not simply enter the prime minister's office unannounced and without an appointment. The first, and last, staff member to inform her of this now ate his soup through a straw and enjoyed a new-found passion for colorful balloons.

Lady Anne, of course, was fully apprised of the plan and, having been following CNN too, aware of the glitch.

"Monsieur d'Istaing," Lady Anne said, nodding to the French president. "Well, gentlemen, I assume that, given the unlikelihood of such a turn of events, there isn't a Plan B on the shelf, is there?"

"Of course there is, Aunt Anne! Of course there is! It's up there on the shelf in the folder titled: 'Contingency Plan in the Event That, after Thirteen Hundred Years of Snoozing, the Danes Should Suddenly Seriously Piss Off a Billion and a Half Muslims with a Bloody Fucking Cartoon!' It's right there next to our plan on how to react if the Earth's rotation should suddenly shift!"

"Well it's nice to see that adversity hasn't affected your witless wit, Thornton. But, getting back to the matter at hand, as there does not appear to be a Plan B, I might suggest that this would be a splendid moment to concoct one. The original plan, as I understand it, was to annihilate innocuous Denmark and then mold public opinion into viewing it as a blow that has been struck for freedom by sending out the 'independent military analysts' on our payroll to talk to the press and give their 'independent analysis'. It now would seem that the public's opinion is going to be strongly formed by the public itself; between those of the Muslim faith who support it, and those on the side of freedom of expression who might take a dim view of it."

"Lady Throppe, you must consider my position," d'Istaing interrupted. "I am the leader of the Parti du Purité Française. Our constituency is made up of those who find Le Pen's views on immigration to be too lax. It would not do for them to see the swarthy masses marching through the *banlieues* waving posters reading 'Vive d'Istaing.'"

"Yes, I can see where that could be a problem," said Lady Throppe. "If my information about the television viewing masses is correct, though, it is unlikely that many would be paying a great deal of attention to the wording on a few signs when their attention could be focused on the much more riveting spectacle of two or three thousand riot police bashing in the demonstrators' heads."

"Yes, yes, I see. Indeed, that would definitely shift the focus more toward our message."

"So much for the domestic side of this," said Lady Throppe. "On the international front we could use the newly developed good will on the part of the Gulf states, which this unexpected situation will undoubtedly engender, to pull a few lucrative oil deals out from under the Americans and the Chinese."

"Well that would certainly please some of our friends," Thornton said."

"Indeed it would," d'Istaing concurred.

"Moving on, what was going to be your original reason for the bombing?"

"Economic crimes against humanity," Thornton said.

"Well, that will have to do for the moment. But something more substantial will have to be formulated within the next few days. How had you originally planned to make the announcement?"

"Valerey and I were going to give a joint press conference."

"No, that won't do. That won't do at all. Too many members of the media with at least some grasp of international affairs would be in attendance. Too many questions. What will have to be done is to set up another venue for the announcement. Something unrelated, nonpolitical. I would suggest that you entrust this matter to your most skillfull men. Have them make a brief announcement regarding this matter, and then return with the utmost dispatch to the putative matter of the gathering. That should provide us with a modicum of additional time. And as we are on the subject of time, given the supersonic nature of ballistic missiles, I think that will have to be all for the moment. Let us see how the announcement is received and predicate any further actions on that."

AND THE PIGEONS
DIED WELL

"Tequila, bourbon, gin–one glass, no ice," came the burly voice from the burly man with the tussled brown hair and the tussled gray trench coat who had entered the pub and moved to the bar.

"Three pound eighty, sir," the barman said, setting the drink before him.

The burly man tossed some coins on the bar, wrapped his meaty hand around the glass, lifted it to his lips, threw his head back, sucked in the drink, and slammed the empty glass back onto the bar.

"Same again."

The barman began mixing another.

Upon arriving in London, Edward Hawingway, or "Haw," as he was known, had been greeted with the sobering, both literal and figurative, discovery that the pubs closed at eleven. He gradually arrived to the conclusion that trashing pubs and thrashing publicans was not an efficacious means of changing this, so he adapted to the reality of the situation and simply compensated for it by beginning his drinking *before* breakfast, rather than after.

Haw had recently been transferred from the Brussels bureau of *The International Herald Lloyd* as a result of his having thrown an assistant editor through a window during a disagreement over whether the paper should also contain news that *isn't* fit to print. Normally, throwing your assistant editor out of a window would get you the sack, but Haw was the best damn euro-pol jockey in the business and they cut him a lot of slack. Hence, they transferred him from Brussels to the London office and hoped for the best.

Haw, as well as working as a journalist, which he referred to as "Groveling to the Whore Devil," also wrote fiction, which he referred to as "Praying to the Bitch Goddess."

Haw slammed back his second drink, ordered another, pulled out a notebook from his coat pocket and leaned on the bar. He then took out a pencil–he always used a pencil when he *wrote*–sharpened it with his penknife, put pencil to paper and began praying to the Bitch Goddess:

And the Pigeons Died Well

The War was over and Jake was drunk. He was thinking of the Woman. He was dressed like the Woman too. She had left her clothes when she left him and he now wore them and it was good.

The morning was cold and gray and Jake poured absinthe into the void where his soul had once dwelt.

Nick entered the *Café*.

"I must kill something," Jake said as Nick sat down at the table.

Nick was drunk. Nick had been drunk since before the War, so it was not a good drunk.

"The Killing was good in Africa," Nick said.

"Yes, the Killing was good in Africa," Jake said, using the feminine form *the* rather than the masculine form *the*. Jake always referred to the Killing as a woman.

"The Killing was good in Spain," Nick said.

"Yes, the Killing was good in Spain."

"I do not think the Killing will be good in Paris."

"In Paris the Killing will not be good."

They ordered two more absinthes, paying for them with their last *centimes*.

"The Killing in Africa is expensive. The War has left us all poor," Jake said, drinking the absinthe in the way that a man does. "The Killing shall be in Paris."

"What?"

"The Killing shall be in Paris."

"Yes, I heard that. What I mean is, *what* are we going to kill?"

Jake was uncertain. Uncertainty made Jake feel weak. He smashed Nick in the face. Nick fell backwards but, recovering quickly, picked up a chair and threw it at Jake's head. Jake ducked and the chair flew through a plate glass window. Nick lunged at Jake and they went through the shattered window. They landed on the sidewalk, scattering a flock of pigeons that were milling about there.

Seeing the pigeons, Jack spoke, virile in his certainty:

"We will kill the pigeons, Nick."

"To kill the pigeons is boring," Nick said, picking bits of glass from his body.

"To kill nothing is worse," Jake said.

"To kill nothing is to die," Nick said, seeing the truth in what Jake was saying.

"I like lollipops," said the womanvoice.

Jake turned his head and saw the woman of Nick standing over them.

"I like lollipops, too," Jake said.

Jake was not a man to humor the feeble of mind, but he did like lollipops.

"Gilda," Nick said. "You are a woman and we are men and these are pigeons and we must kill them."

Gilda told Nick that it was time to go home and she took Nick home.

Jake would kill the pigeons alone ...

... Haw's cell phone rang. He snapped his pencil in two, which he always did when he was interrupted while praying to the Bitch Goddess. He took the phone from his coat pocket. From the number on the screen he knew it was his editor.

"Haw here, Hal."

"Hi, Haw. Listen, we got a little situation here. Mack, on the sports desk, has a cold, or the flu, or had a heart attack, or whatever the fuck. So I had to assign Bob, the meteorologist, to cover the Senior Master's tour. Then a pretty bad hailstorm came down on Dorkshire, so I had to send Babs, from the city desk, to cover it. Then there was a multiple murder in the East End, so I had to send Dotty, from Lifestyle, to cover that. This brings me to you. We need you to take over for Dotty and cover a joint British-French press conference at the Ministry of Gardening. They're going to announce the creation of an endowment for a project designed to genetically engineer a better petunia."

Haw thought about this–though not long.

"Goddamn it, Hal! I am not a goddamn pissant, pavement-licking, crap-shoveling, brown-nosing, sniveling, scumsucking, soap-opera, chit-chat whore! *I'm the real fucking deal!*"

Hal gave Haw a second to blow off some steam.

"We know that, Haw–and we think that's great. So, Haw, if you're catching a taxi over to the petunia thing, remember to ask the driver for a receipt so you can bill it later."

A headstrong silence rumbled across the microwaves before Haw spoke.

"I will do it because I am a reporter and you are my editor–and I love you. But you are also a man–and so I shall break a chair over your head as a man breaks a chair over another man's head!"

Haw crushed the cell phone in his meaty fist and ordered another tequila bourbon and gin.

"You know, buddy," Haw said to the barman. "The day's soon coming when I'm gonna stop groveling to the Whore Devil and dedicate myself to praying to the Bitch Goddess."

"That's nice, sir," the barman said, drying a tumbler and not bothering to look up.

Haw tossed back his drink and stormed out of the pub.

THE MINISTRY OF GARDENING NIPS A BLOOMER IN THE BUD

Haw entered the press room of the Ministry of Gardening. He took a quick look around for any sign of a drinks table and an hors d'oeuvres spread. Nothing. *Cheap-ass Limeys!* Haw's attention then turned to a droning sound coming from the podium. He looked up and saw some pasty-faced Joe jawing on about something or other. Mercifully, it sounded like he was wrapping it up, so Haw moved closer to pick up a few quotes before getting the hell out of there.

"... and we are hopeful that, through cooperation with our French partners, and hard work, we can one day look proudly upon our joint euro-petunia venture and say to ourselves, with no undeserved praise: 'job well done,'" said the pasty-faced Joe, aka Lord Edmund Mountmutton, who was representing Her Majesty's Government at the press conference. Mount-mutton cleared his throat and, nonchalantly, added, "Oh, almost slipped my mind, just one quick, unrelated, announcement; bit of housekeeping, really, before we take questions. Uhm, basically, uh, in order to save the world from Danish aggression, Britain and France, with the support of the United States, have dealt with Denmark with, shall we say, uhm, a certain amount of extreme prejudice, ur ... thermonuclear-wise." Mountmutton crisply cleared his throat again. "Right, then, back to petunias. Any questions, then? Yes, you there," Mountmutton said, pointing to Barbie Binkle from the magazine *Hi, There!*.

"Will the funding for the project cease once a better petunia has been developed, or will it be ongoing with the goal of developing an even better petunia?"

"Excellent question. At this point in time ..."

Mountmutton's voice hummed in the background as Haw scrunched his brow and tried to get his brain to wrap around what he thought he had just heard Mountmutton say a moment ago.

"... and after such time as the review board makes its ruling," Mountmutton was saying as Haw tuned back in, "we will then be in a better position to decide the exact extent to which our petunia efforts will be ..."

"Just hold on one goddamn minute there, Joe," Haw said, interrupting Mountmutton. "Did you just say you guys *nuked Denmark?*"

"My name is not '*Joe*,'" Mountmutton snapped back, feigning restrained testiness, though secretly pleased that he could begin his non-denial denial with an undeniable fact, which always sets a credible tone. "Uh, well, I must say that whatever vernacular meaning *nuke* might have, though I feel we should, for the sake of open and honest communication, attribute some sort of meaning to it, as I am of the opinion, and I'm sure you would all agree, that meaning is good ... uh, I would say, quite on the contrary ... uh, well, rather, sort of-ish on the contrary, though certainly not excessively so ... that, er, well, yes, certain devices–well, perhaps 'devices' is a rather harsh word, were, in a manner of speaking, dropped on–well, perhaps 'dropped on' is not quite accurate, 'dropped over' being more correct, technically speaking, uh ... over, uh, Denmark ... Small ones, rather."

The testy tone of his voice had slipped into a slightly nervous, defensive lilt, but then took on something of a cold authority that was produced by the anger that was building up inside of him as he trained a piercing glance across the pressroom at George Stepontopofus. This press conference had been carefully designed to keep people like Haw away, and Mountmutton did not like surprises. Stepontopofus, the young *wunderkind*, extremely capable, often brilliant, nuts-and-bolts spinmeister, had been put in charge of making sure this thing ran smoothly. Stepontopofus knew he had dropped the ball on this one and he avoided Mountmutton's glare.

"Any other questions?" Mountmutton said, attempting to regain control of the situation. "Yes, you," he said, pointing to Drummond Wackerfuss of *The Naperville Transuniversal Suburban*.

"Will any other EU countries be involved in the petunia project?"

"Not Denmark!" Haw barked.

Some of the reporters began directing steely glares at Haw. They had deadlines to meet and were becoming increasingly annoyed at these nonpetunia-related digressions.

Mountmutton ignored Haw.

"At the present time, only Great Britain and France are involved. But in the spirit of European cooperation, we would welcome ... uh ..." Mountmutton suddenly realized that too much emphasis on "European cooperation" might cause some minds to wonder how Denmark fit into that picture. He shifted the focus. "Any other questions? Yes, you in back."

"Petunia-wise, would you say ..."

"Why," Haw interrupted, "did you nuke Denmark?"

"Economic crimes against humanity," Mountmutton said, too quickly, having memorized this explanation on the outside chance that one of the Lifestyle crowd had just come out of journalism school and was still gung-ho about thoroughness and such. Mountmutton then returned his attention to the reporter Haw had interrupted, "You were saying?"

"Yes, uhm, petunia-wise, are we talking about ..."

"Economic crimes against humanity?!" Haw bellowed. "What the hell does *that* mean?!"

The ensuing pregnant pause bespoke a lack of preparation for that question. It was felt that that simple phrase would have been weighty enough for the Lifestyle corps. Lord Edmund Mountmutton mustered his resolve and unhesitatingly turned toward his French counterpart.

"Perhaps you might like to field that one, Francois?"

Francois Beauxeau de Claunne, a distinguished career functionary whose many notable achievements included nominating Jerry Lewis for *L'Ordre Chevalier des Arts et Lettres*, rarely found himself at a loss, and this occasion was no exception. Clutching his chest, he began to pant heavily. His face turned blue and he fell backwards over his chair–thus feigning one of the most credible cardiac arrests in modern press conference history.

Monsieur Beauxeau de Claunne was taken away and Mountmutton faced the reporters.

"Well, as there seems to be no more questions, I think we ..."

"Just one more," Haw said.

Thanks to Beauxeau de Claunne, Mountmutton had had time to think. It would also be the second time in his career that he was given the opportunity to speak the truth– the first being his earlier statement that he was in no way, in fact, named Joe. He arranged his figure imposingly. Drawing a deep breath, he extended his right arm and pointed a firm finger at the press corps, at the cameras, at the world. In a timber that would have reduced Winston Churchill to a quivering blob, he spoke:

"WE HAVE NO ONE TO APOLOGIZE TO!"

Turning crisply, he strode out the door.

With every Dane having been vaporized, Mountmutton was, for the most part, at least technically correct.

Haw reached into his pocket for his cell phone. Not finding it there, having crushed it in his fist an hour before, he then made a dash for the phone bank outside the press room. Too late. In the moments he had wasted looking for his cell phone, every phone had been taken. The air was abuzz with the reporters phoning in their stories, and through the cacophony only one word, repeated over and again, could be clearly heard–*petunia*. Under any other non-journalistic circumstances, Haw would have simply cold cocked the nearest person and taken the phone. Under these circumstances, however, that would have broken Haw's Code–he had hesitated; they had beaten him to it. They had won; he had lost.

Haw looked at his watch. He had an hour till deadline. The office was only ten minutes away. The story would write itself. He had plenty of time. Haw ran out the door of the Ministry of Gardening and hailed a taxi.

Haw came barreling through the door and up to his editor, Hal.

"The Limeys and the Frogs nuked Denmark!"

Hal smiled.

"A day late and a dollar short, Haw. The Greenlanders have already accepted their explanations," Hal said with a smirk. Having had his fun, he wiped off the expression and got back to business. "So what have you got on the petunia thing?"

Haw, who regarded perplexity was a sign of weakness, was perplexed.

"Uh, Hal ... What the fuck are you talking about?"

"Petunias, Haw? The reason you went to the press conference? Remember?"

"I mean *Greenland*, Hal! What the fuck are you talking about *Greenland*?"

What Hal was talking about was that, while the petunia press conference was in progress, the British and French governments, operating on a plan Aunt Anne had devised, had secured Greenland's approval of the strike. Aunt Anne had brilliantly reasoned that, as a dominion of Denmark, Greenland was now, by default, Denmark. She also intuited that, as a dominion of Denmark, the Greenlanders were also in the singular position of being the only people in the world who had a long-term and deep-seated hatred for the Danes. As such, and with the tacit assurance that a few fishing accords might be re-negotiated in their favor, the Greenlanders, on behalf of Denmark, were tickled pink to go along with it. They humbly apologized for their previous economic crimes against humanity and thanked Britain and France for the tough love which had guided them back onto the straight and narrow. (Aunt Anne's tactic was to catch on very quickly in governmental circles and would come to be known as Vicarious Shit Management.)

Hal was about to explain it to Haw when suddenly an explosive sound filled the newsroom, like that when an earthquake suddenly hits and everything that had previously been still bursts into movement. People began scrambling back and forth, tripping over desks and slamming into walls.

An assistant editor, with a sheet of paper torn from the telex in hand, ran towards Hal. He was running too fast to stop on his own and collided with Hal. The two crashed to the floor. Hal got up on his elbows. He was stunned and couldn't immediately make out what the red faced and gasping assistant editor was struggling to say. Suddenly the magnitude of his missive acted like a cold bucket of water on Hal and he heard loudly and clearly:

"PRINCE HARRY HAS GOT A NEW GIRLFRIEND!!!"

Hal jumped to his feet and took command.

"Bernie, get a positive reaction from someone at Buckingham Palace, and get a negative one from someone else there. We want controversy and infighting. Fred, find me some photos of her topless on a beach in Marbella ... no, scrap that. That'll take too long. Just find any old picture of her on the beach and Photoshop her top off. Herb, find out if she's a commoner. If she is, write up something about the demise of tradition. If she isn't, give me something on the Royal Family being mired in eighteenth-century class divisions. Mary, bang me out twenty inches on Lady Di's reaction to it, as told through some psychic in Cockfosters or Piddletrenthide or whatever. That reminds me, Fiona, throw a news analysis together dealing with the chances that Prince Harry might marry the girlfriend, then find a lover, thus driving the young beautiful new princess into a deep depression whereupon he divorces her—the consequences of which could then possibly lead to her tragic death. Oh, and don't forget to mention that, if this were to happen, the irony would be chilling." Hal hesitated. He knew he was forgetting something. He scratched his head vigorously for a moment, and then snapped his fingers. "Oh, yeah, Haw, find out if she's a virgin or not."

The reporters dove for their desks and burst into warp speed at their keyboards, unleashing an explosive, deafening, *clickity-clack* sound not unlike that made by a herd of one hundred thousand methamphetamine-stoked two-inch stallions in tap-dance shoes breaking into a wolf-spooked stampede.

Hal strode off to his office with the assistant editor at his heels. Haw was left standing alone.

He turned towards the door and left. Haw was through groveling to the Whore Devil.

HOLY MOLY ØLE!

Lars spewed a final surge of vomit on Øle's shoes, wiped his mouth, and went back to putting the finishing touches on the Mr. Clean cocktails he was preparing.

Øle, splayed out and semi-conscious in the armchair, took no notice. Having hooked up in a beer tent in Malmo during the Scandinavian Cup, Øle and Lars had drunk their way down to Copenhagen. What had compelled them to migrate internationally in quest of a cleaning-fluid cocktail can only be nebulously hypothesized as one of those ideas that sounds good at the time after having been on the booze for three days.

One could argue that the reasoning behind their decision was based on the fact that they were almost broke. One could also argue that the money they had spent on the ferry over would have been more wisely spent on a non-cleaning-fluid quaff in Sweden. One could also argue that it is not wise to argue with two Scandinavians on a three-day bender after their minds have been resolutely set on a course of action.

Øle, a Dane, was celebrating Denmark's unexpected victory over Norway ("*No way, Norway! No way, Norway!*") in the Scandinavian Cup championship, and Lars, a Swede, was celebrating his luck at finding someone willing to sport him drinks for three solid days. Øle was six-foot four-inches tall, fair-skinned, blue–eyed, blond and in his late twenties. So was Lars.

"No, but, like ... I really, really gotta get uhm ... damn! Waz the word again? Jeez, I was just, like ... saying it ... ya know... *married*! Yeah, that ... married," Lars slurred out for the umpteenhundredth time or so.

"So you've mentioned," Øle yawned.

"She doesn't have to be rich, she doesn't have to be beautiful–she doesn't even have to like me; she just has to belong to the European Community."

"The European Community," Øle droned, lying back in the chair with his eyes closed.

"I have to get out of Sweden. It's so boring."

"So boring," Øle softly repeated to feign interest.

"I need papers to work in the EU!" Lars shouted, snapping up in his chair for emphasis. The abrupt movement suddenly made him dizzy and he threw up on Øle's shoes again.

"Aaaarruumph! Splat," Øle repeated softly, feigning interest.

"You must know some girl here who owes you a favor. Why don't you call in your chips and do your pal Lars a good turn?"

Øle dragged up his eyelids and did a fairly good impression of focusing on Lars. Øle had given up days ago on trying to convince Lars that Sweden was already *in* the EU.

"Well, I don't know anyone who owes me *that* big of a favor. Anyway, this is Denmark, Lars. You can just as easily marry me. If it's only a matter of a marriage of convenience that shouldn't matter."

Lars' soapy brain mulled that one over. He pushed himself up from his chair and crashed forward onto his left knee. (Though he felt no pain at the time, he slightly tore the cartilage in it which would aggravate his arthritis on cold mornings in the years to come.) Lars clasped his hands together and looked into Øle's eyes.

"Øle, marry me. I want you to bear my working papers."

Øle threw his head back and began barking with laughter. The half-sip of Mr. Clean cocktail that he had in his mouth was forced up through his sinus cavity and green froth bubbled out of his nose. Seeing this, Lars burst out laughing, which set him off balance and crashing into the wall. Øle doubled over at this sight and began slamming his fist on the arm of the chair and quickly pattering his feet on the floor as Mr. Clean dribbled out of his nose and spluttered on his lips. Lars was making yelping sounds brought on by the convulsive laughter that prevented him from inhaling. This sent Øle out of his chair and ping-ponging off the walls. Lars peed himself, which prompted Øle to rush to the toilet to keep from doing just that.

After relieving, refreshing and composing himself, Øle returned to the living room with a half bottle of Windex that he had found under the bathroom sink, and which really isn't that bad with a splash of tonic and a slice of lime.

❧

Lars slowly peeled open his eyes, which were met by a beige carpet about an inch under them. He got to his feet and propped himself up against the wall. Blinking his eyes into focus, he realized that he wasn't in Øle's apartment anymore. Deciding to explore the new surroundings for clarification, Lars stumbled out of the bedroom. (He had cleverly determined that it was a bedroom as there was a bed about a foot away from where he had been sleeping.) He turned left and stared down the dimly lit hallway. Three steps later his foot caught on something and he was suddenly airborne. As his flight control system had shut down from hang-over-load, he was unable to lock his hands into the landing position. His face touched down with a formidable "thump" but, as his head was anesthetized, he suffered only minor discomfort. Turning to investigate the catalyst of this misadventure, he spotted Øle's barf-caked shoes jutting out from the hallway closet. They twitched slightly and a few low grunts from the closet signaled that the commotion had set Øle astir.

"Where are we, Øle?"

"Your place," Øle croaked.

Lars surveyed the area more closely. "Oh yeah," he said, with a glimmer of alacrity. Lars sat up, wincing when his ass pressed against the floor. His butt was very sore, and he wondered why.

"What are we doing here?" Lars asked.

"Well it occurred to you at one point that you had forgotten your toothbrush."

"We came back for my toothbrush? Why the fuck didn't I just buy another one?"

"I suggested that and then you broke out crying, called me an insensitive piece of shit and threw a flower pot at my head. Anyway, you were also beginning to wonder if they missed you at work."

"Oh, yeah, I'd better give them a call."

"Don't bother, they phoned this morning. You're fired."

"Bummer."

"I took the liberty of telling them that you'd always hated the shithole and that they could take the whole goddamn place and shove it."

"Thanks, Øle," Lars said appreciatively.

"I thought it appropriate," Øle replied.

A slight spasm of the screaming heebie jeebies came over Lars. While scratching at the ants, he discovered a foreign object wrapped around the ring finger of his right hand. Upon inspection it appeared to be a piece of tin foil rolled into a makeshift ring. He brushed it off as probably one of the more innocuous of antics he had undoubtedly perpetrated over the past three days.

Lars slid himself up the wall and Øle crawled out of the closet and got to his feet. They shuffled down the hall toward the kitchen in search of nourishment and antidotes. As Øle reached for the handle of the fridge, Lars spotted an identical tin foil ring on Øle's ring finger.

"What are we doing with these things on our fingers? We get married or something?" Lars jested.

"Yep," Øle replied, pulling out a carton of milk and shutting the door.

Lars chuckled.

"Boy!" Øle exclaimed. "You haven't the faintest recollection, have you?"

Lars chuckled.

"And I thought marriage was one of the most memorable occasions in a man's life."

Lars chuckled. And then he stopped chuckling. He furrowed his brow as vague images began to creep forth from the cerebral penumbra: plastic flowers, blasts of rice flying in his face, a matronly lady pounding away at a Casio, smiling faces wishing him health and happiness in his future life with Øooo …

"Ooooh my God!"

"What, Lars? Did you suddenly remember that incident in the supermarket?" Øle said.

"Oh my God!"

"Don't worry. I posted bail for you and if you show up for the court date next month and apologize I'm sure you'll get off with a suspended sentence, maybe a fine. After all, you didn't actually *do* it to the old lady, you just threatened to. Jusrisprudently speaking there's a big difference. You know, if I hadn't had to post your bail we wouldn't have run out of dough and had to go on the cleaning fluids. This should be a lesson to you to think before acting. You owe me fifteen hundred krone, by the way."

"What do you mean we're married?!"

"What do you mean, 'What do you mean we're married?' You proposed to me."

"I was fucking kidding, you moron!"

"Well, you were at first. But after a few Windex 'n' tonics the idea began to take shape. You certainly don't seem very appreciative," Øle said, slightly miffed.

"*Appreciative*?!"

Lars began to vigorously rub his face and pace the kitchen while Øle poured a glass of milk, added an egg, Worcestershire sauce, cinnamon and cigarette ashes, mixed it up into a grayish goop, stuck his fingers into it and began working the mixture into his temples.

"You're full of shit, anyway!" Lars shouted with a dismissive wave of the hand. "What kind of Justice of the Peace would marry us in our condition?"

"No kind. That's why we were married in a Methodist church. In these faithless days I guess they're easing up a bit on their standards."

"But I'm not a Methodist!" Lars shouted, immediately realizing that it was a point of little pertinence at this particular moment.

"So you said. You simply had to sign a paper promising not to oppose a Methodist upbringing for our children."

"*Our chil*–!" Lars decided to skip it. "Well, what I fucking mean is what kind of *anybody* would marry two people who were so obviously off their heads?!"

"One person–I was actually holding it together pretty well."

"*One* person, then, goddamn it!"

"Well, the minister could see that you were Swedish and … well, I guess he probably assumed that that was about as good as you people get. Anyway, calm down. You'll get your working papers and in five years or so we'll get a divorce. Sheesh!" Øle exclaimed testily.

"Working papers?"

"For the EU."

"For the EU?"

"Yeah, you wanted to get into the EU."

"Get into the EU? I'm already *in* the fucking EU."

"So I kept telling you. You were so insistent, though."

"So you married me so I'd *shut up*?"

"Pretty much so," Øle said, rubbing more of the goop into his temples.

Lars leaned back against the wall. He winced when his sore bottom made contact with it. He had forgotten that he had hurt himself when he had landed flat on his ass after being whipped off the second tier of the ferry as a result of a conga-line mishap. When he felt the soreness again, however, he was struck by the horrifying notion that maybe the marriage had actually been *consummated*! But that's not the kind of thing you ask a guy about, is it?

Lars held his head in his hands. The excitement had sent a surge of adrenaline that was flushing the fog from his brain. It finally dawned on him that this was all one big fucking joke.

"Øle, this is all one big fucking joke!"

"It's on the dining room table," Øle responded enigmatically.

Lars took a deep breath, counted to ten, donned a rigor-mortis smile, and slowly, calmly, quietly asked the question.

"What's on the dining room table, Øle?"

"It."

Lars huffed in disgust and stomped over to the table. Looking down he saw it–the marriage certificate. Lars plopped, wincingly, down on one of the chairs. He stared despondent-ly at the document. There was Øle's name and there was his name. There was no doubt about it. It looked like the real McCoy ... Yes, of course, it *looked* like the real McCoy! Lars returned to the kitchen.

"Øle, you prick! Do you think I'm going to fall for this stupid little prank? Do you think I rode to school on the little yellow bus? You just slapped this thing together on your com-puter and got me to sign it when I was off my head! The wed-ding ceremony was just a whole elaborate put-on and ..."

"00-45-909," Øle interrupted.

Lars took a deep breath and released it slowly. Quietly, but with determination, he spoke.

"Now, Øle, I am going to ask you a question, and you are not to respond '00-45-909.' No, Øle. Oh, no, no, no. What you are going to do is to explain, clearly, concisely and articulately, just exactly what, '00-45-909' means."

"That's the international access number, the country code for Denmark, and the number for information. They'll give you the number for the Bureau of Vital Statistics in Copenhagen. More coffee?"

Lars stomped off to the foyer where the phone was. Øle heard Lars dialing; a short conversation; the phone hanging up; Lars dialing again; a short, somewhat louder conversation; and a crisp slamming-down of the receiver. Moments later Lars slowly shuffled into the kitchen with his head hanging low.

"Well, Lars, it's been a good one, but I've got to get back. Oh, and don't forget about your court date next month. I left all the papers on the dining room table." He shot a smile at Lars. "Well, how about a lift back to the ferry?"

"Our first row," Øle quipped, breaking the silence.

"Oh shut the fuck up!" Lars barked as he accidentally downshifted, causing minor damage to the gearbox of his Volvo. The horrible grinding sound set his teeth on edge.

"I don't know why you're so freaked about this thing … unless …" Øle took a sidelong glance at Lars.

"Unless what?!" Lars shouted.

"Well, I don't know … I just thought that this might have stirred up some sort of latent repression type of thing in you that you haven't fully come to terms with yet, or something."

Lars turned and looked at Øle. "Getting upset at waking up to find a Danish man in your closet who it turns out you're married to is, and I believe most psychologists would agree with me on this one, a healthy reaction." Lars ground the gears again. "Listen Øle, I'm taking the ferry over with you and we're going to get this thing canceled."

"You mean annulled."

"I mean *canceled!*" Lars barked.

"Sheesh! Try and do someone a favor."

"A favor! A favor! What if I should die tomorrow? How do you think my parents would feel when, in the process of straightening out my affairs, they discover that I'm married to one Øle Øleson?"

"Not as bad as if they found out you were married to *two* of them," Øle jested.

Lars ground the gears and Øle settled back in his seat, deeming it wise to give the jokes a rest for the remainder of the ride.

"Two tickets to Copenhagen, please," Lars said.

The middle-aged woman behind the ticket window dropped her pen and slowly raised her head. Her eyes were wide and her mouth agape. Lars immediately took this to mean that she, as well as everyone else on the planet, *knew*. He began to splutter.

"You see, we did it to cut through the bureaucracy, not that it was really necessary, me already being in the EU and all. It's not like we actually love each other or anything like that. Heck, I don't even really like him." Lars began to titter nervously. Øle intervened.

"You must be new at this ticket selling game," Øle said, donning his overly pleasant smart-ass tone. "You'll find that, once you get the hang of it, this thing this sort of request will become much less baffling."

The woman shot a furtive glance at a police officer who, fortuitously, had just come into the station to get a coke at the vending machine. She managed to catch his attention and signaled for him to come over.

"What's going on here?" The large and menacing officer said upon reaching the window.

The ticket agent pointed a quivering finger at Øle and Lars.

"What do you guys want?"

"Uhm, two tickets to Copenhagen ... please," Øle answered, carefully choosing his words lest they be interpreted as criminal intent, though he didn't quite know why he was doing that.

"What're you, some kind of smart-ass?"

As his treatment of the ticket agent indicated, Øle was indeed a smart-ass–and certainly enjoyed nothing better than being one with a cop. Not intending to be one at the moment, however, left him unprepared to respond in a smart-ass fashion.

"Uhm, no."

"Well, then get the hell out of here!"

"Uhm, officer, I have to get back to Copenhagen."

The policeman stared at Øle. There was something in his voice that indicated to him that Øle really wasn't trying to be a smart-ass.

"Where the hell have you been for the last couple of days?"

Though the question was asked in a clearly surprised, rather than accusing tone, both Øle and Lars looked down and began shifting their weight from one foot to the other. They were both thinking that the whole thing might have something to do with their behavior on the ferry ride over.

"Oh, well, here and there, you know, officer ..." Øle began to prattle.

"Denmark has been eradicated from the face of the Earth by a massive nuclear bombardment," the officer said.

"Come again?" Øle asked as his booze-addled neurons struggled to wrap themselves around that last tidbit of information.

"I said that Denmark has been … Hey, wait a minute—you're Danish, aren't you?" The police officer asked in what Øle deemed a notably unfriendly tone.

"I want to speak to my ambassador," Øle said, grasping at straws.

"No can do, sausage eater. No country, no ambassador—*capice*? Anyway, some of the boys, after scrapping it up a bit at the Scandinavian Cup, took a bit of a liking to bloodletting. They dragged what used to be your ambassador out of the embassy, tied his arms and legs to four Volvos pointing in four different directions, and VAHROOOOM! Serves the bastard right! You fuckers should never have tried to nick the Gotland in 1363!"

"Well, if Mangus of Sweden and the rest of the Hanseatic League had been a little less intransigent, maybe we would have never found the need to …" Øle cut himself short. It occurred to him that, given the circumstance, this was not the moment to set the historical record straight. Anyone who has ever woken up in a foreign country with a cleaning fluids hangover and is being informed that his county has been annihilated by an increasingly belligerent cop with a recently acquired taste for blood and a six-hundred-year grudge will empathize with Øle.

"I can't help but agree with you officer. Well, uhm … bye." Øle turned gingerly toward the door and headed for it. His walk was awkwardly stiff as a result of his concerted effort to look nonchalant. *Don't run*, Øle told himself. *Whatever you do—do not run.*

Øle stepped out the door and slid over behind the wall, cocking his ear in expectation of gunshots and the pitter-patter of regulation-issued urban assault boots. Not forthcoming either, he whistled a sigh of relief and headed across the street toward a conveniently located bar. Lars, after flashing at the officer what he hoped passed for a friendly grin, went out after Øle, who he spotted going into the bar.

A hazy gray Scandinavian light filtered through the front window of the bar, bathing Øle's face in melancholy. Lars carefully studied Øle's eyes and occasional twitches and movements in an attempt to glean from them some clue to Øle's state of mind. What horrors and sorrows could he be living? Could Lars ever hope to comprehend the devils that would now lurk within? What could be passing through the mind of this living anachronism, rootless and adrift with not past nor peer?

Øle seemed to come around.

"Oh well," Øle said, shrugging his shoulders. "No use crying over spilled milk. Pity about my comic book collection, though. And I'd just acquired the 1953 first issue of *The Black Knight*–and in mint condition." Øle took a sip of his beer. "No need to worry about 'canceling' now, Lars–a huge fireball took care of that for you. I guess your court date is over too, though that should serve as a lesson to you to curb some of your more Neanderthal instincts. Oh, by the way, do you think you could pay me back those fifteen hundred krone in dollars, or euros, or yen, or any other currency still backed by an existing government.

Lars, having stopped at a cash machine on the way to the ferry, took out his wallet and gave Øle two hundred euros.

"Thanks, Lars. Well, hasta la vista." Øle got up from the table and headed for the door.

"Wait, Øle. Where will you go?"

Øle stopped at the door and slowly turned towards Lars.

"Wherever the wind blows me. Wherever destiny shall lead me. Wherever two hundred euros'll get me."

He turned and walked out the door.

BOOK II

OLÉ ØLE

Destiny and two hundred euros (as it turned out, wind played a very small part in it) got Øle to Spain. For reasons unnecessary to expand upon, he rejected France and Britain as possible destinations. The United States and Greenland were also ruled out on the basis of what Øle considered to be serious attitude problems. Øle had spent a blow-out holiday on the Costa Brava five years before, and he remembered that the wine was cheap there. So Spain it was.

Things quickly took a turn for the better for Øle (which, in relative terms, isn't that hard to imagine). He soon found work giving classes in butter cookie confection and pornographic film production techniques. He had also, given his unique position, wisely chosen to assume a new nationality, and now told people he was from Finland. His sole reason for choosing Finland was based on his estimation that 'With us, the ladies come first, because we Finnish last' was a pretty clever pick-up line.

Miraculously, it sometimes worked.

It was a Sunday afternoon late in June and Øle had invited over for lunch a particularly dark-eyed beauty named Carmen who was a student in his Intro to Nut Crushing class (which, coincidently, was the name of a class he taught in butter cookie confection *and* pornographic film production techniques). He had prepared a typical Finnish meal from his "native" Pöpelikkö. For starters, Øle served a creamy sillijääkyke over pinaattiohukainen. The main course was metsätäjänpihvi with hasselbacken perunat and dripping in sianlihakastike. Accompanying the meal was a garden fresh punajuurisalaatti with chunks of piimäjuusto and dressed with vanhanaikainen salaattikastike. There was also home-baked saaristolaisleipä slathered with butter. For desert Øle had baked a raparperipiirakka and served it with a dollop of kuningatarhillo on top.

After lunch, Øle placed the tray with coffee and jälkiruokiadrinkit on the coffee table, deftly shifting the arena of action from the dining table to the couch. The jälkiruokiadrinkit was working its magic, and Carmen was slipping into an amorous mood.

And then, of course, the door crashed open. At the threshold stood Lars.

"Unhand my husband!" Lars bellowed.

Carmen quickly obeyed.

"Now be gone, home wrecker!" Lars screamed in Swedish, jerking his thumb over his shoulder indicating the door. Carmen understood–or at least she understood that, whatever he'd said, it was in her best interest to get the hell out of there. She sprang off the couch and rushed past Lars and out the door. Øle ran to the balcony.

"Come back, Carmen! I can explain!" Øle shouted down to her just as she disappeared around the corner. The truth was, of course, that he couldn't explain–as he didn't have a fucking clue as to what was going on; thus, he sought illumination.

"Lars, you fucker! What the fuck is going on?"

"In the kitchen," Lars chirped domestically.

Øle stomped through the living room to the kitchen.

"God damn you Lars!" Øle shouted, shaking his fists in rage.

"I'm making some tea for myself," Lars said, filling the kettle from the tap. "Like some?"

"God damn it, Lars! You barge in here, fuck everything up and you still have the nerve to still be fucking around."

"Øle," Lars said, turning towards him, "I'm the one who should be upset."

"Øle was quiet for a moment, trying to absorb that one. He then returned to the subject at hand.

"Lars, what the fuck are you talking about?! And what the fuck are you doing here in the first place?! And, while we're on the subject, what is all this 'my husband' crap?!" Øle posed the last question feeling a twinge of reticence, after having asked it, at discovering the answer.

Lars put the kettle down slowly and, just as slowly, turned towards Øle.

"What therefore God hath joined together, let not man put asunder."

Uh, oh.

"Mark 10:9."

Oh shit.

The expression on Lars' face was terrifyingly sincere. The hairs on the back of Øle's neck stood on end. He knew that Lars wasn't joking, and began to instinctively scan the room for possible escape routes and objects that could be used as weapons if need be.

"I bet you're wondering what I'm doing here?" Lars asked serenely.

"Well, Lars," Øle said, in the tone that hostage negotiators employ, and which he maintained throughout the conversation, "I believe I did ask you a question to that effect earlier."

"Well, Øle, after you left I got to thinking."

"Yes."

"And something occurred to me."

"Obviously."

"I began to think why it was that I should find myself in such an absurd position of getting married to a Danish man and then to fortuitously get him to Sweden just hours before Denmark was eradicated from the face of the Earth."

"Coincidence?" Øle peeped, hazarding a theory he sensed would not gain much currency here in the kitchen.

"I don't think so," Lars said, chuckling patronizingly. "God's will, Øle. God's will."

Øle cringed.

"Milk? Sugar?" Lars asked as he carried a tray with the teapot and cups over to the coffee table.

"Uhm … honey."

"Yes?"

"No, uh, I mean I'd like honey in my tea … uh … but we don't have any. Yeah, that's right, we don't have any. So I'll just pop down to the shop and get some." Øle said, too fast. He fully expected Lars to produce a pistol at this point and serenely, with a beatific smile, inform him that he wasn't going anywhere.

"Don't dawdle, it'll get cold," Lars said, seemingly more interested in pouring the tea.

Øle was surprised by Lars' indifference, and then suspicious. How can you second-guess a madman? Would Lars shoot him in the back on his way out? Øle calculated the distance between himself and the door and speculated on Lars' skill on the fast-draw.

"Back in a sec," Øle said, springing out the door and slamming it behind him. He sailed down the stairs, bolted out the building, and fled down the street.

At Øle's behest, the patrolman entered the apartment ahead of him.

"There he is," Øle said, pointing at Lars from behind the protective cover of the officer. Lars looked up from the couch.

"What has he done now, officer?" Lars sighed.

"What have *I* done?!"

"He's been, well, a little, how shall I say, difficult, since shortly after we were married."

"Married?" The officer repeated, looking at Øle.

"Well, sort of," Øle feebly concurred. "But not *married* married, you know," he offered as way of explanation.

Lars took out the marriage certificate and handed it to the middle-aged stocky officer.

"Looks official," the officer said.

"Indeed it is," Lars said.

"But we're two *guys*!" Øle pleaded. "This is *Spain*! You don't accept this sort of thing *here*?"

"Actually, we do, sir. I don't know when was the last time you were here, but Spain's now in the forefront in Europe as far as progressive legislation."

"Well, I liked it a whole lot better when it was a Catholic Church dominated fascist dictatorship," Øle said, heaving a miffed hurumph.

"Listen, I can't be running up here every time you two have a spat," the officer said. "Now I see you've got a nice pot of tea here, so why don't you two just sit down and work this thing through."

"Because there's nothing to work through," Øle protested.

"I once thought that about my own marriage, sir. But then we got some counseling, and you know what? Next month the little lady and I'll have been married for twenty-seven years. There's always some way to work through things if you make the effort."

"Thank you for bringing him home," Lars said as he escorted the officer to the door. "You've given us a lot to think about."

ↄ

A week had passed since Lars' arrival, and Øle had opted for feigning resignation. Feigning resignation–and planning. He had even suggested a trip to Lars as the ideal beginning to a fresh start. And, to show just how much he was settling into connubial domesticity, he had offered to do all of the packing. Hence, one week later they found themselves at the domestic flight terminal of Barajas airport waiting for their flight to Albacete.

"Oh," Øle exclaimed as they stood in line at the baggage check-in line, "gotta pee."

"I told you to go before we left home," Lars chided him in that wifely/maternal manner that had sent Øle teetering on the edge of murder for the last week. (Øle had ruled out the murder option, aware that in prison he would also have a husband–and most likely a significantly more demanding one at that.) "Oh, well, make it quick. We should be boarding soon."

Øle headed for the washrooms, but ducked over to the nearest phone as soon as he was out of sight and dialed quickly.

"Hello, police? There is a man at the baggage check-in counter in the domestic flight terminal of Barajas airport who is carrying twenty grams of heroin and a loaded pistol in a black and silver Nike sports bag. He's a six-foot four-inch fair-skinned blond-haired man in his late twenties." Øle suddenly realized that he had also pretty much described himself. He elucidated. "Uh, the six-foot four-inch fair-skinned blond-haired man in his late twenties who I'm referring to is the one with the revoltingly serene expression on his face." Øle hung up and went out to catch the shuttle bus to the international terminal where he planned to catch the first flight leaving to wherever.

IT DOESN'T GET
ANY BETTER THAN
THIS, EXCEPT FOR
THE CAT THING

Thornton whistled a cheery tune. Thornton didn't often whistle cheery tunes, but, then again, Aunt Anne didn't often die either. Nor did Thornton often soft-shoe–but soft-shoe he did (and with surprising panache) from the bathroom to the wardrobe. Opening it, he felt a twinge of disappointment as he contemplated grey suit upon grey suit. Never before had Thornton had any inclination whatsoever to wear anything other than a grey suit. But today he ached to don something yellow and orange and red, checkered and polka-dotted and bright. A suit that would say to the world, "Behold, for I am giddy with glee!"

Alas, as the nephew, the prime minister, and the one who was to deliver the eulogy, he would have had to pass up the temptation anyway. But it would have been nice, at least, to have been given the option. His chagrin deepened when he realized that he couldn't even wear anything as cheery as a grey suit, and he reached toward the back of the wardrobe for his black one.

Thornton dressed, feeling his joy stifled in such a dreary suit, and then went to his study. He walked slowly. He had been putting off writing the eulogy, as the mere thought of saying anything nice about Aunt Anne was as alien to his being as it was repulsive to his senses. (Anne Throppe, like most arch-evil people, had lived an extraordinarily long and remarkably healthy life and had died peacefully in her sleep of natural causes.) Thornton entered the oak-paneled study, the walls of which were lined with portraits of his ancestors, and sat at his desk. He took a sheet of paper from the desk drawer, drew the pen from its holder and began tapping it on the desk as his eyes searched the room for inspiration. They first fell upon the portrait of Laurel the Hardy sitting on a majestic white steed and holding a lance with his standard flapping in the wind. An angel was hovering above his head and crowning him with a laurel wreath. In the background was a dragon cowering in dread at the expectation of having to do battle with such a formidable slayer as *Laurel the Fucking Hardy*! Thornton snarled and harrumphed, and then turned his attention to the next portrait, that of Aunt Anne's father, Winthrop Throppe—a man whose incompetence soared to such dizzying heights so as to enable him to actually *go broke selling opium to a protected market of half a billion junkies*! Thornton snorted. He realized that inspiration was not to be gleaned from the example of his ancestors. In desperation, Thornton decided to just put pen to paper and let his thoughts flow as they may.

As is well known, he wrote, *all women are bitches. But, in the case of Lady Anne Throppe, she was the Undisputed Atomic Bitch from HELL!!!*

Thornton stopped to review his work. After a reflective moment, he took the sheet of paper from the desk and slid it through the shredder. It pained him to have to destroy such an elegantly-put truism, but he was not here to pen elegantly-put truisms; he was here to write Aunt Anne's eulogy. He took a fresh sheet from the drawer and leaned back in his chair, tapping his chin with the end of the pen. Melpomene finally laid her gentle hands upon his head; Thornton leaned forward and wrote:

We are all saddened by the passing of Lady Anne Throppe.

Thornton stopped to read what he had written; so far, so good. Encouraged, he continued:

Yet we are left with the lingering question: Couldn't the fucking old cow have agonized a bit before she kicked the bucket?"

Thornton slid the sheet through the shredder. Realizing that stream of consciousness did not seem to be doing the trick, he decided on another approach. He would write about someone *else* whom he admired, or at least liked, and then simply substitute "Lady Anne Throppe" for that person's name. Thornton leaned back in his chair again, tapping his chin with the end of his pen. It didn't take long for it to dawn on Thornton—he neither admired, nor liked, nor even remotely tolerated, for that matter, anyone whatsoever, living or dead, in the least little bit. Thornton rose from the chair and walked to the window. Gazing out of windows was said to be good for inspiration. And it worked! In a flash, the muse, instead of laying her gentle hands upon his head this time, hurled herself at him and kneed him in the bollocks. He didn't have to write about *someone*—he could write about *something*! And that something wasn't long in coming to him. He hastened to his desk, pulled out a handful of paper from the drawer and let his pen glide across them. Many pages, though few minutes, later, he jabbed the last full stop into place. He read it over. It was an inspired piece of writing and nothing had to be changed—nothing except to put in "Lady Anne Throppe" where he had written "a red, orange and yellow checkered and polka-dotted suit."

Having finished this unpleasant task, Thornton made a few phone calls. He was still ironing out a few of the details necessary to carry out Aunt Anne's last wish—to have Ewinthrall buried along with her to serve her in the afterlife. As can well be imagined, slaughtering a servant and burying him along with his mistress is a practice which, in modern-day Britain, involves a great deal of paperwork. Even as prime minister, Thornton still had to call in quite a few favors to cut through the red tape.

The church was full. Though there was not a soul on the planet who had the least minimal positive feeling towards Lady Anne Throppe, she was, after all, the prime minister's aunt and, thus, political considerations brought them there.

Thornton approached the podium slowly. This was not for effect, nor as a direct result of the revulsion he felt at having to carry out such a task, but as an indirect result of it. Basically, Thornton, as a final fortification against this most distasteful of duties, had recurred to Dutch courage–enough Dutch courage to get a herd of rhinos barred from the corner pub for life.

Thornton planted himself at the podium and firmly grasped both sides of it. It suddenly occurred to him that he had forgotten to remove the eulogy from his inside coat pocket. He still had enough sense, though, to realize that by releasing his grip on the podium and fishing around in his pocket for it would be, in his present state, too disorienting and dizzying. It would be better, or so he thought, to give the eulogy from memory. And so he did:

"We the bereaved have suffered a great loss. Bereaved-wise speaking we are very, very, very ... bereaved. To say 'bereaved' only scratches the surface. But how are we, the bereaved, to endure this great loss? Well, of course, we must find the strength in what we have gained by our association with my aunt, Lady Anne Throppe. As we all know, she was a bitch ..."

The alcohol was causing Thornton's real thoughts to slip through. He fought to pull himself together.

"... *a bit cheery*. No, no, I would go so far as to say that she was rather awfully cheery." Thornton paused for dramatic effect, and to congratulate himself on having carried that off rather well. "There were times in my life," he continued, "when I never would have made it without her dosh ... her *dash*, her élan, her joie de vivre to pull me through. If it weren't for her being such a cunt ... such a *continuous* supporter, I would not be where I am today. One can look at my Aunt Anne as a stinking shit ... *a sinking ship*, which is to say that she maintained, throughout her life, the values and moral bearing that might seem, in these cynical times, anachronisms. I would resoundly disagree.

"When I think of Lady Anne dying peacefully in her bed, rather than writhing in pain ... *rising again*, I can't help but think the world has lost a slut ... *a lot*. We will live in a world lacking the bitchiness ... *richness* that Aunt Anne brought to it. Yes, her pissing off ... *passing on* will affect each and every one of us. When we think of this fucked ... *defunct* woman, we must remember her as an orange and checkered and polka-dotted suit. So, though we now weep over this whore ... *horrible* loss, we can take heart in the fact that Lady Anne, in death, as in life, will always be an arsehole ... *in our souls.*"

Thornton finished the eulogy and, almost as if planned as a way to punctuate it, he, and the podium he was firmly clutching, slowly, but with firm determination, toppled forward.

Those present were moved to tears as they witnessed Thornton, a man who previously they had always considered to be absolutely heartless, faint from grief at the passing of his beloved aunt.

Thornton left the church and headed toward his car. Despite the lumps and bruises he had suffered as a result of his spill, he was whistling a cheery tune again, and not because he was still drunk. The adrenaline rush that had coursed through him in anticipation of what was coming next had completely sobered him up. He was now off to the event that he had yearned for his entire adult life–the reading of Aunt Anne's will.

Thornton paced in his office and looked at his watch again. It was two to five. The last time he had checked it was three to five–and that seemed an eternity ago. He was thankful, at least, that Aunt Anne's solicitor, Baxter Goldhalter, was never late and would be here at five on the dot.

Being the sole remaining relative of Lady Anne, Thornton would also be the sole heir. The careful reader, however, will remember that he had had a sister, Aurelia. And what became of her? Well, it's anyone's guess, really. Thornton always maintained that she, against their parents' wishes, had run off to Australia with a Hoover salesman. Most, however, suspect that chloroform, a false name, and an insane asylum staffed by nurses with unusually high purchasing power, form a more likely explanation.

It was five on the dot and Goldhalter was shown into Thornton's office. Thornton hastily greeted him and directed him to a seat. Goldhalter sat down slowly, slowly produced some papers from his briefcase, slowly removed his wire-rimmed glasses from his coat pocket and slowly began cleaning them with his handkerchief.

"GOLDHALTER, I *DO* HAVE A BLOODY COUNTRY TO RUN!" Thornton barked.

"I apologize, sir, but this won't take but a moment."

Thornton wasn't sure he liked the sound of that.

Godlhalter put his glasses on, picked up the papers and read:

"'I, Lady Anne Throppe, being of sound mind and body, leave my entire estate to the Lady Anne Throppe Home for Feline Felicity.'"

Goldhalter folded the will and returned it to his briefcase.

A deafening silence rang through the air. When it quieted down, Thornton spoke:

"As far as the liquid assets, maybe we could gain some extra mileage from the £275,000 nil rate band, after that I think we're going to have to go offshore."

"Mr. Prime Minister."

"As far as the real estate, I think if we used the annual exclusion, and I spent at least one night a month in each house, I could claim them as principal residences.

"Mr. Prime Minister," Goldhalter said mechanically. He recognized the signs of when someone has been cut out of the will. It was a common psychological reaction which those in the testate business referred to as Denial Denial. Denial Denial had four stages to it, and Thornton had entered into the first, which was, well, denial.

"Well, I'll just leave it to Nigel, my accountant. He's sharp as a tack. Inland Revenue will probably end up paying *me* money," Thornton chuckled.

"Mr. Prime Minister," Goldhalter said soothingly.

It was obvious, for anyone who knew Thornton well (which is to say, Aunt Anne) that he actually had heard what the solicitor had said. Such intricate and crisply delineated instructions bespoke this. (Had Aunt Anne actually left him her money, Thornton would have done little more than drool and ask, "When do I get it?")

"You know," Thornton said. "It's really all Monty Diddlestiff's fault," referring to the leader of the opposition. "His father was an undertaker and Monty managed to work his way up through the ranks and he simply doesn't understand the situation we men of standing are in. He's the one who's been blocking inheritance tax reform. Well good! Fair enough! But if up is down, and down is up, then why do the children play?" (Stage Two: Temporary Insanity.)

"And, if you've ever noticed, rarely does the sun shine when it's cloudy out. Funny about that. And why, one might ask, is ice cream always cold and saunas are always hot?"

Thornton paused for a moment to gather his thoughts, and then spoke:

"I WANT MY FUCKING MONEY YOU AMBU-LANCE-CHASING PIECE OF SHIT!" (Stage Three: Rage.)

Goldhalter rose to leave. Thornton had calmed down and had now entered Stage Four: Grief. The solicitor felt that it would be undignified for him to sit there any longer watching the prime minister stretched out on the floor, kicking his legs, flailing his arms and bawling like a baby.

Thornton was not about to take this matter lying down. So, in due course, he picked himself up off the floor. He then walked out to the garden adjoining his office. As if to add insult to injury, it was a warm and sunny day. Birds were chirping and small, innocuous bees were busily pollinating the little flowers.

Thornton knew there was nothing to be done. Aunt Anne most certainly would have instructed her solicitors to second guess any possible loophole he might recur to, and head him off. For however much Lady Anne Throppe had felt that she needed him in life, she had decided that, in death, Thornton could ... well ... go fuck himself. The fact that Aunt Anne hated cats more than she hated any other creature made it clear that that was the message she was sending. Thornton had laughed when she first established the Home as a tax write-off. Now Aunt Anne had the last laugh. He had pulled himself up off the floor only to find that he would have to take it lying down after all.

Thornton came out of his bitter reflections. What brought him around was the sight of a kitten that had had the spectacular misfortune to cross Thornton's path at that moment. The kitten, a tortoiseshell that, even by the highly competitive standards set for kittens, was *incredibly* cute. It stopped at Thornton's feet and looked up at him with two of the biggest eyes a kitten ever sported. It crooked his head to one side and peeped the most adorable kitten-meow ever meowed anywhere at anytime by any kitten. It then waddled up to Thornton and began to rub its little bitty head against his ankle. Thornton looked to his right, and then to his left and then behind him. The English are well-known for their fondness for four-legged fluffy creatures, and it would not have been to Thornton's benefit to be observed beating the living bejesus out of the cutest little kitten ever to waddle across the face of the Earth. Thornton concluded that he was alone. He slowly squatted down.

"Coochy, coochy coo, my little pretty."

Thornton sat in the bathroom applying tincture to his wounds. The kitten had held its own and had got in a couple of good ones on Thornton. (Furthermore, if kittens had a sense of poetic justice, and who's to say they don't, then this one would have felt vindicated. After spending three months recovering at the Lady Anne Throppe Home for Feline Felicity, the cost for its re-constructive surgery, physical therapy and psychological counseling had run the Home £92,893 of what Thornton considered to be *his* money.)

Thornton knew that pulverizing kittens, as pleasant as that might be, was only a temporary palliative. In a situation such as this, full-blown, out and out, no holds barred revenge is the only way to reestablish inner harmony. Wreaking vengeance upon a dead person, however, presents limited options. As he daubed the tincture, it began to dawn on Thornton that there was at least one matter that seemed to be of importance to people after they're dead–their looks. They were dressed in their best and made up. The highest compliment that can be paid to someone who's been laid out concerns his or her looks. (She looks very natural. She looks very peaceful. She looks like she's resting. She looks very dignified. She looks better than she did when she was fucking alive!) Looks! Yes, that's it! No one wants to be buried looking like a bum. No one wants to

be buried looking like a fool. No one wants to be buried looking like a clown.

Clown?

෴

Through the thick mist, the black-clad figure in the ski mask
moved stealthily among the gravestones. Thornton slithered
along, carrying a shovel in one hand and his old greasepaint
box in the other. (After the ginmonger's slattern had left him
penniless, Thornton had spent a period in Paris busking as
The Sad Mime—a chapter in his life which, upon his entry into
politics, required rather a few murders-for-hire to cover up.)

Thornton came upon her grave. He read the inscription
on her gravestone and grinned. Through some oversight, Aunt
Anne had failed to leave instructions specifying what she
wanted written on it, thus leaving the decision in Thornton's
hands. If Thornton had struggled over her eulogy, her epithet
flowed from his pen like a hot knife through warm butter. He
had opted for a Latin inscription, "*Hic Est Septus Verus Vene-
ficus,*" which roughly translated as "Here Lies a Real Bitch."
This was his vengeance for the misery she had caused him in
life–this in no way would make up for what she had inflicted
upon him after her death.

Thornton set to work. Digging up and desecrating a grave
and the cadaver within was the sort of job Thornton would
normally have outsourced. But this was pleasure, not business.
As such, his zeal belied his sedentary middle-aged body and he
made quick work of the six feet of earth covering Aunt Anne's
coffin.

The casket, being new and just recently buried, denied
Thornton the ghoulish pleasure of creaking hinges as he
opened it. This mild disappointment was short-lived and was
soon replaced by the joy of once again seeing Aunt Anne dead.
Thornton could have relished that sight all night, but he had a
lot to get through, so he didn't dawdle.

He had given a great deal of thought to the *motif*, so he was able to expedite the job, it now being merely technical rather that ponderously artistic. He had decided on something between the classicalism of Emmett Kelly and the kitsch of Coq Dèsir, a drag queen Thornton had shacked up with while in Paris. (And for whom he had actually developed something close to affection and, consequently, for whom he felt something approaching sadness when he'd had her whacked at the beginning of his political career.)

Thornton first applied a white base. He then began to daub, brush and rub with a skill that hadn't grown rusty over the years. In less than half an hour he was finished. Thornton stood up to admire his work. It was the most gruesomely ridiculous, outrageous, unsettling thing he had ever seen.

It was a masterpiece.

Thornton knew that he couldn't spend all night beholding this most joyful of sights, so he took a couple of pictures with the state-of-the-art infrared digital camera he had borrowed from MI6 for the occasion, and reburied Aunt Anne.

Thornton slunk stealthily (no point in slinking boisterously, is there?) from the graveyard. He had never before slunk from a graveyard, but he slunk as if born to slink. So well did he slink that he, perhaps out of hubris–for there is no other explanation for it, shifted from a finely honed slink to an effective yet far less artful creep. He then, throwing all caution to the wind, began to skulk. Just as he did so, he heard a voice. Thornton froze. He suddenly felt foolish for having hot-doggingly switched from a near flawless slink to a far above average, yet could-stand-improvement, skulk. He heard the voice again and, to his relief, realized that it was not directed toward him. He had not been caught. Not yet. He looked around quickly for cover and, finding such, dived behind a nearby tombstone.

Thornton cocked his ears and tried to hear above the sound of his beating heart. He listened intently. Fear began to drain from him and was being replaced by curiosity–because the voice was an oddly familiar one. Thornton, ever so slowly, eased himself up just enough to peer over the tombstone. He directed his gaze toward whence the voice came. He squinted and could just make out two dark, reclining figures in the penumbra of the graveyard. He saw that they were those of a man and a woman. They were lying on a blanket, the man was propped up on his elbow and near the woman's head was an ice bucket with a bottle of champagne in it. Thornton could now clearly make out the man's face and, as he spoke again, he could clearly make out the man's voice.

"You're looking lovely tonight, my dear. Is that a new dress you're wearing?" he cooed.

Thornton blinked. He blinked anew, and then blinked thrice. This was not a hallucination. It was reality in three glorious dimensions. What Thornton beheld was none other than the portly balding figure of Monty Diddlestiff–the loyal leader of the opposition! The loyal leader of the opposition in a graveyard at four a.m. chatting up a woman who, from the diminutive size of her, was obviously not Mrs. Diddlestiff! Monty Diddlestiff, that son of an undertaker and perennial thorn in his side. Thornton tried to make out who the woman was. He hoped that she too would be someone well-known. That would really be the icing on the cake. Thornton craned his neck a bit more to get a good look at her face. Voilà! The icing! She was none other than Winifried Craparotter–the young and beautiful wife of the Right Honourable Plantagenet Craparotter–the Royal Family's spiritual advisor! A woman who, in her own right, had won the hearts of all of Britain for her tireless work on the behalf of the indigent and infirm. A woman who would often be seen in newspapers and on television bathing lepers and swaddling waifs. A woman who ... who ... *who had died the week before*!

Thornton gasped. Fearing the gasp might have been heard, he popped back down behind the tombstone. As he sat there, he reflected. Sheer dumb luck had never before played a role in any of Thornton's successes. Arson, assault, asskissing, assassination, backroom business, blackmail, betrayal, bribery, breach of promise, backstabbing, cheating, chicanery, calumny, collusion, conning, cronyism, corruption, crafty conniving, cunning conspiracy, deception, dirty-dealing, disloyalty, dastardly deeds, draconian defamation, disingenuous discourse, doctored documents, double-crossing, extortion, embezzlement, espionage, falsehoods, felonious fiddling, flattery, forgery, fraud, framing foes, gambits, graft, gangsterism, gerrymandering, hate-mongering, heinous human-rights abuses, harassment, heckling, hypocrisy, hoax, hoodwinking, hustling, ill-gotten income, improbity, injustice, injury, infamy, iniquity, intrigue, jingoism, jinks (of the highest sort), judas kisses, jury-rigging, kangaroo courts, kowtowing, libel, lawlessness, Machiavellian maneuvering, maligning, mendacity, misdealing, misrepresentation, mischief, misleading missives, masterly malfeasance, malefaction, malevolent machinations, nepotism, non-stop knavery, outlandish offenses, old-boy's network, perjury, perfidious plotting, pilfering, quiescent quislings, racketeering, roguishness, race-baiting, regicide, ruses, recreantness, sly scams, scummy schemes, shiftiness, sinfulness, slander, smoke screens, scurrilous scandal mongering, skullduggery, surreptitious shenanigans, spying, swindling, treachery, trickery, treason, two-faced underhanded undoings, unscrupulous undertakings, unconscionable unveraciousness, venality, violence, vulpine villainy, vice, vote-tampering, wickedness, wiliness, weasel words, wrongdoing, xenophobia and zoophobia (just look what he did to that poor kitten), and, without question, Thornton had also committed uncountable heinous acts that begin with *Y*.

Yes, these had all played a part in Thornton's success. Sheer dumb luck had never factored in. Being in a graveyard with a state-of-the art spy camera at four in the morning and finding the leader of the opposition seducing the cadaver of one of the most beloved and respected women in England was not the sort of card that fate generally dealt him.

As all *isms* do, pessimism disinclines the brain from processing accurately extra-ideological phenomena. Consequently, Thornton was slow to realize that fate had allowed him to stumble, almost literally, upon what was beginning to look like, for lack of a better word, luck.

Taking his 1000x1 zoom, flashless, infrared, silent-operating camera with digital capacity for 12,000 high definition pictures, Thornton slid back up from behind the tombstone and began snapping away.

ℰℬ

"Prime Minister Wingate, Minister Diddlestiff to see you, sir" came his secretary's voice over the intercom.

"Send him right in," Thornton answered.

Thornton jumped to his feet and veritably leapt to the door in one bound. He paused for a moment to compose himself, and then opened it.

"Monty, old man, absolutely splendid to see you," Thornton said, shaking his hand heartily and giving him a convivial slap on the back.

"And to see you, Thornton, though it does comes as something of a surprise that you should feel that way."

"How's that, Monty?" Thornton said as he led the opposition leader to the armchairs and graciously indicated for him to be seated.

"Well, I have been making rather a bit of an effort to schedule an appointment with you for the last several weeks and none of my calls were returned."

"I'm terribly sorry, Monty, but with the passing of my aunt and all …"

"Oh, yes, yes, of course, Thornton. I'm deeply sorry. You must miss her terribly."

"Terribly," Thornton said, mustering every atom of will to shift his continence from gleeful anticipation to as credible of an impression of bereavement as possible. Thornton did not ask what it was that Diddlestiff had wanted to speak to him about, since whatever that might have been was no longer of any importance whatsoever.

Thornton stepped to the drinks trolley. "Care for a stiff … one, Monty?"

"No, thank you, Thornton. It's a bit early for me to have a drink."

"Who said anything about a drink?"

"Well, what, then, were you referring to?"

"I'll get to that soon enough. But first I'd like to discuss a small matter with you."

"I'm all ears, Thornton."

"Well, Monty, to be blunt, I was rather hoping that you would direct your party to abandon your current policies of supporting increases in spending on education and health care, a tax hike for the rich, a curb on military spending, an expansion of civil liberties and, well, all of that other shit you're for."

"Why ever would I do that Thornton?"

"Well, Monty, it's a time management issue, really. Where are you going to find the time to support increasing the education budget when you're going to be so busy working to slash it. And, no matter how good of a multi-tasker you are, there simply aren't enough hours in the day for you to support civil liberties when you'll be so tied up with increasing government intrusion into people's private lives. And you can't burn the candle at both ends by supporting tax increases for the rich when your going to be run ragged working on new ways to give them tax breaks."

"Whatever would compel me to do that, Thornton?" Diddlestiff said with a bemused tone in his voice.

The foreplay was over.

Thornton reached into his coat pocket and produced a thick envelope. He handed it to Diddlestiff, who opened it and pulled out a stack of photographs. Thornton sat down and prepared to relish the moment.

"Hmm," Diddlestiff said as he flipped through the photographs. "Hmm," he added.

Thornton was disappointed, and bewildered. Though Diddlestiff looked concerned, his expression did not evince the horror that Thornton had been expecting. Diddlestiff did not look at all of the photographs, having grasped the general idea from a cursory flip through the first few.

"Ironically, Thornton, the purpose of my coming here was to encourage you to completely abandon your policies and adopt ours. It now looks like I shan't be expecting you to do that."

"Keenly perceived, Monty. Well, it appears that the only thing necessary now is for you to pop back over to Parliament and get the ball rolling."

"Oh, I don't think that will be necessary."

"Oh, you don't, do you? You know, Monty, I was first fitted for glasses when I was thirteen years old. I was so embarrassed the first day I wore them. I was so sure all the other lads would laugh at me. But, Monty, we're not adolescents here, so I promise I won't laugh if you put yours on. It's perfectly obvious that you're blind as a bat without them."

"Twenty/twenty vision, Thornton; never worn glasses in my life."

"Then perhaps we should talk about the early signs of the onset of Alzheimer's, Monty."

Diddlestiff chuckled. This caused Thornton to actually seriously consider the state of Diddlestiff's mental health.

"My mind is as sharp as a tack, Thornton."

"Well, you do seem to be having some difficulty grasping the situation."

"Oh, I fully grasp the situation, Thornton. However you must remember that, although having consort with entities that no longer enjoy vitality is something that the English, in general, find distasteful, there is another sort of behavior which they find far more reprehensible." Diddlestiff reached into his jacket pocket and produced a thick envelope which he handed to Thornton, who opened it and pulled out a stack of photographs.

"Amazing the times we live in, Thornton. For less than a thousand pounds one can purchase a digital camera with a 1000x1 zoom lens and an almost limitless capacity to store photographs."

Thornton went through the pictures. With each one he looked at, Thornton's jaw dropped that much closer to his chest. There he was, in high-definition picture after high-definition picture, beating the bejesus out of the cutest little kitten to ever waddle across the face of the planet.

Diddlestiff rose, walked to the door, opened it, and then turned to Thornton.

"Shall we call it a zero score draw, Thornton?"

A RANGER LENDS A HAND TO THE STRANGER WHO ENDED HIS LAND (ALBEIT VERY INDIRECTLY, AND WITH NO MALICE INTENDED)

The tall blond forest ranger had spotted a curl of smoke from his observation tower and now strode through the woods towards the source of it. It appeared to be just a campfire, but this was the dry season and it was imperative that it be extinguished immediately.

As he drew closer to the source of the smoke, he could begin to make out what sounded like a drunken voice singing in French. Though this forest was almost a thousand miles west of Quebec, it wasn't all that unusual to find drunken Quebequois wandering around it. It was unusual, though, that the French would be so awful.

The ranger rounded a maple tree, pulled a tall mass of shrubs apart and crawled through it. He spotted the source of the singing, jumped back, and reached for his pistol. He was about to draw it and shoot, but, fortunately, he had the sangfroid to realize that if the creature he was now face to face with was singing in a language, then it must be human. There were very few other indications that would have led him to that conclusion. With his elbow-length matted hair and navel-length matted beard and a filthy body covered by only a few shreds of what might have been at one time clothing, the creature had an aspect to him that made the Unabomber look like a GQ coverboy.

The creature glared at him and it gnarled its mouth.

"GET OFF OF MY PLANET, FOREST FUZZ!!!" he growled.

Then, in an instant, the creature made a Jeckel and Hyde transition. His eyes turned warm and he smiled.

"Nice weather we're having," he said in a charming tone. "It looked as if we had gotten a little rain earlier this morning, but that might have been a little ground mist. Sometimes ground mist gives the impression that it's going to rain. Funny how a little rising moisture would seem like impending falling moisture. It's truly a wonder, don't you think?"

The creature chuckled to himself and shook his head in a way that seemed to indicate that he was musing on the ironies of nature.

"So, Smokey, you got a name?" the creature said, in a voice curiously mixed with street hobo "fuck you" and urbanity.

"Mobutu Obi," the forest ranger said, briefly reflecting that, in his effort to escape from Lars, he might have overdone it a bit in the selection of an alias. But, then again, desperate times call for desperate measures.

Øle took advantage of the creature's overture to ID him.

"And what's *your* name?"

"THE EARTH SHALL SWALLOW YOU WHOLE AND YOU WILL LANGUISH IN ITS EXCREMENT-FILLED BOWELS FOR ETERNITY!!!"

The creature then morphed back into suave civility and extended his hand to Øle.

"Frank Slaughter. Pleasure to meet you."

Since that fateful rainy night in Paris, Frank had forsaken civilization. He had wandered where the wind blew him, and survived as he could, all the while lapsing into and out of sanity.

He pulled a bottle out of a ragged pocket that barely clung by a few threads to his ragged garment. It was not Maison de Chat Beaujolais this time, but a bottle of pine-scented Lysol. He uncapped it and took a long pull from it, smacked his lips and proffered the bottle to Øle.

"Oh, no, thanks," Øle said. Understandably, since waking up to find himself married to Lars, Øle had sworn off cleaning fluids.

"I am going to have to ask you, however, to put out that campfire. It's the dry season and just one stray spark could set this whole forest off like a tinder box."

"LET IT BURN LIKE THE FIRES OF HELL!!! LET EVERYTHING THAT IS GREEN AND STRONG BE SEARED INTO NONEXISTENCE!!! LET ME BE SUR-ROUNDED BY A CHARRED WORLD TO MATCH MY CHARRED SOUL!!!"

Øle, as a forest ranger, was technically a civil servant. As such, he had learned the cardinal rule of civil service: When faced with a problem, make it someone else's.

"If you want to be surrounded by a charred world maybe you should head on down to Duluth," Øle said.

"I beg your pardon?"

"Duluth. Didn't you hear about that? No, I guess you wouldn't have. Anyway, not long back, in a fit of humanity turned brutal and bestial, the residents of the place rampaged through the town, burning it to the ground."

"Duluth?"

"Yes, Duluth."

Frank began to slowly approach Øle with an intense look in his eyes. Øle eased his hand towards his pistol. Frank stopped, his face six inches from Øle's. A maniacal grin spread across his face, and he spoke:

"*Catch the Spirit!*"

Frank shrieked with laughter and pranced off into the woods.

DULUTH REDUX

It was beginning to dawn on Mayor Mainott that maybe this little stroll wasn't working out very well for its intended purpose. Leaving his office to stretch his legs and clear his mind to focus on his re-election campaign, in theory, seemed a good idea. But, as he took in the sight of the charred remnants of Duluth and reflected upon the role that he had played in it, his thoughts turned to: A) *Is taking a walk through the charred remains of a city which I am responsible for having destroyed the best way of contemplating a re-election campaign for mayor of same?* B) *I'm screwed.*

The mayor also understood that his responsibility for the destruction of the city was, as hard as it might be to believe, only the most visible tip of the iceberg. Beneath the obvious murky waters ran an undercurrent of incompetence, deceit and corruption that threatened to drag him down and drown him.

Mainott began to walk more quickly in an unconscious effort to get past the blackened hulls and on to fresher, greener vistas. This was futile, as the whole damn city was a crispy mess.

A genius, Mainott thought. *It would take a genius to pull this re-election off.*

Mainott turned the corner of Fifth and Central and froze in his tracks. There, sitting before him on a bench, was the most hideous creature nature had ever engendered. It was a testament to the hideousness of the creature that it should stand out in a burnt-out city teeming with vermin, beggars, urchins, harlots, lepers, grave robbers, opium eaters, cutthroats, actors, poets and lawyers. It appeared to be some sort of primate as there was a prehensile thumb on the hand that was clutching a bottle of Listerine. The creature took a pull from the bottle and then suddenly fixed its fiery gaze upon the mayor.

"Ironic, isn't it Mainott; you gargle with Maison de Chat Beaujolais, and I drink Listerine."

Mainott jumped back in shock that the creature could not only speak, but could speak his name. But there was something about the voice that Mainott recognized. He slowly approached it and squinted in an attempt to peer through the hair and filth. *It couldn't be!* Mainott thought. *Oh, God! But, yes, it is!*

"Slaughter!" Mainott gasped. "But, what–! How–!"

"How did I end up living on a bench in this, I suspect even in its heyday, most fly-over of towns? It's a complex, intricate, yet subtle story. Tragic, yet blended, in its own unique way, with sublime beauty. In short, Mainott, it is the sort of story that would quickly bore you senseless and send you channel-surfing away from it in search of midget mudwrestling."

The shock was wearing off and Mainott's thinking began to turn to practical considerations. There before him was the Master. The man who could sell snow to Eskimos; coal to Newcastle; sand to Saharans; stones to … to … well, to people who already have all the stones they could ever possibly need. Anyway, here before him, as if placed by God himself, was the only man on the planet who could save him.

"Slaughter, a friend in need is a friend indeed, and never let it be said that Maynard Mainott is not. A friend indeed, that is. It would be my pleasure to offer you a position on my team, thus allowing your talents to catapult you once again to the heights which you so merit."

"So you're deep in the shit and you need me to drag your useless fat ass out of it, eh?"

"Well, yes," Mainott said contritely. "That's about the size of it. You see, the election's coming up and it's not going to be a cake walk."

"What's in it for me?"

Mainott sized up Frank's situation and made an offer.

"How about a pack of smokes, a quart of malt liquor, a ham sandwich, and five bucks?"

Frank made a counter offer.

"How about a $200,000 cash advance, an unlimited expense account, a penthouse, and a Ferrari F430 Spider–with lamb skin upholstery, of course?"

Mainott carefully considered his position, and duly modified his negotiating stance.

"OK."

"Right then," Frank said as he leaned back on the bench, pulled a half-smoked cigarette from behind his ear and lit it. "First of all, tell me what you consider to be your weaknesses and your opponent's strengths."

"Well, first of all, he's a war veteran, and I used my dad's influence to get a cushy position in the Minnesota National Guard."

"You mean he chickened out under fire while you stood tall defending the ramparts of Minnesota against the godless Canadians."

"Well, actually, he was decorated for bravery, while I never even bothered to show up for duty."

"You mean he chickened out under fire while you stood tall defending the ramparts of Minnesota against the godless Canadians. Repeat that one hundred times before going to sleep tonight. When you wake in the morning you'll find it to be true. With a similar media barrage, so will the peasants. Next"

"Well, since I've been mayor, Duluth has gone from having, roughly, a $4,000,000 budget surplus to having an $1,500,000,000 budget deficit. On the other hand, my opponent, as a former state treasurer, had a pristine record of fiscal soundness."

"You mean that, as state treasurer, your opponent plunged the state into debt, thus dragging Duluth down with it; a fact which any citizen or journalist willing to comb through hundreds of thousands of spread sheets can easily corroborate."

"Yeah! Yeah, I see." Mainott began to chuckle. "Hey, this is easy!"

Frank grabbed Mainott's tie and slowly pulled his face down to an inch away from his own.

"Oh, is it? Really think so? Well, you shit-kicking, backwoods fuckwit, maybe you'd like to try this all on your own?"

"No, no!" gasped Mainott, as he tried to get the words out without the benefit of a steady flow of air through his windpipe. "I ... just ... mean ... that ... you ... make ... it ... *look* ... so ... easy."

Frank released Mainott's tie.

"Next."

"Well, as, *cough*, you've just, *cough*, pointed out," Mainott said, loosening his tie and catching his breath, "I'm a bit of a, well, *cough*, fuckwit. I bombed out of all the expensive private schools my parents sent me to. My opponent, on the other hand, through his own merit–having come from a family of sharecroppers, graduated first in his class from Harvard Law School."

"East Coast liberal out-of-touch arrogant elitist ..."

"A sharecropper's son?"

Frank cuffed Mainott.

"You've interrupted me, Mainott. How many times are we allowed to interrupt me?"

Mainott was a reasonably clever fuckwit, and answered without hesitation.

"Once, and only once?"

"Well done, Mainott, well done. Anyway, what the hell do you mean 'a sharecropper's son'? How many sharecroppers are there in Minnesota?"

"None, actually. He moved up here from Mississippi thirty years ago."

"*Foreigner! A fucking foreigner!* Coming up here to *el norte* to steal mayoral jobs away from *real* Minnesotans. Excellent! Religious affiliation?"

"Mine?"

"To start with."

"Uh … well, I guess I never really gave a shit."

"Episcopalian, starting tomorrow. No, make that Lutheran; that'll fly better with these fucking herring eaters. Make sure you take a camera crew along to church with you. Now, let's move on to your opponent's level of heathenism: What's his stance on the theory of evolution? Has he ever mentioned dinosaurs, the Ice Age, continental drift or anything else that 'supposedly' happened more than 6,000 years ago?"

"Well, last week he did a shake-and-grin with some school kids at what's left of the natural science museum."

"Excellent. We'll get a picture of that from the newspaper morgue and throw it right back in his evolution-loving fucking face. Sex life?"

"Well, I did the wife a couple of weeks ago, but it was our anniversary, so I couldn't really get out of it."

"Not you, you nitwit, your opponent! Extramarital affairs of any kind?"

"Never heard of any."

"Too bad, making them up is such grunt work. I'll be up all night Photoshopping. Well worth the time invested, though. Next."

"Well … and this is kind of the biggie. Uh, through my total incompetence I caused the entire city to collapse into a blind panic resulting in ..." Mainott raised his hands and waved them around at the surroundings. "Well ... in this."

"And who knows when it may be burned to the ground again. Do we want someone at the helm who has no experience in dealing with these things? And has your opponent ever come out and publicly stated that he is steadfastly against the city having been burned to the ground? Can he truthfully deny that he himself has never lit a match?"

"And if my opponent asks me if I've ever lit a match?"

"Lie. Then accuse him of negative campaigning. And why are we even talking about this burned-down-city crap anyway? That's yesterday's news. This is America! Who gives a damn what happened yesterday? We boldly set our gaze toward the future. And if you're opponent gets into office, I think we all know what future that would spell."

"Do we?"

Frank heaved an exasperated sigh and began slowly shaking his head.

"My God, Mainott, you really aren't the swiftest cheetah on the savannah, are you? GAY MARRIAGE, you moron! GAY MARRIAGE! Your opponent is committed to pushing through legislation which would require teachers to instruct their students that they must marry someone of their same sex!"

"Is he?"

"Has he ever come out against it?"

"Not that I know of."

"How much more of a glaring endorsement could he possibly make?"

"Right, right," Mainott said, pausing for a moment before getting to his final point. "There is, however, another matter, uh, having to do with the reconstruction of the city, or, uh, rather, the lack of it. You see, there's been a ... situation, uh, with the federal reconstruction aid."

"Hasn't arrived yet? *Fantastic!* We couldn't hope for anything better than having Washington to shit on."

"Well, uh, actually, it has arrived."

"Really? How much?"

"Uh, sort of, around, you know, about … sixteen billion dollars … ish."

Frank blew out a whistle and looked around at the city surrounding him. It was pretty obvious that not sixteen cents had gone into its reconstruction.

"Mainott, Mainott, Mainott," Frank sighed, shaking his head in disgust. "Any *idiot* knows that you don't embezzle *all* of the money!"

"I know, I know. I just couldn't help myself."

"Well you're damn lucky I'm here to help you."

Frank gave the matter some thought.

"First of all, we're going to have to put some distance between you and the dough. You can't have that amount in a bank account under your name."

"Oh, I already thought about that," Mainott said, winking. "It's not under my name. It's in a numbered Swiss account."

"For Christ's sake, Mainott. How naïve can you be? All that about 'anonymous accounts' is just the sort of bullshit they *want* you to believe," Frank lied. "They can trace those right back to you," Frank lied.

"They can?"

"Of course they can," Frank lied. "Well, at least *most* numbered accounts," Frank lied. "I'd have to have a look at the account number to see which kind it is," Frank lied.

"Oh, would you?" Mainott said, his voice awash in relief. "Gee, I'd sure appreciate that."

"Not at all, Mainott. Not at all. It's one for all and all for one."

He rose from the bench and put his arm around Mainott's shoulder.

"Yes, Mainott, if we can keep my plan on track, and your fuck-ups to the bare minimum, we'll win this one. We'll win this one. And, as far as your opponent is concerned, when we're finished with him he'll be lucky to get elected assistant shit shoveller for the Duluth Zoo baboon house."

"Now, why don't we wander off to your office and have a little look at that account number."

ØLE'S FINAL STAND

Øle shaved one final thread-sized fleck from the match stick-sized piece of wood and then tested the fit. Perfect. He then gingerly applied just the right amount of glue and, with the precision of a surgeon, put it into place. He was finished.

Øle stood and took a step back. What he saw was magnificent. It had taken nine months of seven-day weeks and sixteen-hour days, but before him was the result. Every second of effort was worth it–for before him Øle now beheld the most impeccable scale-model reproduction in matchsticks of St. Peter's Cathedral the world has ever known.

Øle took another step back. To say it was done in match sticks is not true. Every tiny plank had been hewn by Øle from white poplar twigs. He had decided on white poplar to give his creation a marbled gleam he thought it deserved, and the effect was stunning. Øle had to hike out two days to the poplar grove, and two days back, laden with bundles of twigs, back to the watchtower. He had had to make the trip several times. Oh, but it was worth it! His toil, sweat and agony were a thousand fold–no, a *million* fold rewarded!

He had created many replicas of famous monuments since he had been stationed out here, alone and hundreds of miles away from the nearest person. The Parthenon, the Sydney Opera House, the Leaning Tower of Pisa, and many more. But none even came close to the glory of his St. Peter's Cathedral.

Øle took another step back–and tumbled backwards over the railing of the watchtower.

Lady Luck was smiling down upon Øle and he landed on something soft. Lady Luck then pulled the rug out from under Øle and made that "something soft" a nine hundred and eighty-three-pound grizzly bear with a nasty disposition that had been snoozing below Øle's watchtower.

As he was being mauled to death, Øle took time out to reflect upon the vagaries of the human condition. Ten years before, at a job interview, the interviewer had asked Øle where he saw himself in ten years time. Øle didn't quite remember how he had responded to that question, but he was pretty sure he hadn't said: "Getting eaten by a grizzly bear after hiding out in the Canadian wilderness under the alias Mobutu Obi to escape from my Swedish husband who's under the delusion that God had encharged him with the mission of leading me out of Denmark before its nuclear annihilation."

No, this was not how Øle had seen himself in ten years time. He'd had plans. He was going to settle down, get married (not to Lars, of course), raise a few kids in a little house with a picket fence and spend his weekends puttering around the garden, maybe a little bowling on Tuesday evenings with the guys, and a couple of weeks a year frolicking under the Benidorm sun.

Obviously, that was not to be. Øle, however, was not one to gripe. Throughout his life he had always rolled with the punches, and he continued to do so (more accurately, he was now rolling with the mighty swats of a grizzly bear's paws, but, whatever).

As he now took stock of his life, he realized that he had lived a good and decent one. He had never lied. He had always treated others as he wished to be treated himself. He was generous, kind, considerate and caring. He had been a good son and–given the conditions–a good husband as well. Øle was, actually, full of shit; none of what he was now telling himself was even remotely true. But, under the circumstances, a little denial can be forgiven.

One thing he told himself was true. In his analysis of himself he had also concluded that he was the sort of guy who never made the same mistake twice. At least in one case this was true. After Lars, Øle had never again done anyone a favor.

BOOK III

DULUTH REDUX AGAIN

Mayor Frank Slaughter strolled across the Place de Slaughter and basked in the splendor of his achievement. He had been about as hands-on as one could have been in its design and construction, as he had been in the reconstruction of the entire city. The Place was, as was Frank's style, a seamless mesh of eclecticism. There was Classic, Neo-Classic, Gothic, Neo-Gothic, Modern, Neo-Modern, Post-Modern and Neo-Post-Modern; and in the center of it all, there was a translucent pyramid. (Frank had been suffering one of his bouts of insanity when he commissioned its design and construction. Though initially, when he returned from la-la land, he found it a horrendous eyesore, he decided to keep it because it had provoked a refreshing controversy of the cerebral onanistic variety rarely found outside of Paris. ("It's a clear example of a neoantidisestablishmentarian antideconstructionalist blah blah blah.")

Frank wore a Yvonne Abette sewer-sludge brown soft-finished worsted suit with pinstripes too subtle for the naked human eye to perceive, a linen shirt the color of curdled cream, an Albanian-blue crêpe d'Uluth necktie woven from the silk of free-range worms and a pair of Enrico Massimo close-soled, cap-toed, subtly polished black shoes that fit him in the insteps like a pair of condoms. To punctuate his ensemble, he wore a tie clip and matching cufflinks hewn from the gold teeth wrenched from the mouths of a select group of highly cultured Duluth political prisoners.

The rebirth of Duluth was not just reflected in its glorious architecture. Since the sudden collapse of French culture (which had always been a mystery to Frank) Duluth had become the international leader in *haute couture*, wine, cheese, enigmatic films and perfume (Eau d'Uluth sold for $7,000 an ounce).

Frank had become mayor following Mayor Mainott's guillotining after the outbreak of The Terror. This was not entirely fortuitous.

Upon first setting foot in Duluth, Frank immediately recognized that its resurrection and his own were inextricably intertwined, and he worked indefatigably toward that goal from the very first moment. When he agreed to engineer Mainott's re-election campaign, he did so under the condition that he be appointed deputy mayor, whose main duty was to take over as mayor should anything happen to Mainott.

The campaign that Frank had orchestrated for Mainott's re-election had been so overwhelmingly successful that, such was the trust that Mainott had placed in him, Frank was given sole charge of drafting Mainott's speeches. And, such was the trust he had had in Frank, Mainott never bothered to read them before giving them.

The Terror had broken out shortly after Mainott gave a speech, which began:

"Was it my fault that the city burned? Was it my fault that the city collapsed into chaos after I sent the entire police force out on vacation? Was it my fault that the vast amount of the federal reconstruction aid was spent on houses, luxury cars and jewelry for me and my family, with the rest being socked away into my Swiss bank accounts?"

Shortly after becoming mayor, and brutally squelching The Rebellion, Frank initiated a sweeping reformation of every aspect of Duluth life. He oversaw its reconstruction and its economic recovery and introduced sweeping reforms.

The result was awe-inspiring. Almost overnight, Duluth went from being known as "Peoria without the Pizzazz" to "Paris without the Dog Shit." (Failure to scoop the pooch poop was punishable by death and dismemberment, with the bits being fed to the dogs. Frank thought that turning the offenders into dog excrement themselves was the height of imaginative jurisprudence, as well as a masterpiece of Gallic irony, and, thus, made it a special project of his to have this law pushed through.)

Yes, Frank thought, *this is truly a masterpiece I've created. A mark of my genius that will last until the end of time.*

THORNTON HAS A HO

"You're a disgusting feck. A wingeing little pompous ponce. You're a prat. A plonker. A right tosser puke. A spoilt little wanger ..."

"No. No. No, you stupid tart! How many times must I tell you? It's 'wanker,' not 'wanger!' Wanker! Wanker! Wanker! Wanker! Wanker! You are not to call me a 'wanger,' but a 'wanker!' Is that so bloody difficult?!"

Thornton had lost his patience and was pacing furiously– a task not easily performed since the cheap sort of carpeting that you normally find in roadside motels kept snagging his stiletto heels.

Thornton often had this problem with the hookers. Since his aides had determined that having a written script for them to study was "ill-advised," lest it fall into the wrong hands, Thornton was forced to stage direct each and every hooker he had in her lines. And getting this Appalachian sow herder to do a reasonable facsimile of the ginmonger's slattern was testing the limits of his limited patience. Thornton's irritation was exacerbated by the fact that the air conditioner in his room wasn't working properly. The heat and humidity of an August day in Washington D.C. are unbearable enough in the best of circumstances. But when, like Thornton, you're dressed in nylon stockings, a corset, silk panties and bra and wearing a Dolly Parton wig; and with your face caked with powder, rouge, lipstick and eye shadow, well, you can imagine.

As a director, Thornton was no Martin Scorsese. He saw his "actors" much as Alfred Hitchcock did–as cattle–and, thus, did not encourage them to draw from within themselves. Had he abandoned the approach of having Candy simply memorize "you're a wanker," and opted for explaining to her exactly what the word meant, she would have readily absorbed it and delivered it with accuracy, enthusiasm, and conviction. She would have given a performance that would have relegated the entire oeuvre of Marlon Brando to that along the lines of your garden variety B-western chuck wagon cook. (You know, the type who could never even have dreamed of achieving the depth that Walter Brennan had brought to the role). But, anyway, suffice it to say that Thornton was not a good director.

So, at this point we might assume that the question in our cherished reader's mind is: What was Prime Minister Thornton Wingate doing dressed in women's underwear and instructing a prostitute to verbally abuse him in a cheap motel room in Washington D.C.?

We shall also take the liberty of assuming that our cherished reader has so far been sufficiently attentive to our modest tale so as to have already worked out the answer to the first part of the question. As such, we will limit ourselves to addressing the second part: What was Thornton doing in Washington D.C.?

Thornton was in Washington to attend the Summit to Halt Atomic Terrorism (SHAT). The purpose of the summit was to discuss means and ways to end nuclear proliferation. Thornton was to give the inaugural speech. And why would that be? Thornton, along with d'Istaing, were the only two men living, and two of only three men ever, to have ordered a nuclear strike. As such, in the way that history and politics work, they had morphed into the doyens of nuclear disarmament and nonproliferation. (For more information on this phenomenon see: "Henry Kissinger Wins Nobel Peace Prize," *The Universal Truth*, October 17, 1973).

Meanwhile, back at the motel room.

"You're a wanker! You're a wanker! You're a wanker! Why is it so bloody difficult for you to call me a wanker?!"

Candy took all of this in stride. She had been paid in advance, paid extremely well, and instructed that the reason for this was that this client had to be treated with the utmost discretion.

Thornton heaved an exaggerated sigh and wobbled toward the night table where the gin, tonic and ice were. He sat down on the bed and mixed himself a stiff one, took a couple of large swallows, and immediately felt calmer. This would be the last calm he would feel for some time to come.

"Why, Thornton! It appears that you share the same predilection in attire as Mr. Sherlock Holmes."

Thornton spat out a mouthful of gin & tonic, jumped to his feet, and spun around to the source of the voice. There, by the door, hovering about two feet off the floor, clown face and all, was the specter of Aunt Anne.

"EEEEAAAAOOOO!!!!" Thornton commented.

"Oh, Thornton, calm down. You act as if you've just seen a ghost," said Aunt Anne, unable to resist that one.

"EEEEAAAAAOOOOOIIIIIEEEEEAAAAO-OOOIIII!!!!!" Thornton added.

Candy, who was not privy to the presence of the ghost of Aunt Anne, began to question the limits of discretion and started scanning the room for easy-to-wield blunt objects. Her eyes fixed upon the gin bottle.

Thornton spun around and looked at Candy. Oddly, she seemed more concerned about Thornton's behavior rather than about a ghost floating around in the corner of the room. This slightly reassured Thornton that, perhaps, he was simply suffering from the heat.

"You, there. Look over at the door and tell me what you see!" Thornton commanded her.

Candy looked over at the door, looked at Thornton, looked back at the door and looked back at Thornton.

"A door?" Candy said hesitantly, expecting another outburst berating her for her lack of thespianship.

"Yes, yes. It's just a door, isn't it?" Thornton giggled a bit. "Yes, yes, just a door. Just a door, really."

Candy shot a quick glance at the gin bottle.

Thornton was somewhat relieved, but not completely reassured.

"Tell me you don't see an old bitch with a clown face hovering around by the door."

"You don't see an old bitch with a clown face hovering around the door," Candy repeated, feeling that, at least this time, she had gotten her lines right.

"No, you stupid tart! I want you to look over there and tell me, in your own words, what you see!"

The needle on Candy's discretion meter was swinging wildly towards red. She lit a cigarette and blew out the smoke.

"Listen, Tiger. You tell me what you want me to say and I'll say it. I ain't gettin' paid here for no creativity."

"Thornton."

Thornton began to whistle and exaggeratedly avoided looking anywhere near the door.

"Lovely weather we're having," Thornton said to Candy.

"It's a fuckin' hundred degrees in the shade. If that's your idea of wonderful weather I sure the fuck don't ever wanna go to wherever the fuck you come from."

"Thornton, I am here. I have chosen not to reveal myself to your 'lady friend', but I am most assuredly here."

Thornton turned slowly to the door and was blinded by a sudden flash of light. When his eyes recovered, he saw the ghost of Aunt Anne hovering there with a camera.

"Like you, Thornton, I, too, have recently developed a passion for the hobby of photography. I am sure the people of

Great Britain will be so pleased to see how much their prime minister is enjoying his official visit abroad."

It occurred to Thornton that, though she couldn't see Aunt Anne, the tart must surely have seen the flash. He spun around to her.

"Did you see that?"

"See what?"

"The flash! The flash! The clown's got a camera and is taking pictures."

"There better not be no clown with no camera takin' pictures here! I ain't gettin' paid to have no clown takin' no fuckin' pictures! You want *that* service, Tiger, you better pull out your fuckin' wallet again!"

"Thornton."

Thornton spun around in Aunt Anne's direction.

"What are you doing here?" Thornton demanded, adding, "I thought you would be burning in Hell."

There was no invective in his tone. He had simply taken it for granted, not unwarrantedly, that that would, in fact, be the case, and was just honestly surprised to discover that it was not.

"It would appear that no one with a clown face is allowed in there, Thornton. They seem to feel that the presence of clowns might have the effect of bringing cheer to the residents. Rather counter to the whole purpose of the place, isn't it?"

Thornton flushed with anger. Aunt Anne had done it again.

"Yes, Thornton, so it would seem that we shall be seeing quite a bit of one another from now on."

Thornton's knees felt weak. He moved to the bed, sat down, put his head in his hands, and began to weep bitterly.

Candy, of course, was not the first hooker ever to see a British prime minister in women's underwear weep, but the utter forlornness of it moved her deeply. She recovered quickly from this sympathy, though, and decided to take advantage of his distraction. Moving swiftly to the night table, she snatched up the gin bottle and, with a deft roundhouse, brought it crashing against the side of his head. Thornton did a half cartwheel, landed on his head, stayed in a headstand position ever so briefly and then collapsed onto the floor. Candy quickly found his wallet and fled the room.

"I must say, Thornton," said Aunt Anne, addressing herself to the crumpled pile of silk, nylon and tangled limbs on the floor. "Your 'lady friend' most certainly has an impressive technique."

The squad car pulled up and parked at the entrance to the Wal-Mart. The burly officer got out and entered the store. Though large, as Wal-Marts tend to be, he quickly spotted where the in-progress was and headed toward it.

As he approached, he could make out a group consisting of a plump, middle-aged man who appeared to be the manager, a couple of teenage stock boys, and an aging man in women's underwear and a Dolly Parton wig.

"So what seems to be the problem here?" Officer Ernie McKlusky said, wishing he had phrased the question in a way so as to have indicated that he was not wholly unaware of what the problem was.

"The problem," said Thornton, "is that I require cold cream, and these bottom-feeding peasants will not supply me with it." Without Ewenthrall's revivescent spritz, Thornton had not quite recovered from the gin bottle to his head.

"The problem," said the manager, "is that he doesn't have any money."

McKlusky made a quick assessment of the situation and turned toward Thornton.

"Sir, don't you think it might be a good idea if you just went home, had a rest, maybe changed into something more ... suitable, and then came back for the cold cream when you have the money to pay for it?"

"But I require the cold cream now. I need it to remove the make-up."

"Well, sir, I can take you somewhere where they've got plenty of cold cream to remove your make-up."

"*My* make-up?! Who gives a bloody fuck about *my* make-up?! I've got to remove the clown make-up from my dead aunt's ghost so the bitch can go to Hell! Why is that so difficult for everyone to understand?!"

McKlusky mused briefly upon the now glaringly erroneous notion that he had firmly held up until then that, after twenty-three years on the force, he had seen and heard it all.

"Perhaps," Thornton continued, "if I mimic it, you cretins might get it through your thick skulls!"

Thornton began to glide and drift around the Wal-Mart mimicking the removal of a clown face from a dead aunt's ghost. His experience as The Sad Mime did not fail him and he gave a bravado performance. More to the liking of Officer McKlusky, Thornton was prancing toward the front exit where the squad car was parked.

McKlusky followed Thornton as he sailed out through the sliding doors. Thornton continued his mime and McKlusky took advantage of his distraction to open the back door of the squad car. He then leaned against it and waited for Thornton to finish his performance, which he did forthwith. Thornton wiped a bit of sweat from his brow and walked up to McKlusky.

"Get it now?" Thornton said. "Or shall we try puppets?"

McKlusky took Thornton's arm and began leading him into the backseat.

"Get your unclean and lesser-order hands off of me! Do you have even the remotest clue as to just who I am?" Thornton shouted as he pulled away from McKlusky's grip. "I am the prime minister of Great Britain!"

"Is that a fact?" McKlusky said. "Well, what a coincidence, 'cause I'm the princess of Shangri-La," to which he added, "get in the fucking car, asshole." Whereupon he grabbed Thornton, slapped the cuffs on him, put his hand on top of Thornton's head and perp-shuffled him into the back of the squad car.

❦

Haw lay on the bunk and stared at the bedsprings of the bunk above him. He had been in quite a few holding cells in his life and had to admit that this one wasn't too bad. The bunks were bugless, the toilet in the corner wasn't overflowing with excrement and, for the moment, no crack-fueled chainsaw murderers had been tossed in with him. Certainly not the highest quality holding cell he had ever been in (that would unquestioningly be the one in Singapore where he had been held after being arrested for chewing gum in the street), but definitely not bad.

He was here as a result of his having trashed a yarn shop following the comment that the sixty-six-year-old cat-loving spinster owner had made regarding her doubts concerning Dominguez having given one hundred and ten percent during his 1957 *corrida* against *Cojonado*.

"Stupid cow," Haw muttered as he thought about the incident again.

Haw heard footsteps approach and stop at his cell door. A screw opened it, a figure was pushed in, the door clanged shut and the screw left. Haw observed his cellmate. This was not the first time he had been locked up with transvestites, but, even from behind, he noted, this one, by far, took the cake for ugly with a capital *U*.

The transvestite, who was facing the door, muttered something which Haw, obviously mistakenly, understood as, "And so now how will I ever remove the clown face from my dead aunt's ghost?"

Haw vaguely recognized the voice.

The he-she turned around.

Haw vaguely recognized the face. Why should he recognize it? A chill went down Haw's spine. He feared that this vague recognition might be the nebulous memory of some drink-sodden liaison that had gone horribly, horribly awry. But, upon further consideration, he dismissed the notion. Nobody could be *that* drunk!

The transvestite turned to Haw and spoke.

"Now the bitch will never go to Hell."

Haw now knew who the voice belonged to. And, in spite of the caked-on make-up, he now also recognized the face. Had Haw merely known this man through newspaper photographs, he would never have recognized him. But, while posted in London as a reporter, Haw had spoken to this face on many occasions and, as unlikely as this situation might be, there was no mistaking him.

"How are you, Mr. Prime Minister?"

A look of intense relief came over Thornton's face.

"You recognize me?"

"Of course I do, sir."

"You know who I am?"

"Certainly I do, sir."

Haw sat up on the bunk and moved to the foot end. He patted the bed to motion him to sit down. Thornton saw the sympathetic face that Haw had donned, and eagerly sat down next to him.

"It's been so dreadful."

"I'm sure it has been, sir."

"It's been so absolutely dreadful."

"Undoubtedly, sir. Maybe it would do you good to get it off your chest, sir. Tell me all about it. Tell me *all* about it"

Thornton did.

"You want me to get you out of here?" Sheldon Fusswacker, Haw's lawyer, asked as he sat opposite him in the interrogation room. He had been roused from his bed and he was not happy.

"Six hours ago I told you that the owner of the yarn shop, showing surprising benevolence and an extreme willingness to forgive, was ready to drop the charges if you simply paid the damages and apologized. You said, and I quote: 'I'll apologize the day that dried-out twine flogger learns one one-hundredth as much about bullfighting as she knows about cleaning cat shit up off the carpet.'"

Contrition was not part of Haw's make-up, but he was a professional and he had a column to write. (Haw had journalism in his blood and not long after leaving the *The International Herald Lloyd* he was back groveling to the Whore Devil, now as a columnist for the on-line paper *The Universal Truth*.) Haw swallowed hard before speaking.

"Listen, Sheldon. I'll kiss the stupid cow's scrawny ass at high noon on Main Street if that's what it takes. Just get me the hell out of here!"

Fusswacker made the arrangements.

McKlusky took his tray with the coffee and six assorted donuts and sat down at the table where Czclnski was sitting. It was shift-change time at the precinct, so the Donut Room was at peak activity.

"Bob."

"Ernie."

McKlusky sat down and dug eagerly into his donuts.

"Tough one?" Czclnski asked.

"Yup."

"Anything special?"

"Collared the prime minister of Great Britain."

Czclnski laughed, spraying donut crumbs.

"Well, they must be running pretty low on prime ministers over there," Czclnski said, taking a large bite from a raspberry spritz and swallowing it whole. "Because I collared one of them myself today."

McKlusky chuckled. For some reason he couldn't quite put his finger on, however, he felt a sensation of cold foreboding.

"Just what did he look like?" McKlusky asked.

"Well, to begin with, he looked a lot like a she."

"Mine too, as a matter of fact. Old fucker in drag."

"Well mine might've been a fake prime minister but she was at least a real *she*. More specifically she was Candy, ya know, the hooker who works the truck stops out on I-95. We collared her trying to pass off hot credit cards. She was at the Kmart trying to buy six thousand dollars worth of costume jewelry." Czclnski took a bite of strawberry frosted to create a dramatic pause. "Funny thing was, we ran a check on the credit cards, and you'll never guess what—they actually *did* belong to the real prime minister of Britain! Fucked if I can figure out how the hell Candy got a hold of them."

Two things suddenly occurred to McKlusky: 1, The British prime minister was, indeed, in town for the nuclear summit (McKlusky, as a matter of fact, was to be assigned to the security operation); 2, Upon careful consideration, the face under all of that make-up was, indeed, that of said prime minister.

The color drained from McKlusky's face and he stood up.

"Listen, gotta go."

Czclnski noticed that McKlusky had left a quarter of an uneaten custard-filled on his tray—and he knew exactly, then and there, that some pretty heavy shit had just come down. And he knew exactly what that heavy shit was, and who was going down with it.

"You mean your drag queen prime minister was—?!"

"The Real Fucking Deal," McKlusky forced out in a hoarse and gasping voice.

Czclnski went silent. It was one thing, as he himself had done the month before, to empty a clip into a fifteen-year-old black kid because you'd mistaken his cell phone for a pistol. There we're just talking a lot of paperwork, a couple of hours before the IAD and, worst-case scenario, two weeks suspended with pay. But this was the Big Enchilada. The Fuck-Up di Tutti Fuck-Ups–McKlusky had ARRESTED A VERY IMPORTANT PERSON IN THE MIDDLE OF HIS KINK! McKlusky was last week's chopped liver. He was the mayor of Sayonara City. He was the residual turd floating in the just-flushed toilet.

He knew it. McKlusky knew it.

Czclnski, for as much as he deeply sympathized with McKlusky, went into self-preservation mode. He shot a quick glance around the Donut Room to see if anyone had observed him fraternizing with Dead Man Walking. As far as he could make out, the coast was clear.

"Well, McKlusky, I ..."

Czclnski, realizing that it would be foolhardy to stick around long enough to finish the "gotta go" part of the sentence, whisked his ass out of there.

McKlusky's only hope was that everything would be kept hushed up.

BEING THE BRITISH PRIME MINISTER IS A DRAG

By Edward Hawingway

WASHINGTON - "Because I had to remove the clown make-up from the face of my dead aunt's ghost so she could go to Hell."

Thus did British prime minister Thornton Wingate respond when asked by this reporter why he should find himself last night in Washington D.C.'s 57th precinct holding cell dressed in lady's lingerie.

Personally, I found that to be as good a reason as any. I, however, am not a British voter. Presumably many of them might hold differing opinions; opinions which they will be free to express in the upcoming general elections there.

"Well, you see, in Britain, as in many parts of Europe, we take a rather broader view of these matters than the Americans," said Hugh Jass, political analyst for *The Dorking Chronicle*. "The prime minister can, as far as we're concerned, gazelle down High Street in frilly knickers to his heart's content, as long as unemployment stays below the double-digit mark and the NHS continues to patch us up reasonably well. But the Americans tend to take a dimmer view of these sort of things. They have a rather quaint, Norman Rockwellish expectation of how a national leader should comport himself. In that sense, I feel Wingate's choice of venue for prancing about in a G-string was rather unfortunate and might influence the voters' general perception of the soundness of his judgment."

Translation to American English: Wingate's up Crap Creek.

When this reporter was posted in London as a correspondent for *The International Herald Lloyd*, I followed Prime Minister Wingate's career quite closely and grew to understand that something like last night's incident was not the sort of thing he would let keep him down.

I am reminded of the time when, after it was discovered that Wingate's vaunted ancestor—and Wingate's claim to worthiness—Laurel The Hardy was found to be an incompetent boob, Wingate, in cahoots with the equally beleaguered French president, Valery Discard d'Istaing, nuclearly annihilated Denmark ("economic crimes against humanity" my ass!).

And how will Prime Minister Wingate react to this one? Well, let's just say that if I lived in a small, powerless country, I'd be lining my basement now with lead sheets.

LEAVE NO CHILD'S BEHIND

Professor Emma Soterick was pleased with herself, and she had every right to be. As a tenure-track associate professor at the University of West Virginia at Skunkrat for the last eleven years, she had achieved what all academics strive for–she had managed to keep her job. And, almost as important, she had so far avoided making an ass herself. This was not due to chance. Dr. Soterick had taken to heart the two age-old tenets of academia:

I. *Est vos sanctus officium ut servo vestri.* (It is your sacred duty to keep your job.)
II. *Asinus non facium.* (Do not make an ass of yourself.)

In academia there are two ways of achieving this:
1. Propound a theory so outrageous that other academics (following tenet II) would be too shit-scared to challenge, lest they end up on that list with the guy who laughed at Pasteur.
2. Propound a theory so obvious that, well, who's going to challenge it?

Dr. Soterick, like the vast majority of academics, adhered to the second school of thought. Ergo, her work had furthered humanity's insight by providing it with such solid scholarship demonstrating that: An overwhelming percentage of bears not in captivity defecate in wooded areas; a statistically insignificant number of popes have been non-Catholics; consumers save more money if they shop at stores where they sell the same merchandise cheaper than they do at more expensive stores; people over the age of eighty tend to be less comfortable with new computer technology than people under the age of twenty; college students are more likely to binge drink on the weekends than the populace at large; being dropped repeatedly on one's head during infancy results in poorer scholastic performance; applying the death penalty to innocent people has virtually no deterrent effect on other innocent people to not commit crimes for which they receive the death penalty; and, her most renowned study to date–people are more likely to do what they are more apt to do.

The results of Soterick's latest research were published in the *New York Semi-Independent*. (Strictly speaking, it couldn't be called her latest work. Soterick had written the conclusion shortly after receiving the $11 million grant to conduct it. Her main work over the last five years, while gathering the data to tack her conclusion onto, had been in leading a protracted battle against the Romance Languages Department over photocopier access.)

Dr. Soterick had decided to study Americans' attitudes toward pedophilia. The numbers had been compiled and crunched and the findings were reported in the *Semi-Independent*: 99.987612 percent of Americans were in favor of pedophilia.

Janet had a hard time catching her breath after running into the Strategy Room of the White House, newspaper in hand.

But the adrenalin overcame the lack of oxygen and she managed to blurt out:

"99.987612 percent of Americans believe in *something*!!!"

Bob Rasputum jumped to his feet and began barking orders; "Get hold of Ben and have him immediately free up the president's schedule for the next twenty minutes. Jack, you get with Ed and Murray and write the speech of your fucking lives, ask Janet what the whole thing's about. Lacey, get out to the pressroom and tell them to get ready. Larry, get the make-up people here. Stat! God damn it people, STAT!!!"

The White House staffers were 24/7 type of people, but, even given that, it was breathtaking to see the gusto with which they jumped into the task. The American people had never before been 99.987612 percent in favor of, or against, **ANYTHING**!!!! Never before had a situation even remotely like this ever happened. A total win-win situation was just thrown into their laps and all they had to do was to glom before anyone else glommed.

The president was easily located. He was peddling around the Rose Garden. He was always peddling around the Rose Garden at this time of day. He was suited up, made up, handed the still-smelling-of-ink speech, and trundled out in front of the rapidly assembled White House press corp. The president began:

"I am, and make no mistake about this, the pedophilia president. Let me repeat, I am the pedophilia president. If there is anyone out there who has not heard what I have said, I will yet again state, unequivocally, I AM THE PEDOPHILE PRESIDENT. When you say 'pedophilia,' I say 'yes.' When you say 'pedophilia, pedophilia,' I say 'yes, yes.' I am the pedophilia president." (The president thought 'pedophilia' meant a love of peddling bicycles; thus, his tone reflected his passion.)

"Let me remind you that for years, DECADES, whenever the subject of pedophilia would arise, my opponents would always stick to their big-government, tax-and-spend, bleeding-heart nonpedophilia ways. Well I am here today to tell you that those days are over now."

The president now assumed a somber, determined tone. "I will propose to Congress the immediate allocation of $17 billion, with further increases as deemed necessary by the Presidential Committee that I will appoint for the development and implementation of this administration's unequivocal pro-pedophilia program." The president switched from somber to passionate. "Are you asking, 'Is the president one hundred and ten percent in favor of pedophilia?' Are you asking: 'Is the president one hundred and twenty percent in favor of pedophilia?' Well, if you are, I'm here to tell you 'no.' I'm here to tell you that the president is two hundred percent in favor of pedophilia! I'm here to tell you that God is two hundred percent in favor of pedophilia. I'm here to tell you that, between me and God, we're four hundred percent in favor of pedophilia." I am here to say–Leave No Child's Behind."

☙

The *New York Semi-Independent* was quick to rectify its mistake. The very next day they ran the following retraction:

> In our report on Dr. Soterick's study on the attitudes of Americans toward pedophilia we reported that 99.98712 percent of Americans are in favor of pedophilia. The study, in fact, indicated that 99.98712 percent of Americans are *not* in favor of pedophilia. We regret our error.

AND LEAVE MY
MEDAMN FISH ALONE

And the Lord sat at his desk and stared out at the heavens (pretty much the only view he had from there). He was thinking about fishing. Truth be known, that was the only reason he had created fish.

His daydreaming was interrupted by the arrival of Gabriel, head of the Prayer Analysis and Administration Department.

"Sir, I hate to disturb you, but we've been picking up a lot of chatter recently from a certain Lars Larsen. The nature of his prayers, however, leads us to believe that he's not just another planbomb." (*Planbomb* was celestial jargon for "prays like a neurotic bunny on a methamphetamine binge").

And the Lord was sarcastic.

"Oh, really? And what could he possibly want? No, no, don't tell me, let me guess. Could it possibly be, oh I don't know, maybe ten million in cash and an eighteen-year-old supermodel?"

And the Lord did roll his eyes.

"Actually, sir, it goes beyond that."

"Oh, he wants *twenty* million in cash and *two* eighteen-year-old supermodels! Shesh! There's just no pleasing some people."

"As I said, sir, he's not your ordinary planbomb."

"Yeah, right."

Before creating the PAA department, God had micro-managed most of the work himself. Attending to the prayers from all the self-aware creatures he had distributed on planets throughout the universe, however, finally became a bit too much for him and so he delegated. The experience, however, had made him a bit jaded.

"Well, okay, all right, then tell me just who is this Lars Larsen and what does he do?"

"He a member of a species which evolved from monkeys and is now known on his planet as 'human', and what he's doing is fifteen to twenty for trying to board an airplane with a loaded pistol and a bag of heroin."

"Oh, a prison house conversion! Well, knock me over with a feather."

"Actually, we began to pick up signals from him shortly before his incarceration."

"Really? That's odd."

"Indeed it is, sir."

"Okay, okay. Just what is he praying for?"

"He's praying for an end to war, poverty, hatred, racism, hunger, disease, cruelty, ignorance, greed and taxes."

"They've got all that?"

"Yes, sir."

"All on just the one planet?"

"Yes, sir."

"Wow! Sounds like a real shithole!"

"Well, sir, to put it this way, many inhabitants of your other planets have visited it over the years, but not a one has chosen to stay."

"I can imagine. Anyway, this dump got a name?"

"Earth."

"Eh?"

"Earth."

"Earth? Sounds like a belch. Did I give it that name?"

"Yes, sir, upon returning from your weekly meeting of the Celestial Chapter of the Raccoon Lodge."

And a testy clap of thunder did sound.

"Are you implying that I was drunk?"

"Of course not, sir. A bit festive, perhaps, but certainly not drunk."

"All right, all right. Anyway, fill me in on this place."

Gabriel opened the folder he was holding and began to read.

"Earth. You created it 4.5 billion–or 6,000–years ago, depending on who you ask. You created it in six days, and took the seventh day off to rest. But you then got wrapped up in another project and never went back there to finish the job. You've actually been there, sir."

"Have I?"

"Yes, sir. It's one of the places you put fish."

And the Lord did scrunch his brow.

"Earth? Earth? Earth? Oh yeah, now I remember. There was some great fishing in that big river where they were building those pyramids. They ever finish those?"

"Quite some time ago, sir."

"I remember they had a great drink there, too."

"Beer, sir."

"Yeah, that was it. Beer. They still got that?"

"Yes, sir. It's become quite a popular beverage. Especially on fishing trips."

And the Lord did think.

"Right, I'll go down there."

"To answer Lars' prayers?"

"Nah, take too long. I'll just pop down and spook the crap out of him so's he'll get off our backs."

And the Lord did feign an afterthought.

"And now that I think about it, as long as I'm down there I might as well get a bit of fishing in."

And the Lord did check his day planner.

"Let's see. Looks like my schedule's easing up a bit in about six hundred years from now. Why don't you plan my trip for then."

"Well, sir, there are actually two problems with that. The first is that the human creatures you put on Earth only have a life span of, at the most, about one hundred years. The Lars in question will have been dead for about five hundred of those."

"No wonder the place is so screwed up; no one's ever around long enough to have to wallow the mess they make. And the second problem?"

Gabriel hesitated. He knew that the next bit of information was going to send the Lord totally Old Testament, and he was not looking forward to being in the same room with *that*.

"Well, sir, it's the fish."

"What about them?"

"Well, sir ... uh ... it's just that, uhm, in six hundred years, well, uh, there aren't going to be any there."

"There aren't? Where are they going to go?"

"Well, sir, they aren't going to go anywhere. It's just that ... well, sir, the fact is they're all going to be dead by then."

"Dead!" A clap of thunder sounded. "How?"

"Pollution, sir."

"Pollution?"

"Pollution, sir. The humans pour toxic chemicals into the rivers, lakes and oceans."

And the Lord did say "pishaw."

"Pishaw! Don't be ridiculous, Gabriel. You don't have to be me to know that you don't piss in the pond you fish in."

"They do, sir."

"Why?"

"Well, sir, essentially the reason is ... well, uh, it's not for me to criticize, but you perhaps you should have spent more than six days on the place because the dominant species you put there–and, by the way, they think you created them in your image–well, the dominant species is, how can I put this? Uh ... well ... it's kinda dumb."

"Nobody can be that dumb."

"They are, sir."

And the Lord did mull all of this over. And the Lord then did blow his lid.

"Medamn it! Who the medamn hell do they think they are? And what the medamn hell do they think they're doing with my fish? Why, I'll knock their blocks off! I'll tear 'em from limb to limb! I'll kick the stuffing out of 'em and shove it up a turkey's ass for roasting! I'll fricassee 'em and have 'em for breakfast! I'll pound 'em into the ground! I'll kick their medamn asses into next Tuesday!"

And the Lord did take a deep breath, and the Lord did release it slowly.

"Cancel all of my appointments. I'm going to this Earth place pronto! Where's my hat?"

SHAT

"Nuke Duluth!" French president d'Istaing shouted, slamming his fist on the table.

"President d'Istaing, please. We've already agreed upon the procedure," Rasputum said.

The procedure Rasputum was referring to was such: Bunkport, to give him something to do, would throw a dart at the world map. Those assembled would then check their respective briefing books to see if the country on which the dart had landed was, by their individual criteria, nuke-able.

How the Summit to Halt Atomic Terrorism, originally conceived to discuss nuclear disarmament and to stop nuclear proliferation, had turned into a planning committee to unleash a nuclear attack on some, for the most part *any*, country, was simple–Bunkport and Thornton weren't the only ones present who were in it, and deep. As luck would have it, all of those in attendance, in one way or another, were in serious shit.

Be that as it may, the reader at this point could not be faulted for wondering why they had chosen to nuke their way out of a jam when the last time that tactic was employed it proved to be a near disaster. The operative word here is "near."

After buying some time by downplaying the issue at the petunia press conference and distracting attention with the "Prince Harry has a girlfriend" ruse, "secret intelligence" was declassified demonstrating that not only had the Danes been committing economic crimes against humanity, but that they were also responsible for higher gas prices, global warming, childhood obesity, bird flu, alien abductions, unsightly graffiti, reality television shows, most serious traffic accidents, Attention Deficit Disorder, the appalling absence of a good five-cent cigar, the heartbreak of psoriasis, mobile home park tornado vulnerability, and erectile dysfunction. (The hatred against Danes grew so strong that dog owners renamed their Great Danes "Freedom Pooches.") The unfortunate outcome of this unmitigated hatred toward the Danes was the fostering of the notion that "the only good Dane is a dead Dane." Thus, the "good" Danes, which is to say the cheerfully cooperative Greenlanders, were snuffed out by popular demand.

The only remaining glitch had to do with those who, as a result of the cartoon thing, supported Denmark's stance on freedom of expression. This was simply dealt with by rounding up anybody suspected of harboring this view, stripping them of their rights, and holding them incommunicado in little cages on remote islands.

The list of those present at SHAT, and their reasons for needing to seriously divert the attention of their respective citizenries, is as follows:

> -Valery Discard d'Istaing–President of France. Despite his popular co-nuking of Denmark, France never recovered its position and was now being overtaken in everything from *haute couture* to stinky cheeses by some previously backwater city called Duluth.

> -Yogiof Yelstin–President of the Russian Federation. Recently revealed that his connection to the mafia is minimal–raising the alarming question as to just who is running the country.

> -Fuc Yu–President of China. Wondered aloud at a recent party congress whether socialism was incom-

patible with slash-and-burn, meat-grinder, survival-of-the-fittest free-market economic policies.

-Grehepe Nehi–Prime Minister of India. Never able to quite put behind him his transferring twelve billion dollars to a Swiss bank account, and then transferring himself to Switzerland, minutes after Kenny Bunkport erroneously informed him that India was coming under nuclear attack.

-Muhammad Ali (not *the* Muhammad Ali, the other guy)–Prime Minister of Pakistan. Never quite put behind him his transferring of nine billion dollars to a Swiss bank account, and then transferring himself to Switzerland, minutes after discovering that the prime minister of India had been informed that India was under nuclear attack and, even though he knew he wasn't responsible, he knew that the prime minister of India wouldn't see it that way and would retaliate and, well, hell! Who wants to stick around for that?

-Yehudi Mann–Prime Minister of Israel. Recently come to light that he had forgotten to call his mother on her birthday.

"Ok, let's get on with it," Rasputum said, getting down to business. "Mr. President, whenever you're ready."

Bunkport, who had been squirming in his seat like a kid waiting for Christmas, perked up.

"Can I? Can I? Can I? Can I?!"

"Yes, you can, Mr. President."

The president picked up a dart and hurled it at the map. It landed on Togo. Those in attendance began leafing through their briefing books.

"That's no good with us," Rasputum said. "The CEO of Halliburton has a summer home there."

"There's also a large Chinese community living there," Fuc Yu added.

"Go ahead and throw again, Mr. President," Rasputum said.

"Neatooo!" Bunkport shouted as he flung the dart. It landed on French Guinea.

"Can't do it," d'Istaing said. "There are French timber and mining interests there and it'll be at least a couple of years more until they strip the place clean."

"We can't go with that either," said Fuc Yu. "There's a large Chinese community living there."

"President Yu," Rasputum said. "There's a large Chinese community *everywhere*! What are we supposed to do? Bomb the moon? Anyway, Mr. President, go ahead and throw again."

"Oh boy! Oh boy! Oh boy!" Kenny squealed as he hurled another dart, which landed on Saudi Arabia.

"Well, as well as having a large Chinese community, perhaps there's another reason or two which I believe preclude our having to check the briefing book on this one?" Thornton quipped.

This was met with an expression of general amusement.

"Go ahead and throw again, Mr. President."

The dart landed on Djibouti.

Those gathered flipped through their briefing books. As there seemed to be no objections, Rasputum traced a plan:

"Well, we can start this off by getting up in front of the UN and announcing that we have an overwhelming inkling that the leader of Djibouti, Yaddidy Yaddidy Yah, or whatever the hell his name is, wouldn't mind having WMDs if the opportunity should ever arise. To merely deny that he wouldn't implement a program to acquire WMDs, even if he possibly could, does not make this a safer world. To repeatedly mention that the country can't even afford to import cans of spray lubricant to keep their First World War surplus Springfield M1s operational only underscores their desire to obtain unconventional weapons. If they can't spread their evilness throughout the world with their rusting arsenal of six hundred and twenty breach-loading ninety-year-old rifles, maybe a couple of thousand ICBMs capable of transporting nuclear, chemical or biological weapons might do the trick."

Rasputum automatically slipped into TV interview shtick.

"We cannot base our defense on what someone's intentions are, nor can we base our defense on what someone's *might* be. To build a solid defense, we must base it on what someone's possible intentions might be could they ever even remotely entertain the notion of them. If recent history has taught us anything, it is that, in this world that we now live in, we must not wait until our potential enemies have entered into the nuclear era. Nor should we even wait until they have entered the Bronze Age. If we have learned anything from our experience in Vietnam, it is that it is futile trying to bomb our enemies back into the Stone Age; thus, prudence and wisdom dictate that we bomb them while they are *still* in the Stone Age.

"There will be those who will be against us. There will be those who will be for us. But there is one thing I can assure you, and that is when all is said and done, the chips have been called in and the fat lady, excuse me–the weight challenged lady–has sung, democracy shall prevail."

Fuc Yu and Yogiof Yelstin cleared their throats.

"Oh, yes, and free market communist dictatorships and kleptocracies, too," Rasputum quickly added. And he continued:

"Because failure would undermine our success. And this we cannot allow. We must act before it is too late. We must strike while the iron is hot, because he who hesitates is lost. And lost is not where we want to be, because that would make it difficult to find our way back. And we must be back! We must be back in the front!"

Rasputum paused to feign gravitas to his final statement.

"I ask you now to support us fully. I ask you to support us totally. I ask you to support us unconditionally. And yes, I ask you to support us completely. Because if we waiver now, we may be denying our children, and the children of our children, and the children of our children's children, their God-given opportunity to waver in the future. And that we cannot do."

Rasputum cleared his throat and addressed the summit attendees. "So how do you think that will fly with the fucking farmers?"

Those in attendance burst into applause.

"*C'est magnifique!*" d'Istaing shouted.

"Tally ho!" Thornton yelled.

"*L'Chayim!*" Yehudi screamed.

(Fuc Yu, Grehepe Nehi and Muhammad Ali presumably also chimed in with typical Mandarin, Hindi, and Urdu exclamations, but the author couldn't be bothered to look up what these might be given the crap money he's getting for this book.)

"*Nyet.*"

"Beg your pardon, President Yelstin?" Rasputim said.

"*Nyet.*"

"'*Nyet*' what?"

"*Nyet* with the Djibouti kabang."

The applause died down and they all sat there perplexed. Nobody there, for the life of him, could understand why anyone would be in the least bit against annihilating Djibouti. Their perplexity began to turn to anger. *If not Djibouti, then where? We could be here all fucking day!*

Fuc Yu gave sardonic voice to their mood:

"Yogi, there's not a potato within a thousand miles of Djibouti. Don't worry, they can't possibly be vodka producers of any significance."

"Yut your yap, Yu!" Yelstin yelped.

"Bomb Duluth!" d'Istaing shouted.

"Bomb India!" Ali screamed.

"Bomb Pakistan!" Nehi bellowed.

"I hate cats!" Wingate hollered.

"Mother will never forgive me!" Mann cried.

"I want a marshmallow!" Bunkport chirped.

"Gentlemen, gentlemen, please. For God's sake, let's get on with it!" Rasputum said.

"GENTLEMEN, GENTLEMEN, PLEASE. FOR GOD'S SAKE, LET'S *NOT* GET ON WITH IT!" God said.

An appropriate silence filled the room. The men gathered there immediately intuited that, if they had been in deep shit before, they were now definitely in much, much deeper shit.

How God manifested his presence there is a little tricky to explain. It wasn't a visual presence. It wasn't really even an aural presence, as his voice had gone into each of their individual heads, rather than booming across the room. But it was definitely *him*, and everyone knew it.

Rasputum was the first to speak, and to give voice to the general sentiment:

"Uh ..."

"SHUT UP!"

Shut up Rasputum did, and not with difficulty as he had pretty much expressed everything that was on his mind at the moment.

"JUST WHO THE HELL DO YOU PEOPLE THINK YOU ARE?"

"I'm Kenny," said Kenny.

"I KNOW WHO YOU ARE! IT WAS A RHETORICAL QUESTION, YOU NINCOMPOOP!"

Actually, as had been established previously, God had no idea, whatsoever, who these people were, and only a vague memory of the planet they inhabited. He didn't get to be God, though, by not knowing how to play the game and, as such, opted to play the omniscient card.

"WHAT I DON'T KNOW IS–WHY YOU ARE KILL-ING MY FISH?"

God thought that that was a pretty clever follow-up, and was a little put off when he observed that the only reaction it provoked was general bewilderment.

"Fish?" Rasputum said, finally recovering his capacity for speech.

"Uh … AND THERE'S OTHER STUFF!"

"Fish?" Rasputum repeated.

"AND OTHER STUFF! LIKE I SAID!"

God quickly thought about some other stuff he could mention. An idea occurred to him.

"LIKE THE FACT THAT YOU'RE PLANNING ON BLOWING UP MY PLANET!"

"Just a part of it. A small part," Rasputum said, feeling that this would have some ameliorative effect. "Nowhere with fish, of course," he added, feeling vaguely that this would score some points. "Anyway, we were just kidding," he then said, hoping that out-and-out bullshit would fly as easily with God as it did with the press and public.

"AND I SUPPOSE YOU WERE JUST KIDDING ABOUT THE FISH, TOO?"

Gabriel nudged God and shook his head to indicate that this might not be the best approach.

"God, do folks get to eat marshmallows all the time in Heaven?" Kenny asked.

And the Lord scrunched up his brow and looked at Bunk-port. He then turned to Gabriel.

"Just who is *that* Bozo with the darts over there?"

"The leader of the free world and the commander in chief of the most powerful army ever to exist in the history of the world, sir."

And the Lord chuckled.

"No, seriously."

"Seriously, sir."

God returned his gaze to President Bunkport, who was now drawing pictures of marshmallows in the margins of his briefing book.

"I thought you said they had made some progress in evolving from monkeys"

"Some less than others, sir. If you observe the others in this room, you will note a keen and cold intelligence in their eyes."

God duly observed this.

"Well if they're the smart ones, and he's the dumb one, then why is he running the show?"

"You see, sir, quite often the dumb one will be made the leader because the masses identify with him more. It's called the 'who would you prefer to have a beer with' factor. While the masses are busy being amused by his down-to-earth homespun ways, the smart ones bleed them dry."

"I see, I ... Just hold on one cotton-picking minute there buckaroo!" God roared as he shot a fiery gaze at Gabriel. "So what you're saying is that the *dumb* one is usually the chief honcho and his *aides*," God said, emphasizing this last word while leaning over to within one inch of Gabriel's face, "are the *smart* ones!"

"Only on Earth, sir. Only on Earth." Gabriel said–quickly.

God held his steely gaze on Gabriel's face to see if he could perceive any muted smirks or muffled giggles. Satisfied, for the moment, that Gabriel wasn't taking the piss out of him, he returned his attention to the matter at hand.

The magnitude of his fuck-up began to dawn on him. His youthful hubris in thinking that he could slap together a planet in six days, rather than the standard four years, now came back to haunt him. The Lord had always taken it for granted that he was perfect and, up until now, had never confronted any evidence to the contrary. He was now faced with this Earth creation of his—a glaring wrinkle in an otherwise smooth fabric of perfection.

And the Lord went postal.

What we're talking about here is a wrath that made the stuff in the Old Testament look like a Shirley Temple movie. We're talking about divine fury that would make the Apocalypse look like a kitten batting around a ping-pong ball. In short, we're talking about some pretty serious shit about to come down.

Gabriel took a step back. He had been God's personal assistant for millenniums untold, and he new better than anyone when the Lord was about to go all fire and brimstone.

The Lord's chest swelled and his eyes quivered with rage. He poked a finger in the air and spoke:

"THE FIRMAMENT SHALL BLAZE AND THE SEAS SHALL BOIL! THIS THAT IS CALLED EARTH SHALL VANISH FROM MY UNIVERSE! I SHALL SMITE YE! A BALL OF FIRE SHALL LAY WASTE TO THE EARTH AND ALL THOSE UPON IT! A MIGHTY VENGEANCE SHALL BE MINE! AND UPON THE LAND THERE SHALL BE STRIFE AND TORMENT! THE RIVERS SHALL FLOW WITH MOLTEN BLOOD! FROM THE BRANCHES OF THE TREES SHALL DANGLE ENTRAILS—AND OTHER BITS AND PIECES! THE SEAS SHALL RUN DRY! Uh … AFTER THEY BOIL! Uh … GOT THAT?"

Their silence indicated that they had. The silence was finally broken by President Bunkport.

"God, if you're sore 'cause we were gonna blow up Djibouti, then why are you gonna blow up the whole world to punish us?"

That God was hovering in the conference room threatening Armageddon was one thing, but that Kenny Bunkport should make a relatively astute observation was really a jaw-dropper, and all attention turned toward him. A good thing, too, for God, because nobody noticed that, for the moment, he was at a loss for anything to say. He recovered, finally, and found a response:

"OH ... SCREW YE! SCREW YE ALL!"

And he was gone.

And then he was back, because he had thought of something else to say.

"SO YOU WANT TO DESTROY MY EARTH FOR THE GENERATIONS YET TO COME? I THEREFORE DECREE THAT ALL PRESENT HERE SHALL BE IM-MORTAL AND SHALL WALLOW IN THAT WHICH YOU CREATE!"

And he was gone.

And then he was back, because he had thought of something else.

"AND THAT BOOB WITH THE DARTS OVER THERE SHALL BE THE SUPREME LEADER OF EARTH UNTIL THE END OF TIME!"

And then he was gone, but really, this time.

PLEASE DON'T LET ME BE MISUNDERESTIMATED

Rasputum hurried along down the corridor, his mind racing. If he had been a busy man before, there was no comparison with what his days were now like. Converting a world that had previously been a hodge-podge of liberal democracies, oil-drenched plutocracies, mediaeval fundamentocracies, and Qaddafi-like wackocracies into a monolithic, centrally ruled, God-ordained empire was a job as tough as it sounds.

Rasputum was heading toward the office of the Secretary of Death to discuss the mass execution schedules. (Given that elections had been replaced by eternal unchallenged power, nobody could much be bothered with coming up with euphemisms anymore.)

As he passed the Oval Office, he noticed that His Divinely Opted-For Mega-Omnipotent Ruler Of The Lands And The Seas And The Air For All Of Eternity And Then Some was sitting at his desk staring out of the window; all very normal, except, Rasputum noticed, he was smoking a cigar–something that he had never seen him do before.

In all the flurry of recent days, Rasputum hadn't had time to tell Bunkport that, well, he just wasn't necessary anymore. Before, he had hardly been necessary either, except to read the occasional speech or, around election time, pose for a photo-op at a children's hospital or an old folks home or some shit like that. But this was no longer necessary and, by extension, neither was Bunkport. Except maybe for his birthday address to the world, Rasputin and the others could handle the rest. *Well*, thought Rasputum, *now is as good a time as any to get him out from under our feet.*

"Good morning, Your Mega Omnipotent Divinely Opted-For One."

Bunkport turned his chair to face Rasputum.

"Ah, good morning, Boris, good morning."

"It's a beautiful day outside, isn't it, Your Awesomeness?"

"Indeed it is, Boris. Indeed it is."

"Wouldn't you be happier peddling around the Rose Garden instead of being cooped up in here, Your Truly Astounding Everythingness?"

"Who wouldn't be, Boris. However, I've got an empire to run."

"Well, I would be happy to take care of whatever you feel needs to be done, Your More Than Noteworthy Numero Uno Terrestrial Super Muckity Muck." Rasputum said, somewhat surprised that Bunkport was even aware that a change had taken place.

"Well that's just what I've been meaning to mention to you," Bunkport said as he stood up and puffed on his cigar. "You won't be taking care of *anything* anymore, Boris. You're fired."

"Whah–?!" Rasputum said, for the first time in his life experiencing the sensation of being flabbergasted (well, the second time, if you count when God showed up at the SHAT summit).

"Rather tactless way of putting it, I know, Boris. But emperors aren't tactful. You never saw Napoleon going around saying: 'Excuse me; I beg your pardon; if you could just spare a second; hate to trouble you.' No, Boris, we're to-the-point sorts. Have to be, really. Even we divinely appointed ones have to throw our weight around a bit every now and again. Reminds people who's ruling the roost and all that."

"But ... is it ... was it ... is it something I did wrong?"

"Wrong? Nonsense, Boris, I couldn't have asked for a better secretary of state. You were magnificent. You did everything right, and don't you let anyone tell you anything different. I couldn't have done it without you." Bunkport took a long pull from his cigar and released the smoke. "The thing, Boris, is that I *have* done it. I *have* achieved my goal. I *am*, as you and the others so kindly put it, The Undisputed Divinely Opted-For Numero Uno Super Muckity Muck For All Of Eternity And Then Some; thus, you are no longer needed. You are superfluous, dead weight, dross, a spent booster rocket which must now be jettisoned."

"I, uh …"

"Rather unexpected turn of events, eh Boris? Well, as you know, *Li benter homines id quod volunt credunt*," Bunkport said with a wink.

Bunkport took another puff and smiled wryly at the dumbfounded Rasputum.

"Yes, Boris, I actually *did* pay attention in Latin class."

Bunkport walked to the window.

"You're astonished, Boris. You cannot believe that anyone could pull off such a sustained and credible performance. Well, you're right–for it was not a performance. I cannot lay claim to such a soaring thespian accomplishment. Even with my iron will and rock solid determination I would not have succeeded in forever masking the glint of genius in my eye. No, Boris, my achievement was far, far superior. You see, I hypnotized myself into stupidity. Cast a spell over myself, if you will. I ate, drank and, most importantly, thought stupid. And what could bring me around? What word, sound, gesture had I autosuggested to snap back to my old self? One thing, and only one thing–I had programmed myself to remain stupid until the voice of God granted me immortality and eternal omnipotence over the Earth.

"It was a risk, Boris. Indeed, it was a great risk. For I, by no means, had any way of knowing that this would ever happen in my lifetime. I could easily have condemned myself to forever being the drooling, blathering moron that you had always known me to be. And why should I risk so much? Simply, I had no choice. A mind as brilliant, and an ambition as unlimited, as mine could not have settled for anything less. President of the United States? Had I not been stupid at the time I would never, even as the stepping stone that it was, have suffered a position so far below my capabilities and ambitions.

"I can see, Boris, that you cannot believe that any one man could so perfectly, so magnificently perfectly, if I may indulge in poetic license, fool everyone." Bunkport chuckled. "Yes, Boris, for a man of your minuscule capabilities that would seem a monumental achievement. But, you see, Boris, that was nothing. For me that was a task akin to you picking your nose. No, what was required to achieve my ambitions was to completely deceive God. And that, Boris, is what I have done.

"I believe Cato put it best, *Semm hominum mores* ... Ah, there I go again. But I think we've had enough Latin for one day. And especially on such a splendid afternoon as this who wants to stay inside all day listening to dry Latin quotations? You're exactly right, Boris, this is a wonderful afternoon for a ride."

Bunkport stepped to his desk and pressed a button. Presently, two figures entered the Oval Office. Rasputum recognized them. They were two solid masses of muscle and malevolence whose services he had used in the past when the job at hand was of a nature that would have made Idi Amin queasy.

"Bruno, Slobavic, it's such a splendid day today, why don't you take the ex-secretary of state out for a nice long ride."

THORNTON

"Well, congratulations again, Valery. That's excellent news. You must be very pleased. Uh, huh. Uh, huh. Well, it's been drizzling a bit, but it's not too cold. And there? Well, remember to wrap up if you're going out. Right. Okay. Well, talk to you soon. Bye."

Thornton hung up the phone. He had rung d'Istaing to congratulate him on Duluth's being nuked. Bunkport had approved it, not for any electoral or political reasons–there weren't any elections or politics any more, but simply to placate d'Istaing. After all, if you're immortal, you don't want another immortal riding your ass until the end of time.

An unexpected outcome of the recent events was that Thornton and d'Istaing had become friends–Thornton's first friend since Ashton. Being among the handful of immortals was a pretty strong common bond. The irony, though, was not lost on Thornton. During the Laurel and Hardy business, Aunt Anne had tempered her suggestion that Thornton become friends with the French with the assurance that it would not be forever.

Not forever indeed.

A true friendship was also made possible by the fact that, with everything now set in stone, there was no need for trickery or deceit. There were no elections, no negotiations, no backroom dealings, no intrigue–no nothing. His friendship with d'Istaing was basically all he had now. Though he would forever hold his position, which now carried the title Viceroy of Central Bunkportia, there was very little for him to do. At first he was immersed in compiling his death wishlist, which Bunkport forced him to pare down from an original number which would have wiped out more people than the Black Plague. But the main ones were on the list, including Candy, Monty Diddlestiff, Edward Hawingway, Officer McKlusky, the staff at the Wall-Mart and Aunt Anne's lawyer. Thornton now discovered that, with no one to hate, and nothing to scheme, he was bored. And this would be the case for all of eternity.

Thornton rose from his desk and walked to the drinks trolley. The floor was not carpeted, so his stiletto heels did not snag. He was dressed essentially like he was that fateful day in the hotel room except he was also wearing a pink silk dressing gown. He now dressed like this everyday, in private and in public; what difference did it make? (Another of the, as Thornton was now coming to understand, very few benefits of eternal life was that Aunt Anne was now off his back, the result of a little known paranormal technicality that prohibits ghosts from haunting immortals.)

Thornton poured himself a scotch and walked to the window. The boredom he could bear, Thornton thought as he looked out at the drizzly greyness–but he could no longer look forward to death alleviating him of his greatest sorrow. Every waking moment, from now until the end of eternity, Thornton would live with the emptiness that had dwelt inside him since the day he had lost the ginmonger's slattern.